W9-BVA-597

MARION COUNTY PUBLIC LIBRARY
321 MONROE STREET
FAIRMONT, WV 26554

JUN 2 4 2010

KNIGHTLEY ACADEMY

KNIGHTLEY ACADEMY

BY VIOLET HABERDASHER

ALADDIN

NEW YORK   LONDON   TORONTO   SYDNEY

This book is a work of fiction. Any references to historical events, real people, or real locales are used fictitiously. Other names, characters, places, and incidents are the product of the author's imagination, and any resemblance to actual events or locales or persons, living or dead, is entirely coincidental.

ALADDIN

An imprint of Simon & Schuster Children's Publishing Division

1230 Avenue of the Americas, New York, NY 10020

First Aladdin hardcover edition March 2010

Copyright © 2010 by Robyn Schneider

All rights reserved, including the right of reproduction in whole or in part in any form.

ALADDIN is a trademark of Simon & Schuster, Inc., and related logo is a registered trademark of Simon & Schuster, Inc.

For information about special discounts for bulk purchases, please contact Simon & Schuster Special Sales at 1-866-506-1949 or business@simonandschuster.com.

The Simon & Schuster Speakers Bureau can bring authors to your live event.

For more information or to book an event contact the Simon & Schuster Speakers Bureau at 1-866-248-3049 or visit our website at www.simonspeakers.com.

Designed by Lisa Vega

The text of this book was set in Bembo.

Manufactured in the United States of America

0110 MTN

2 4 6 8 10 9 7 5 3 1

Library of Congress Cataloging-in-Publication Data

Haberdasher, Violet.

Knightley Academy / by Violet Haberdasher.—1st Aladdin hardcover ed.

p. cm.

Summary: In an alternate Victorian England, fourteen-year-old orphan Henry Grim, a maltreated servant at an exclusive school for the "sons of Gentry and Quality," begins a new life when he unexpectedly becomes the first commoner to be accepted at Knightley Academy, a prestigious boarding school for knights.

ISBN 978-1-4169-9143-4 (hc)

[1. Orphans—Fiction. 2. Knights and knighthood—Fiction.
3. Boarding schools—Fiction. 4. Schools—Fiction.] I. Title.

PZ7.H11424Kn 2010

[Fic]—dc22

2009023443

ISBN 978-1-4169-9901-0 (eBook)

For Edward,
who gave a little girl the wrong sort of books.
And for Ted,
who encouraged her to write them.

ACKNOWLEDGMENTS

In a rarely explored hallway of Knightley Academy, beneath decades of dust and generations of cobwebs, there hangs a puzzling little plaque, inscribed with sincerest thanks to the following people:

Ellen Krieger, the editorial quill that could do no wrong; Mark McVeigh, who loved the story even from his exile; Ted Malawer, who asked why the world wasn't at stake; Kate Angelella, who inherited the project with enthusiasm; Robyn Gertner, a fellow scribbler and writing companion; the girls of Primrose Hill, who put up with an author for a boarder; the East London café society; Mary Bell, for her enthusiasm; Professor William Sharpe, who ignited my Victoriana research; Julia DeVillers, for encouragement; the Philolexians, for encouragement; the Five Awesome YA Fans; and, of course, my family.

And at the bottom, most curiously of all, are the initials VH, which have bewildered historians for the past century.

1

THE FIVE YEARS' CURSE

The *Midsummer School for Boys sat on top of a steep but rather flat hill,* staring down its nose at the village below. You see, the Midsummer School for Boys was a grand place, where sons of Gentry and Quality learned how to stare down *their* noses at anyone beneath *them*. They also learned mathematics and science and history and how to steal food from the kitchens and torment the serving staff. But I'm getting ahead of myself.

Come to think of it, you probably know all about the Midsummer School for Boys, and are at this moment rolling your eyes and muttering, "Yeah, yeah, nothing new here, get on with the story." In fact, if I asked, you would most likely tell me that *everyone* already knows about the Midsummer School for Boys, and what they know are the following three facts:

1. All of the Midsummer students inherit titles more impressive than those of the first edition volumes in their vast school library.

2. All of the Midsummer professors routinely turn down jobs with prestigious universities, preferring instead to keep teaching secondary school algebra and dining at the High Table in Midsummer Hall.

3. The Midsummer School for Boys is probably cursed, since no student for the past five years has gained acceptance to Knightley Academy upon graduation.

But curses, unlike pocket watches and bicycles, are meant to be broken. And what you *don't* know about the Midsummer School for Boys is that its curse will break two days after our story starts, in the most scandalous and extraordinary way.

For the past five years, always on the fourth of May, the chief Knightley examiner and his silent assistant have urged their expensive black automobile up the hill from Midsummer proper and through the iron gates of the school. And every May the students have gathered solemnly in their full academic dress, bowed in unison, and returned to their dormitories, each thinking that *he* will be the one to break the Midsummer Curse.

The year in which our story takes place is no exception. The night before the examiners arrived, Valmont and Harisford, two popular, if somewhat brutish, fourteen-year-old boys, skulked through the darkened corridors of the Midsummer School. They carried with them (along with the fuzzy contents of their bathrobe pockets) half a chocolate cake stolen from the kitchen, and they were discussing the exam.

"What about Hobson?" Harisford demanded, licking some fudge off his index finger.

"Hobson? Riiiight," Valmont sneered. "He stutters when he's nervous. 'Oh, m-m-my lady, allow m-m-me to defend your honor.'"

Both boys snickered.

"Leroy, then," Harisford said, now having licked a small patch of cake completely bare of frosting. "He's brainy enough."

"And wants to study physics at some specialized school in *France*, for God's sake."

"So who else is there?" Harisford asked as they turned a corner and passed by the great wooden doors to the library.

"No one." Valmont shook his head. "Worthington's an idiot, Porter weighs more than the whole kitchen staff combined, and Crewe's a coward. Of course *I'm* not worried, what with all *my* family connections. So I suppose, if you're not quite as dim-witted as usual when we sit the exam, it would be down to you and me."

Actually, it *wasn't* down to Harisford or Valmont, who, by the way, knew far more about the origin of the so-called curse and his intended role in breaking it than he professed. No, the most likely candidate was at that moment just ten feet away, on the other side of the library door, feverishly memorizing a stolen textbook.

Henry Grim awoke two hours before morning announcements and, yawning, dressed in his uniform. Tiptoeing past the still sleeping Sander, he collected the all-too-familiar bucket and towel and, starting with the astronomy tower, began cleaning the blackboards.

After the tower, he tackled the science laboratories,

frowning as he remembered falling asleep every night over the bone-dry biology textbook last term. Next he moved into mathematics, where complex equations filled each blackboard with their exponents and limits. He'd suffered through this subject too. After that was history, all dates and names, and then languages, repetitive phrases written across the board in a half-dozen tenses. And finally, English. Usually, Professor Stratford was not awake before chapel, and often he dozed into his teacup at breakfast, but that morning, Henry found him sitting at his desk, nose deep in a popular gossip magazine.

"Erm, Professor?" Henry knocked on the doorframe, not wanting to interrupt.

"Oh, Henry!" Professor Stratford looked up from his magazine—the front page of which screamed: DEADLY PIES! DAILY GOSSIP! AND SECRET ARMIES OF THE NORDLANDS REVEALED!—and smiled warmly. "Come in, come in! I was just, well—oh, no need to erase the board today. We're continuing yesterday's discussion of Marlowe. Now, what was I saying?"

"You were going to tell me about the article you're reading," Henry said, biting back a smile.

"Quite right." Professor Stratford held his copy of the *Tattleteller* aloft. "'Secret Armies of the Nordlands

Revealed.' The most significant political news of the last century, right here, opposite an advertisement for wart removal cream."

"Really, sir?" Henry asked, failing to hide his smile. "Should we be expecting an invasion before tea?"

"Probably not. But you never can tell." The professor shrugged and grinned good-naturedly.

Professor Stratford wasn't yet thirty and, despite being a celebrated expert on the modern eighteenth-century poets, was largely regarded by the other masters as something of an overgrown schoolboy.

"I'll challenge you to raise the alarm, sir. This is serious news, indeed."

Professor Stratford nodded gravely, playing along. "Challenge accepted, Sir Henry."

Henry rolled his eyes at the professor's sarcasm. "Well, tomorrow's the exam. We'll find out who's accepted then."

"I have a feeling about this year," Professor Stratford said. "Sixth time's the charm."

"*Really*, sir? Where did you read that? In the *Tattleteller* as well?" Henry joked.

Professor Stratford burst out laughing and then nervously glanced toward the doorway, as if he really were a schoolboy and at any moment would be chastised for his outburst.

Reflexively, Henry looked too.

"There's no one coming, sir," Henry said, relieved.

Although he read the textbooks, Henry was not a student, and his friendship with Professor Stratford was dangerous to them both. For a moment, Henry thought the professor might change his mind and call off their secret tutoring sessions—taking away the only happiness that Henry knew. The silence hung there for an uncertain moment until Professor Stratford cleared his throat and, trying to pretend he was cross, grumbled, "Oh, get out of here, Grim! Same time this evening? And don't forget that essay I set you on the Greeks."

"If I forget, will you punish me by making me scrub the blackboards?"

"Don't be silly, Grim. We have *servants* to do those sorts of things."

Smiling at the joke, Henry said, "No, sir. I won't forget."

And, realizing that Cook might throw away his breakfast if he was any later, Henry dashed off to the kitchens.

* * *

At half past eleven that morning, a small black dot appeared in the distance. Upon further scrutiny, this dot gradually took the shape of an automobile, and finally the automobile began its clanging, spirited assent of the hill upon which the Midsummer School was perched.

"Move your arse, Porter!"

"Shove off, Hobson, you're standing on my foot."

"S-s-sorry, Valmont."

The year-eight students jostled their way into line, elbowing and pushing for the best positions. Each of the boys wore full academic dress, which itched in the heat. They sweated beneath formal tailcoats, pin-striped trousers, starched white shirts, high collars, black bowties, and traditional Midsummer School top hats.

The headmaster and professors stood behind the boys, pretending they were deaf to the complaints and bullying.

Suddenly, the chrome front of an expensive black automobile nosed its way over the top of the hill and through the centuries-old iron gates.

Everyone tensed.

A driver hopped out and ran around the front of the car to open the door.

The examiners had arrived.

A couple of the boys exchanged looks out of the corners of their eyes, not quite daring to stop facing forward. Instead of imposing, crusty old windbags, the examiners were cheerful-looking men in plain black suits, almost as young as Professor Stratford.

"Welcome," Headmaster Hathaway said, stepping forward to greet the examiners.

"Welcome, Sir Examiners," the boys chorused, touching their right hands to the brims of their top hats.

Valmont's hand trembled as he lifted it to the brim of his hat. These examiners weren't the ones he had been told to expect. But that was no reason to panic . . . right?

"Thank you," the shorter of the two men said, crisply shaking the headmaster's hand as his companion stood silently by his side. "We're glad to be here at the Midsummer School."

Examiner the Shorter's silent companion snapped to life and, reaching into his leather briefcase, pulled out a sheet of paper and began to read in a sonorous baritone.

"Grand Chevalier Winter extends his warm greetings to you, the Midsummer School for Boys. Sir Frederick, his appointed chief examiner, has come to evaluate any and all desiring residents of this school for admission to Knightley Academy this approaching August. The examinations, to be held on fifth May at promptly eight o'clock in the morning in the Great Hall, will test both physical and intellectual accomplishments and aptitude. If granted admission to Knightley, a student will spend the next four years studying military history, medicine, languages, ethics, protocol, diplomacy, and fencing. Upon graduation, a student will become a Knight of the Realm and be assured a prestigious career as a police knight, knight detective, or secret service knight."

Examiner of the Baritone promptly folded this paper and placed it back inside his briefcase, which he closed with a snap. As he surveyed the faces of the boys and their teachers, he was puzzled to find a broad smile on the young, mustachioed professor's face.

Henry took his usual seat at the long mahogany table near the reference books in the library and waited for Professor Stratford to arrive. He'd finished his essay an hour earlier, after helping Cook wash a mountain of dishes. Henry's fingers had been so wrinkled from the hot water that he could barely grip his pen. Now he frowned at his essay, wondering if his usually elegant penmanship looked too sloppy.

The day had been thick with excitement—for everyone else. There was a new grand chevalier (a sort of headmaster) at Knightley for the approaching year—and a new chief examiner—and no one knew if this meant that the exam would be different from previous years.

Henry privately thought not.

After all, there had been only one change at Knightley Academy since its founding nearly five centuries ago, and tradition was tradition. Anyone familiar with the Midsummer School could tell you that.

Three short knocks sounded on the great cedar door to the library, marking Henry and the professor's secret code, and Henry unlatched the lock and heaved the door open.

Professor Stratford, in his chalk-stained trousers and rumpled shirtsleeves, slipped through, juggling an armload of books.

"I'll be finished tidying up in a moment," Henry said loudly, in case someone might be passing through the nearby corridors. "Are you returning some overdue library books, sir?"

Henry followed the professor to the antique table where he'd left his essay.

"Tout les livres sont les livres de la biliotheque," Professor Stratford said, raising an eyebrow as he waited for a response.

"Er, *mais c'est tort, maitre, lorsque la conaissance dans les livres ne s'appartient a une place, mais s'appartient a la monde,"* Henry replied nervously.

"Bien."

Professor Stratford switched to Latin next, then Italian, before finally returning to English.

"Excuse me for asking, sir, but why are we reviewing languages?"

Professor Stratford sighed and slumped in his chair, looking every minute less like a teacher and more like one of the year-eight boys.

"I've been tutoring you every night for almost nine months, Henry."

"Yes, sir."

"Ever since I caught you returning that copy of Milton to my desk last September."

Henry cringed. "I'm still sorry about that—"

"Never mind the past, Henry. I'm not sorry about it. No, it's rather the contrary."

Professor Stratford pressed his fingers to his temples for a moment, and then began again. "You're by far the cleverest boy at Midsummer. I want you to know that."

"Thank you, sir," Henry said, flushing from the unexpected compliment.

"But all of this sneaking, all of these late nights spent reviewing material far beyond my own boys' curriculum, it has to add up to something."

"I'm not sure I'm following you, sir," said Henry.

"One must benefit from one's risks, Henry. And you never know when we'll be found out. That's why I want you to sit the Knightley Exam tomorrow."

"Sit the exam?" Henry nearly shouted. "Are you mad?"

"Hardly. I listened carefully to that proclamation the examiners made this morning, and it appears you're eligible. They did say 'All *residents* of the Midsummer School.'"

"Excuse me for being rude, sir," Henry said through clenched teeth, "but I highly doubt that they are going to let a *servant boy* sit the exam for becoming a knight."

"They have to," Professor Stratford said, emphatically thumping his fist against a textbook. "And so do you. I swear on my folio of *Twelfth Night*, if you don't take that exam I'll . . . I'll report you myself for sneaking into the library every night and borrowing books."

"But," Henry said, his brain spinning to make sense of what was happening, "it'll never work. Even if I pass—and no Midsummer boy has passed in five years, in case you've forgotten—they'd never let me go. I'm a commoner. A ward of the Realm. I'm—"

"A perfect candidate," Professor Stratford finished. "They'd be mad not to take you. Unless, of course, you *want* to scrub blackboards for the rest of your life?"

Henry sighed. Of course he didn't. Why else had he struggled through math and history and that horrible Latin in his precious free hours? But Professor Stratford was only trying to help. They both knew that there weren't many prospects for a fourteen-year-old with a birth certificate that read, *baby boy found on church steps on the grimmest day of the year.*

"I'm sorry," Henry said, "but I *am* trying. I'm putting away money for proper schooling, and maybe one day I'll have the chance to make my life less unfair, but until then I'm not going to aim for the impossible."

"I think that's a brilliant plan," Professor Stratford snorted. "Why don't you tell it to Galileo, to Milton, to Michelangelo? Tell *them* they shouldn't have aimed for the impossible. Because, Henry, the most terrible thing in this world is to be haunted by those two little words 'What if?' until the end of days."

Henry sighed. He stared at his tutor, so determined to force the world into a new way of being, where hard work was valued and rewarded in the place of social standing. But the only meritocracy that Henry knew of belonged to their northern neighbors, and there were dark whispers of what price the Nordlandic people really paid for their so-called equality. For Henry, the world had always been divided into commoners and members of the aristocracy, with an unbreakable line between the two.

But times were changing—everyone said so. There were electric lights now and telegrams and steam engines and even the occasional automobile. It was nearly the turn of the century, and that alone was cause enough to wonder what novelties the future would hold. And what if Professor Stratford *was* right—what if he *could* sit the exam? He might fail. But he might pass. Would they really let him attend Knightley? To learn medicine, fencing, and diplomacy? To sit as a real student in the lectures at the most elite academy in the country, and not scramble for scraps of leftover lessons in darkened corridors, a mop over his shoulder?

"Professor, do you truly think this is what I should do?"

Henry and the professor stared at each other, fully aware of the consequences this decision might have. Both of them could lose their jobs. The late-night tutoring sessions they'd worked so hard to hide over the past nine months would be instantly obvious. But despite all this, Henry still hoped Professor Stratford would say yes. Henry tensed, waiting for his tutor's answer.

"Je ne le pense pas, Henri. Je le connais."

Translation: "I don't think, I know."

2

THE KNIGHTLEY
EXAMINATIONS

Ten students stood nervously inside the Great Hall the next morning, awaiting the exam. Despite the early hour, they appeared immaculate, not a hair out of place, not a wrinkle in their trousers.

Henry, having rejected his staff uniform and donned instead his rumpled, secondhand trousers and badly patched shirtsleeves, tried not to fret that his brown hair spilled past his collar or that he hadn't been able to locate his necktie. He peered through the doorway at the students inside the hall, none of them commoners. These were the boys whose dormitories and classrooms he had scrubbed for the past year, whose suppers he had served. But more important, none of them wanted to go to Knightley as badly as he did. For these boys, getting into Knightley would be an honor to boast about, like getting picked first at sport, but for Henry, it would mean *everything*.

And so he took a deep breath and stepped into the Great Hall.

The boys, thinking it might be one of the examiners, looked up.

But it was only that odd serving boy, the one with the too-long hair and falling-apart work boots, probably on his day off.

"You're not supposed to be in here," Valmont said sneeringly to Henry. "They're giving an exam."

It was then or never. Chalkboards or swords. What could be or what if.

"Yes, and I intend to take it," Henry said coolly.

"You?" Valmont's lip curled. "Do you even know how to *read*? And aren't you supposed to be fixing that clogged toilet up on the third floor?"

The venom in Valmont's voice stung, and Henry took an involuntary step back.

A couple of boys laughed. And then the perfect retort popped into Henry's head.

"Why so defensive?" Henry asked. "Are you afraid of some competition?"

"Competition?" Valmont laughed uproariously. "You?"

"Yes." Henry took a step forward, his brown eyes boring into Valmont's blue ones. "Me."

Valmont glared.

Henry smiled.

"Even if you pass the exam, they won't have you," Valmont said, and for a moment, Henry's smile wavered. "So go on, keep wasting everyone's time. I hope they fire you for this. In fact, I think *I'll* see to that personally, once I get into Knightley, which I *will*, because I'm a Valmont."

A couple of boys yelled their approval, and Henry forced himself to keep calm. Fighting wouldn't solve anything—except making sure that he *did* get fired. But Valmont's words were poison darts landing a little too close to the target for comfort. What if he *was* wasting everyone's time? What if Professor Stratford had believed in him, and risked his place as English master, for nothing?

Trying to quiet these thoughts that thundered through his head, Henry reached into his dirt-smudged satchel, pulled out a book, and leaned against the wall, losing himself in the text.

All too soon the carved wooden doorway at the far end of the hall swung open, and Examiner the Shorter strode forward, hands thrust into the pin-striped pockets of his dark suit.

"Morning, boys."

"Good morning, Sir Examiner," the students called in unison, straightening up as though they were already students at Knightley.

Henry closed his book and held it at his side, trying not to fret over how grubby he looked compared to the carefully turned-out students.

"Are all residents of the Midsummer School for Boys who wish to sit this exam present?" the examiner asked.

"Yes, Sir Examiner," everyone chorused, Henry included.

"Excuse me? Sir Examiner?" Valmont asked, tentatively raising his hand.

"Yes?"

"This boy here"—Valmont pointed at Henry—"is a school servant. He shouldn't be allowed."

"I see," the examiner said coolly, jingling the coins in his pockets. "You, in the shirtsleeves, what's your name?"

Henry gulped. "Henry Grim, sir."

"And how old are you, Mr. Grim?"

"Fourteen, sir."

"And where might you live?"

"The servants' quarters in the attic rooms, sir."

"Then it would appear that, this year, you are indeed eligible to sit the exam. And whether or not you should be allowed to do so is not up to the discretion of mere schoolboys."

Valmont frowned, and Henry tried not to smile.

"And now, if there are to be no more disruptions," the examiner said, "you will follow me into the anteroom, where you will take the written portion of the exam. You are allowed three hours. To complete the exam in full would take five hours. And so, you must choose which questions you will answer, and think hard about what your choices will reveal when the exam is scored. Follow me, please."

Henry swallowed nervously and followed the whispering boys through the doorway and into the small anteroom, where four rows of desks had been set up. On each desk sat a thick booklet and a pencil stub without an eraser. Examiner of the Baritone sat at a master's table facing the rows of desks.

Henry chose a seat in the back. There were sixteen desks, and the other boys avoided him, leaving Henry surrounded by empty seats. This was fine with him. At least no one could accuse him of cheating.

"Before you begin, are there any final questions?" asked Examiner the Shorter.

"I have one," Harisford said, without bothering to raise his hand. "Sir. Where are the erasers?"

"You will not be permitted to use erasers," the examiner replied with just the faintest hint of a smile. "In life, your actions and words are permanent. You may remove the ink, but they are indelible."

"So it's part of the test?" Harisford asked.

"Yes, it's part of the test. Any last questions? No? Very well, time remaining will be given every fifteen minutes. You may begin."

Henry stumbled out of the anteroom with the rest of the boys, his left hand cramped from writing. He was exhausted, and had no idea whether he had passed or failed. The exam had been full of baffling questions, pages of personal inquiries such as "Please describe your childhood home," "What is your most shameful memory from when you were young?" "Please describe the sorts of presents you receive on your birthdays and for holidays," and "If you misbehaved as a boy, what were your punishments like?" And then there were the typical math/science/history/English questions. But there were also odd questions written in foreign languages with instructions to answer these questions in different foreign languages. The last three pages were hypothetical questions: "If you accidentally insulted a foreign dignitary, how would you recover from this faux pas? Please describe a scenario in your answer."

Henry had mostly answered the school subject questions (he avoided the math ones, as he was terrible at math), the language ones, and the hypotheticals.

Anyway, he didn't really think it was anyone's business that his childhood home was the Midsummer Orphanage or that his most shameful memory was the time he visited the City and someone mistook him for a beggar, offering him a spare penny. Or that he sometimes received a pair of new (to him) shoes or trousers on his birthday, and that, when he misbehaved, he was given extra chores to perform on an empty stomach.

He didn't feel like writing about how the orphanage priest had taken Henry under his wing for a while, teaching him to read and write and hoping that Henry might become a man of the church when he grew older, but all that had stopped when Henry got into a pile of philosophy books and declared that he didn't believe in God.

And so Henry had waited until he turned thirteen and could leave the orphanage, then hiked up the steep hill to the Midsummer School, with its vast library and gilt-framed portraits, where he worked as a servant boy and studied stolen books at night.

This story, he knew, wasn't the story of a knight.

Even so, that didn't stop him from wanting to get into Knightley. Not for the glory of passing the exam and breaking the Midsummer Curse, like so many of the other boys, but because if he did, it would be the first thing to go right in his life in a long while.

Henry's stomach grumbled, and when he looked at the clock, he realized it was nearly noon and all of the boys were heading in the direction of the dining hall. Cursing under his breath, Henry opened a shabby little door that lead to a servants' staircase and raced to the kitchen.

"Yer late, boy," the cook grumbled when Henry arrived, panting, in the clammy kitchen, which smelled of stewed vegetables and roasted meat.

"Sorry," Henry said, trying to catch his breath.

"'E was takin' the exam," one of the maids said, pointing a wooden spoon at Henry. "Fer that fancy school. Wasn't yeh?"

"Yes, I was," Henry said quietly, staring at his falling-apart boots.

"Mr. High an' Mighty thinks 'e's gonna be a knight," the maid cackled.

"Well, 'e ain't," said the cook. "Now git out there an' serve yer superiors, boy, no time teh put on yer livery."

The cook shoved a heavy tray with bowls of savory soup into Henry's hands.

Henry staggered over to his assigned table, which, just his luck, was filled with boys who'd taken the Knightley Exam.

"Oh, this is priceless," Valmont said, smirking. "*Now* do you remember your place, servant boy?"

"You can never step into the same river twice," Henry said, slamming a soup bowl onto the table in front of Valmont.

"What's that supposed to mean?" Valmont sneered.

"It's from the Greeks," Henry said. "And it means that things change."

With that, Henry plunked the last soup bowl on the table and headed back toward the kitchen to wait for the next course.

Maybe it was Henry's imagination, but the meal that afternoon seemed unusually filling. After the vegetable soup, there were roast beef sandwiches and roasted potatoes, then chocolate cake with thick frosting.

Henry nibbled at one of the leftover sandwiches, his stomach a heavy pit of nerves. The exam wasn't finished, of that he was certain. Why else had the examiner called that morning's test the "written portion"?

As Henry cleared the dessert plates (which the boys at Valmont's table had deliberately smeared with frosting, and then coated with a disgusting layer of salt and pepper all the way to the edges) he spotted the two examiners seated at the High Table. Professor Stratford also sat at the High Table, and he caught Henry's eye, clearly wanting to know how the exam had gone.

"Did you need something, sir?" Henry asked, approaching the High Table.

Professor Stratford looked at Henry blankly, and then his face broke into a sheepish grin. "Good heavens, I've already forgotten it! No matter. *Everything's going well, then?*"

"*Excellent*, sir," Henry replied, playing along that he and the professor didn't know each other, and that their conversation really was as innocent as it sounded.

"That'll be all, er, Harold," Professor Stratford said, his eyes twinkling.

"Yes, sir," Henry said, balancing the dirty dessert plates on his serving platter and heading back toward the kitchen.

"If yeh want supper t'night, yeh can help wash these," the cook grumbled as Henry brought the plates over to the sink.

Henry sighed and began to roll up his sleeves. But the dining room sounded oddly quiet, and then he heard the boom of a single voice.

"I'm sorry, Cook," Henry said, dashing back through the swinging door.

"—students who took the written portion of this morning's exam meet on the back lawn in five minutes. That will be all," Examiner the Shorter said, standing behind his chair at the High Table.

Henry pushed open the door to the kitchen. "Cook? I can't help with the dishes now. Can I do it this evening instead?"

"Yeh better. And don' think I won' be reportin' yeh for this."

"Go ahead," Henry challenged, his hand still on the door. "It's not my job to wash plates, anyway. I do chalkboards and Sander does dishes, so make him do what he's paid for."

Henry thought he'd be the last one on the back lawn, but when he arrived, he was the first.

That didn't bode well.

After a minute, all of the other boys approached slowly, in a line, and there was a nasty smile on Valmont's face.

Silently, the line of boys surrounded Henry in a menacing circle.

Valmont made a sound as though he was going to cough, but then he spat a large glob of saliva. Henry stepped out of the way. But then another boy cleared his throat, and another, and Henry realized what was going on.

He closed his eyes, waiting for it.

And then a familiar voice demanded, "What's going on out here?"

"Nothing, Professor," a couple of the boys muttered, reluctantly breaking the circle.

"I should hope not," Professor Stratford said, and despite his cheerful grin, his eyes were threatening. "I wouldn't want to have to discipline anyone. Good gracious, I came out here to cheer you boys on."

"*All* of us?" Valmont demanded.

"Yes," Professor Stratford said, raising an eyebrow. "*All* of you."

"Oh, wonderful, every one of you is punctual," Examiner the Shorter called, walking briskly across the grass with Examiner of the Baritone.

"Hello, Sir Examiners," everyone said.

"Hello, boys. We'll be running some physical tests this afternoon, so for your sake, I hope you've not stuffed yourselves full of sandwiches and cake."

Henry suppressed a smile. Everyone at the table he'd served had practically gorged themselves.

"Well," Examiner the Shorter continued, "in any case, let's begin with, shall we say, four laps around the perimeter?"

Each lap was a kilometer, Henry knew.

"Sir?" a boy asked, hand in the air. "What are we to do with our jackets and ties?"

"A good question, and I'm sure you'll think of an answer quickly," the examiner replied. "Now, on my mark."

The boys scrambled out of their neatly pressed coats and ties, flinging them onto the grass.

"Please begin."

By the end of the first lap, Henry noticed that a few of the boys looked like they might be sick. By the end of the second lap, three of them were.

"Run it off, boys," Examiner the Shorter called cheerfully, waving his pocket square.

Running in heavy work boots wasn't the best idea, and Henry finished fifth. His feet ached, and he needed to catch his breath, but he wasn't too tired, and he *definitely* wasn't going to be sick.

"Wonderful effort," Examiner the Shorter called. "Please line up for cups of water."

The boys sighed gratefully and shuffled into line, with Henry at the rear.

"Shouldn't the servant do that?" Valmont huffed as Examiner of the Baritone handed out cups of water.

"Possibly," Examiner the Shorter conceded, as though the thought had not occurred to him until that very moment. "Now, another lap, please, and try to spill as little of the water as possible while you run."

A few boys looked up at the examiner in surprise, having already drunk greedily from their cups and having assumed that the ordeal was finished.

"And begin," the examiner called.

Placing his palm flat over the cup, Henry ran slowly.

It wasn't about finishing first, he knew, it was about the water. Henry was starting to understand that no portion of the exam was exactly as it seemed, that there were tests nestled within tests.

After the lap, the boys were told to line up and give their names. Examiner of the Baritone recorded the amounts of water left in their cups. Henry cast glances out of the corners of his eyes. As far as he could tell, his cup was the fullest.

"Drink up, now," Examiner the Shorter advised. "You've had a long run, and I won't keep you any longer. You're free to leave."

"That's it?" Harisford asked.

"That's it," Examiner the Shorter replied.

One by one, the boys picked up their jackets and ties and headed indoors, leaving their cups in the grass.

Sighing, Henry began collecting the cups.

"I'll take these to the kitchen, sir," Henry said to Examiner the Shorter.

"You can't carry all of those by yourself," Professor Stratford said.

Henry had forgotten that he was there.

"It's fine, sir," Henry said.

"Nonsense, my boy, you must be exhausted. You've just run five kilometers. I'll help."

Professor Stratford swept up an armload of cups and started toward the main building.

"Thank you for letting me take the exam," Henry told the examiners, and then hurried to catch up with Professor Stratford.

"Nice touch, there, collecting the cups at the end," Professor Stratford said. "I'll bet anything that was part of the test."

"I thought it might be," Henry admitted. "And Cook would just send me back out here to collect them anyway."

"So it seems fortune would favor the unfavored," Stratford said, smiling to himself.

"Who said that?" Henry asked, not recognizing the quote.

"I did. Just now."

"Thank you for rescuing me earlier," Henry said.

They'd passed into the main building and Henry led the professor down one of the servants' stairways.

"I've seen it happen before. This isn't the first time these boys have tried that spitting trick."

"How chivalrous," Henry said with a lopsided smile.

"Isn't it?" The professor's face broke into a wry grin. "So how do you think it went today? The exam?"

"Well, it was odd. I mean, it was as though half the exam was secretly buried in other tests, and what you didn't do counted as much as what you did."

Professor Stratford nodded.

"I think I did well," Henry said. "But I'm not certain. I wish they'd tell us already."

"Tomorrow, my boy. Tomorrow."

They reached the back entrance to the kitchen.

"I can take everything from here," Henry said.

"Don't be ridiculous," the professor said, barging into the kitchen before Henry could protest.

"Sander, yeh rascal!" Cook yelled, and then took in the scholar's cap of the man who had just entered the kitchen with an armload of cups. "Sorry, sir. Didja need sumthin'?"

"Just returning these cups," Professor Stratford said. "And I'll be borrowing young Henry to help me for the rest of the afternoon. Hopefully he won't be missed."

Without waiting for an answer, the professor smiled and sailed out the swinging door.

Henry quickly deposited his armload of cups in the

kitchen and followed Professor Stratford. "What do you need me for, sir?"

"Oh, nothing," the professor said, smiling. "I thought you could use a few hours to yourself."

"Too polite to tell me I need a bath?" Henry joked, grateful for the unexpected kindness. Although, now that the professor mentioned it, a bath wasn't such a bad idea. His shirt was sticky with sweat.

"You've found me out, Grim. And no lessons tonight. But come find me if you need me."

"I will. And thanks again."

The prospect of an afternoon free was a wonderful thing, and Henry headed off to the washroom to clean himself up.

Evening came all too soon, and Henry climbed out of bed, where he'd fallen asleep with a mystery novel on his chest. His legs felt rubbery from running, and his feet had blistered, making every step pinch painfully.

"Where's Sander?" Cook asked, pulling a roast from the oven.

"Haven't seen him," Henry said. "I was, er, helping Professor Stratford all afternoon."

"Well, now yeh can help me. These need teh be served." Cook waved a beefy hand in the direction of a table covered with salad plates. "An' since Sander ain't bothered teh come down an' do 'is job, yeh'll be servin' his table as well as yer regular."

"Wonderful," Henry muttered, hefting a large platter of salads.

The boys at his usual service table were the same crowd from that afternoon, and instead of ignoring him, as they had in the past, now the boys took a special interest in Henry.

They had him running back and forth to the kitchen to fetch a pot of mustard, which Harisford insisted he must have on his salad, or clean cups, as Crewe and Porter had noticed nonexistent flecks of dirt on theirs.

And then there was Sander's usual table, occupied by an unruly group of eleven-year-olds, one of whom dared an unfortunate-looking boy in too-large spectacles to drink a disgusting concoction of salad dressing, milk, pepper, and gravy. Thankfully, the boy didn't throw up, but he did spill most of the gross-out potion down the side of the table, and Henry was expected to mop it up.

The meal couldn't end soon enough. And when it did, Henry found himself rolling up his sleeves to wash dishes, even though *that* was Sander's job as well.

Sander was sixteen, the eldest of the four serving boys, and the most reliably unreliable. He left half his work for Henry to do and was careless with the duties that he did perform. But he was Cook's nephew, and so he got away with it, much to Henry's annoyance.

Finally, Cook dismissed Henry, whose hands were now raw from the hot water and soap. Henry nearly dropped his plate of supper as he staggered up the stairs to the attic. After bolting his cold food, Henry lay on his cot, staring up at the sloping ceiling.

He didn't want to get his hopes up. He'd certainly learned that lesson at the orphanage. And yet . . . what if he *did* get in to Knightley? Henry closed his eyes, imagining the heft of a practice sword, the well-cut uniform, the essays he would write and the things he would learn.

Knightley . . . he'd grown up knowing the school's history; after all, it was the history of his country. For the past hundred years, all of the Britonian Isles had been at peace with one another. This was because of the Longsword Treaty, named for the famous knight who had inspired the first draft. Back then, Knights really *did* ride around on horses, fighting in service of their overlords. Back then, there were bloody wars to fight, with thousands of men drafted into the common service every week and shipped overseas or overlands to certain, gruesome death. But with the Longsword Treaty, all that changed. As long as no citizens were trained in combat, peace would remain among the countries. And so Knightley Academy closed down its archery fields and tilting courses, concocted a written admissions examination in place of their annual jousting competition, and hired masters to teach history and languages and medicine. Knighthood modernized—to be a knight was to keep the law and the peace, to be a man of letters before most boys their age ever set foot into university, to swear an oath of chivalry and, with that oath, be given a title in gratitude for one's service to the realm.

There was no military, and no need for one, not with all of the neighboring lands bound fast by the same treaty. But the treaty had not stopped revolutionaries in the Nordlands from overthrowing their monarch thirteen years earlier and installing their leader, Yurick Mors, as high chancellor. Lately, Chancellor Mors's decrees had been the subject of many whispered conversations that Henry often overheard in the kitchen. The new laws levied outrageous taxes against all imports, forbade the employment of foreigners, and set a mandatory curfew for all citizens. It was only a matter of time, most people said, until the Nordlands self-destructed and Mors fell from power. After all, they whispered, that's what happens when a country does away with its class system. And yet . . . some people whispered that Mors was more powerful than anyone could imagine, and that an army was gathering, one with new weapons that they could use without violating the treaty—without being trained in combat. But these rumors were just legends and lies, the stuff of tabloid writers who read too many adventure stories, passed around by those with a flair for paranoia. Professor Stratford read them for a laugh, and anyway, there was no proof.

Closing his eyes, Henry tried to derail his train of thought into something resembling sleep. After all, he was only thinking of these things because he was nervous, and nerves played off one's fears.

But right then, Henry's greatest fear was quite personal. He feared that he had failed the professor and himself. That he had failed the exam. But a tiny voice inside him insisted that there was hope. Hope that if he went to Knightley, he would have a life filled with opportunity, leading to an assured future. A life in which he would be surrounded by people who would become like a family, something he had never known. And he wouldn't be just Henry anymore. In four years he would kneel and become Sir Henry Grim. It sounded so grand and yet so . . . impossible.

3

THE BOY WHO PASSED

When Henry awoke the next morning, he noticed with some relief that Sander had slunk in during the night and was curled up fast asleep in bed.

Henry buttoned his shirt and gave Sander a nudge. "Wake up. You're on for breakfast."

Sander groaned.

Henry laced his shoes. "Up, Sander. Come on. You'll be late."

Sander opened an eye and rolled over, his cheeks sunken and peppered with stubble. "Don' feel so good."

"Stop faking," Henry said sharply. "Five minutes."

"Uuuugh, I shouldn'ta bin gamblin' at the pub las' night."

Henry yanked the blanket off Sander. "No, you shouldn't have been at the pub in the first place, much less gambling there. Now stop laying about and do your job. I'm not getting stuck with your work two days in a row."

Sander groaned but swung his feet over the side of the bed. "I los' at cards again," he moaned. "This week's wages an' the last."

"You'll lose more than your wages if you don't watch it," Henry said, his hand on the doorknob.

Henry performed his morning tasks without thinking, mechanically scrubbing the blackboards and laying out fresh pieces of chalk. It wasn't until he reached Professor Stratford's classroom that he snapped out of his fog.

But the professor wasn't at his desk.

Henry quickly washed the blackboard, his heart pounding. It was nearly time for morning announcements, and for the first time, he was impatient to hear them. He'd tried to put thoughts of Knightley out of his mind that morning, but they had taken up permanent residence and stubbornly refused to budge.

"Even if I pass," Henry murmured to himself as he wrang out his washrag, "they won't let me go. I never really thought that they would."

But this was a lie, and not a very good one at that. The examiner had seemed so kind yesterday, and why else would he have allowed Henry to take the exam? Furthermore, why would Professor Stratford have urged him to take the exam if the results didn't matter? They *had* to matter; after all, they mattered to Henry more than anything.

Henry slipped into the dining hall just as breakfast ended, glad that he wouldn't be forced to take care of the dishes. The large hall smelled of sausage and egg and strong tea, and Henry's empty stomach grumbled. Sander, pale and sweating, cleared the last of the plates from the High Table and staggered back toward the kitchen.

Suddenly, Henry felt dizzy. He didn't want to know the results. Not like this, in front of everyone, his disappointment on display. Why couldn't there have been a list posted quietly outside the library?

Headmaster Hathaway rose from his seat, and Henry gulped, leaning back against the wood-paneled wall for support. His heart thundered, and he felt as though he had flu, or maybe one of Sander's hangovers.

"Students," Headmaster Hathaway said, clasping his hands in front of his large belly, "this day's announcements are brief, as our term draws to its close at the end of next week. We have only one announcement, and I hope you will give a warm welcome to Sir Frederick, chief examiner of Knightley Academy."

Henry watched nervously as Examiner the Shorter—Sir Frederick—rose and walked to the lectern next to the High Table.

"Thank you, Headmaster Hathaway. As you boys are no doubt aware, eleven of your own took the Knightley Entrance Exam yesterday, and my colleague and I have spent the night evaluating their performance. Admission to Knightley Academy is not granted lightly, and for those of you who did not make it, do not despair. But for any of you who did"—at this, the hall filled with curious whispers—"congratulations."

Sir Frederick paused for effect and stared at the whispering students until they quieted.

"Yes," Sir Frederick resumed. "This year there are congratulations in order—to one boy. I would like to extend my sincerest admiration and welcome to the newest pupil at Knightley Academy . . ."

Smiling apologetically for the interlude, Sir Frederick

reached into his pocket and pulled out an envelope bearing the Knightley Academy crest. Valmont had half risen in his seat, a look of smug triumph on his face.

". . . Henry Grim."

Instead of filling with applause, the hall remained silent. The Midsummer School for Boys had fifteen students per year, and every boy there could tell you that no one in year eight was named Henry. Valmont's look of triumph had changed to one of unbelieving rage.

And then, in the awkward silence, Professor Stratford stood up at the High Table and began to cheer. "Huzzah, Henry, m'boy! I knew you could do it! Get up here!"

Shocked, Henry walked numbly forward.

There was no applause, just whispers and accusing stares. Henry didn't dare to look over at Valmont again.

Henry approached the lectern, and Sir Frederick smiled, stuck out his hand for a brief handshake, and gave Henry the envelope containing book lists and school instructions.

"Is it my imagination," Sir Frederick mused, "or is there a decided *lack* of congratulations?"

"It's not your imagination, sir," Henry muttered, his face growing hot.

Professor Stratford sank back into his chair, his silence heavy with meaning.

"Ahem," Headmaster Hathaway said, his mustache twitching in fury. "Might I see the three of you in my study? *Now.*"

Henry had never been in Headmaster Hathaway's study, and for this he was thankful. The room was large and filled with expensive-looking sets of books, their spines immaculate, as though they had never been read. Most of the room was occupied by a large, imposing desk and three chairs.

One of the maids had lit a fire in the grate, which blazed hellishly, enveloping the room in stifling, smoky heat.

Henry ran a finger around the inside of his collar, trying not to sweat. There were only three chairs. He stood against the back wall as Professor Stratford, Sir Frederick, and Headmaster Hathaway settled into the seats.

The dangerous silence held, and then suddenly broke as Headmaster Hathaway exploded. *"What is the meaning of this?"*

"The meaning, Headmaster?" Sir Frederick said

calmly. "I should think that would be self-evident. Young Henry here has passed. Congratulations to you all!"

"But this is absurd!" the headmaster thundered, his face a horrible shade of puce. He took a few calming breaths. "I mean, this boy is not a student; he is a servant."

"He's a resident of the school," Professor Stratford put in. "And as a resident was eligible to take the exam."

"No doubt this is *your* doing," the headmaster accused, his finger pointed at the young professor in warning.

"Yes," Professor Stratford said. "I told him to sit the exam."

"No, he didn't," Henry interrupted. "It was my idea. The professor didn't—"

"Hold your tongue, boy!" Headmaster Hathaway roared.

Henry nodded meekly.

"Nevertheless, the boy has passed," Sir Frederick said. "With very high marks, I might add. We would be happy to have him. I don't understand the trouble."

"Servants," Headmaster Hathaway said, straining to keep calm. "Do. Not. Become. Knights."

"I'll admit it is a bit unusual," Sir Frederick conceded. "But then, so is Henry. And for a servant, he's remarkably educated."

Professor Stratford slumped in his chair, chewing nervously on the corner of his mustache.

"Jonathan Stratford!" the headmaster boomed.

"Yes, sir?" Professor Stratford gave the headmaster an innocent stare, although a telltale wisp of his mustache was darker than the rest.

"Have you been *helping* this boy?"

Henry had never before heard the word "help" sound so contemptible.

"I have been tutoring him in the evenings, yes."

"So you decided to help a *servant* pass the exam while you let all of your *students* fail?" the headmaster accused.

"Now hold on a minute. You can't blame *me* for Valmont and Harisford and the rest."

"I most certainly can, and I *will*," Headmaster Hathaway roared. "In fact, I think it would be a very good idea if you resigned. *Today.*"

"You can't be serious," Professor Stratford protested, but they could all see that the headmaster meant what he had said. "Fine. You have my resignation. I'll pack my things directly."

With a sidelong glance at Henry, Professor Stratford strode toward the door and threw it open, his footsteps echoing along the hallway.

"Have a seat, Henry," Sir Frederick said, motioning toward the empty chair. ·

"I forbid it," the headmaster threatened.

"I'm fine standing, sir. Thank you," Henry said, still in shock.

The last ten minutes had been like something out of a bad dream. He'd passed the exam. Gotten into Knightley. But it didn't feel exciting or wonderful. It was horrible. Professor Stratford had practically been fired for helping him—and why? Because awful boys who didn't deserve to go to Knightley in the first place had been rejected. Henry didn't know what to think. He just knew that the conversation in this stifling room was far from finished.

"Now, Headmaster, was that really necessary?" Sir Frederick asked.

"It has nothing at all to do with you, Sir Examiner."

"Ah, but it does. I feel responsible. You are saying that the professor's teaching is at fault here, but did you ever consider that the fault might lie"—he paused—"in the exam?"

"The exam?" Headmaster Hathaway echoed.

"Yes, the exam. Perhaps the professor taught the boys extraordinarily well. But none of your students has passed the exam in five years, and surely Professor—Stratford, was it?—can't have been teaching here for more than a few years."

"Two years," the headmaster grumbled.

"So perhaps the exam is to blame, and *that* is why it's been so long since a Midsummer boy has passed."

Henry bit back a smile. He was certain the examiner wasn't saying what he really meant—that the exam was designed so that horrible boys like the ones at Midsummer would not pass, that none of them was chivalrous enough to gain acceptance to Knightley.

"Perhaps so," the headmaster begrudgingly agreed.

"Now, you've been headmaster here a long time, if my memory serves." Sir Frederick paused for just a tiny moment. "I'm sure a man as secure in his position as yourself would find no harm come to him if he showed a young colleague some compassion and offered him back his job."

"Professor Stratford has already resigned," the headmaster said. "It's in the past."

"The *recent* past," the examiner said.

"The *past*," Headmaster Hathaway corrected firmly.

"I see," the examiner replied, his tone implying that he didn't see at all. "Well, there is another matter on the table. Henry here."

"He. Is. Not. Going," the headmaster said.

"I'm afraid that isn't up to you, Headmaster. It's up to Henry. Henry, do you plan to reject my offer?"

Henry looked up, hardly daring to believe it. "No, sir, I don't."

"Clear as rain," Sir Frederick said. "Now, Headmaster, it appears the boy will indeed be attending Knightley. And so, if he's going to continue working here until the fall term, I wonder if you might afford him a few hours each evening to properly continue his studies? We wouldn't want him to fall behind."

"But he isn't a student!"

"You can bill Knightley Academy for his tutor. He *will* be needing a new one, now that our dear Professor Stratford has resigned."

"Bill . . . Knightley . . . tutor . . . I . . ." the headmaster stuttered.

"Yes?" the examiner urged.

"You're fired!" the headmaster shouted at Henry. *"Fired! Get Out!"*

"Now, that *really* isn't necessary," Sir Frederick soothed. "In fact, I think everything has gotten a bit out of hand."

"Six years!" the headmaster moaned. "For six years

now my boys have failed your ruddy exam, and a servant boy passes."

"An ex-servant," Henry said coldly. "Seeing as I've just lost my job."

Sir Frederick stood. "And, Headmaster, you might want to return to the dining hall. I believe the boys are waiting for you to end the morning announcements."

"What am I going to tell them?" the headmaster said with an odd little laugh, as though thinking aloud.

"What you wish," Sir Frederick said. "Come along, Henry. I believe we're finished here."

4

AN EXPLANATION,
OF SORTS

Upon the occasion of being called into the head-master's office, and especially upon the occasion of being fired from one's job, there is rarely a reason to rejoice. And yet, as Henry followed Sir Frederick down the narrow hallway with its flickering gas lamps and portraits of past headmasters, Henry certainly felt like rejoicing.

He was going to Knightley!

But . . . he was also fired, and worse, Professor Stratford was in trouble and it was all Henry's fault. Henry might never see his tutor again, never have the chance to thank him or to apologize.

"Sir? Where are we going?" Henry finally asked.

"To my room, so we can speak in private. I believe I owe you an explanation."

An explanation? As they walked, Henry's mind began to churn out possibilities of what Sir Frederick wanted to explain. Maybe—maybe Henry wouldn't be able to attend Knightley after all. That had to be it. Glumly, Henry followed Sir Frederick up the grand staircase and down the lavishly wallpapered East Corridor on the second floor. The East Wing rooms housed visiting scholars.

Sir Frederick's room was one that Henry had never before entered. It was a grand bedroom with an elegant four-poster bed, colorful tapestry rugs, large windows overlooking the front drive, and a marble mantelpiece.

Sir Frederick motioned toward two plush chairs on either side of the fireplace and Henry felt his cheeks redden.

"Is something the matter?" Sir Frederick asked, settling into one of the chairs.

"It's just . . ." Henry didn't know how to explain that members of the serving staff didn't usually sit down in the presence of a superior, much less across from them in comfortable, expensive chairs.

To his credit, Sir Frederick seemed to guess this. "Henry, please. You're going to be a knight. You'll have to stop acting like a serving boy sooner or later. Now sit."

Henry sank into the luxurious chair, his left leg bouncing nervously.

"I've promised you an explanation, my boy," Sir Frederick began, "and that will come in time. But no doubt you have questions, and we'll tackle those first. For all that you held your tongue in the headmaster's office, you seem an inquisitive sort. So ask away."

Henry stared at the examiner in disbelief. Of course he had questions. Come to think of it, he was bursting with them. But Henry was used to taking orders from adults, to being told things rather than given the opportunity to find them out himself. And so Henry asked his question, the one he had been wondering ever since the dining hall had gone silent a half hour earlier.

"Sir, am I truly to attend Knightley?"

"Of course," Sir Frederick assured him, as though it were the most natural thing in the world and not an exception that flew in the face of five hundred years' tradition.

Sir Frederick began patting the pockets of his pin-striped vest and pulled a carved wooden pipe out of his left hip pocket and a book of matches out of his right.

With the flare of a match, a bit of smoke, and a few contented puffs, the examiner leaned back in his chair, smiling at Henry.

"Anything else?"

Emboldened, Henry asked, "I don't suppose it's usual for you to allow *anyone* to take the exam—not just the students, I mean."

Sir Frederick smiled, and his eyes glazed over as though he were not staring at Henry through the haze of his pipe smoke, as though his thoughts were very far away indeed.

"No, not usual. But not unusual either. You see, my boy, this is my first time as an examiner. I'm the medicine master at Knightley, and the new headmaster wanted to appoint his own examiner from among the willing faculty members."

Henry frowned. He hadn't known that Sir Frederick was one of the schoolmasters—and of medicine, no less—but Sir Frederick hadn't answered his question at all.

"But—"

"But why, you mean?" Sir Frederick smiled wryly. "There *is* an explanation, you know. Quite simply, I grew up in a position similar to yours."

"*You* were a servant?"

Henry doubtfully scrutinized the examiner's well-cut suit and elaborately carved pipe, looking for traces of a kitchen boy or apprentice gardener.

"Similar, not identical," Sir Frederick conceded. "I was the chaplain's son at a respectable upper school, and they let me study there without fees, a sort of hanger-on student. In the evenings, I had to run school errands, and I lived with my father and not in the dormitory with the other boys. There was a famous exam at this school as well, for a prestigious scholarship to Camwell University. One of my schoolmasters wrote to the proctor and asked him if there mightn't be a loophole to allow me to sit the exam, even though I was not listed as a proper student on the school register. The proctor took pity, and I won the scholarship. Of course, this was many years ago, but I've always wanted to do the same for another boy."

"So that's why you said any *resident* of the school was eligible," Henry mused.

"Precisely," Sir Frederick agreed, puffing on his pipe only to realize that it had gone out while he spoke. With a shrug, he tucked the pipe back into a waistcoat pocket. "I thought there might be another charity boy allowed to sit in the backs of the classrooms, perhaps a sick matron's son or a cook's nephew."

"You wouldn't want Cook's nephew, sir," Henry said, trying not to grin at the thought of Sander becoming a knight. "I'm afraid he took sick at the pub last night."

Sir Frederick frowned for a moment, and then his face brightened. "You mean that older boy from breakfast who looked as though he had flu? Is *that* what was the matter with him?" Sir Frederick chuckled, delighted.

Henry stared at Sir Frederick, understanding what the examiner had wanted to explain: his past. And his motives for letting Henry take the exam.

Henry smiled weakly. A new thought was nagging at him, whispering doubt into the dark recesses of his mind: the students at Knightley would all be important. Elite. And Henry would still be Henry, a nobody orphan. They might treat him the way the Midsummer boys had when he had shown up to take the exam.

"Sir?" Henry asked. "What do you think it will be like for me at Knightley?"

"Academically," Sir Frederick said, "it's a difficult place, challenging for even the most disciplined scholars. That's not to say the lessons won't be fascinating, or even useful. But I'm certain you'll have no trouble keeping up and will probably earn good marks. The boys there are the best we can find from the country's finest schools, and perhaps you're worried whether or not they will accept you."

The examiner paused knowingly.

"In truth," he continued, "I don't know the answer to your question. The boys at Knightley are not cruel, but they are privileged, and they have a sense of entitlement and loyalty to their own kind. In order to protect the common good, you must consider yourself in a position elevated from that of a common citizen, and many of these boys have considered themselves thus elevated from birth. I don't think the other students will welcome you with open arms, but I don't think they'll treat you horribly either. Then again, chivalry can stretch only so far against the rigid structure of centuries-old tradition, even if this is a time of great change."

Henry nodded. Sir Frederick's answer had been honest.

"Everyone keeps saying that this is a time of great change, sir," Henry mused. "But do you truly believe it?"

Sir Frederick considered this, his brows furrowed together, and just when Henry thought Sir Frederick might not answer him at all, the examiner cleared his throat and said, "Equality is contagious. What Chancellor Mors has done will undoubtedly have irreversible echoes throughout the Isles, and perhaps not the echoes we immediately suppose. But you can't dwell on perhapses, Henry. You can only wait and see."

Wonderful, Henry thought. Another evasive answer, another adult afraid to speak the truth about everyone's fears, no matter how unfounded those fears might be. Wait and see. He could do that.

"Well, if equality is catching, it's too bad there won't be other boys with backgrounds like mine at Knightley," Henry said finally, reflecting on how much pressure was upon him to succeed, not just for himself but for boys in positions similar to his own who might be able to take the exam in the future.

In fact, Henry was so deeply caught up in his thoughts that he failed to notice a gleam in Sir Frederick's eye.

Five minutes later, Henry was running down the second-floor corridor when his feet slipped out from under him and he took a spectacular fall, landing facedown on a plush carpet.

"Ugh," Henry moaned, climbing to his knees.

"Servant boy," a voice drawled, and Henry looked

up to find Valmont and Harisford leaning against the striped wallpaper, holding a length of rope between them, with nasty, satisfied smiles on their faces.

Henry stood, resisting the urge to rub his sore knees and elbows. He wouldn't give Valmont the satisfaction.

"What do *you* want?" Henry grumbled.

He and Valmont were the same height, both of them tall for their age. Valmont glared, and Henry raised an eyebrow, waiting.

"Here, servant, I've spilled a glass of juice a ways down the corridor, so you should get the mop," Valmont said.

"I'm not a servant," Henry said, crossing his arms. "I don't work here anymore. So go clean it up yourself."

Henry shoved past Valmont and tried not to limp from his fall. After a couple of steps, Henry turned around. "I'll send you a letter from Knightley," he called, "to let you know what you're missing."

"Like you're really going," Valmont sneered.

"Why else would I be leaving the Knightley examiner's room just now?"

"Unclogging the toilet?" Valmont suggested. "You certainly smell like it."

"Well, if I do," Henry returned, "that's probably because I've just done *your* laundry."

Harisford snorted, and Valmont turned red.

"That was *my* place you took at Knightley, servant boy," Valmont mumbled, trying unsuccessfully to recover from Henry's verbal blow. "You took it from me, and you don't deserve it, and don't you think for a moment that I'll forget or let it drop."

Henry didn't dignify Valmont's empty threat with even the tiniest of responses. Instead, he turned the corner and took the stairs up one more level to the corridor where the schoolmasters kept their lodgings.

A door with a brass plaque that read JONATHAN STRATFORD, ENGLISH was ajar. Henry knocked, and then, without waiting for an answer, pushed the door open.

Professor Stratford's suitcase sat on his bed, and the professor stood over it, folding an armload of shirts and trousers.

"Hallo, Henry," Professor Stratford said, trying to smile cheerfully although he had just lost his job. "What did I miss?"

"I've been fired too," Henry said glumly, staring at his shoes.

"But what about Knightley?" the professor urged.

Henry looked up and allowed himself to smile. "I begin in August."

Professor Stratford let out a cheer, his armload of clothing tumbling into the suitcase in a wrinkled heap. "That's wonderful! Fantastic! Henry, you're going to be a knight!"

"I know," Henry said, closing the door. "But I've nowhere to go until the term starts, and Sir Frederick's worried that I won't get on with the other boys once they find out about my background."

"That's easily solved," Professor Stratford said, piling an armload of books into his suitcase.

"It is?"

"Certainly. I'm leaving on this afternoon's train bound for Hammersmith Cross Station to try and find work as a tutor. You could, er, I mean, you're welcome to join me."

Henry's face broke into a huge grin. Go to the City with Professor Stratford? Perhaps the next few months would not be so dark and doubtful after all!

"Let me just call a servant boy to pack my trunk and we'll depart directly," Henry joked, imitating a ridiculously posh accent.

But even though he'd meant it in jest, Henry couldn't

help thinking that his new classmates would have accents just like the one he had mocked and that, at the start of next school term, he *would* be in a position to order around servant boys.

Everything in his life was about to change—no, not about to; it already had. And so Henry climbed the rickety old stairs to his attic room and packed his few belongings into his falling-apart suitcase without a second thought to Sir Frederick's peculiar forecast.

5

ARRIVALS AND DEPARTURES

Henry stared out the window of their compartment, watching the grass-covered Cotswolds wobble past. Clutched in his fist was a rumpled ticket labeled *Midsummer Station–Hammersmith Cross Station*. He'd been on the train for two hours, and in just an hour more, he and Professor Stratford would reach the City.

Eight years had passed since Henry last left the town of Midsummer, and indeed, this was the only route he'd ever traveled. When Henry was six, his orphanage had taken a day trip to visit some museums and monuments in the City, and Henry, fascinated by a famous painting he'd once seen in a book, had been left behind.

A gentleman had mistaken Henry (with his threadbare coat and worn-thin shoes) for a beggar and given him a penny "so he mightn't go hungry." Embarrassed, lost, and afraid, Henry had sat down on the curb outside the museum and cried.

When Henry had looked up, a police knight stood over him, wearing a coat with buttons made of brass, a gleaming peacekeeper's sword at his side. The knight had bought Henry a hot cider to warm him up and helped him find the orphanage matron.

And now, eight years later, Henry was heading back toward the same city, no longer just a grubby orphan boy who lagged behind in the museum and got mistaken for a beggar but a soon-to-be student at Knightley. Perhaps one day *he* would be the kind face that comforted a lost boy, the honest police knight who settled a dispute between customer and shopkeeper, or the trusted guard of a member of the royal family. Perhaps even King Victor himself.

Next to Henry in the cramped train compartment, Professor Stratford dozed, chin tucked against his chest, a thick and scholarly book pages-down across his lap.

Henry turned his gaze back toward the passing landscape, watching the fields become smaller and the houses clump together as though they were afraid of open spaces. He watched the roads become more trafficked and the churches grow grander, with spires that seemed to stand on tiptoe, reaching toward the heavens like children stretching for the top shelf.

It was nearly six o'clock when the train shuddered into the station and Henry gently shook Professor Stratford awake.

"Kumquats or hobgoblins, please," Professor Stratford mumbled sleepily, and Henry bit back a laugh.

"Professor? We're here."

As if in agreement, the train's shrill whistle blew and a conductor out in the hall yelled, "Hammersmith Cross Station, end o' the line. All passengers alight here."

Professor Stratford gave an enormous and rather loud yawn, then lurched to his feet, eyes still half closed. In a sleepy stupor, he groped blindly in the air for his suitcase, which sat stubbornly out of his reach on the overhead rack.

Henry snorted with laughter. He'd seen Professor Stratford fall asleep at the High Table over a plate of jam and toast, but he had clearly underestimated the professor's ability to wake up and function. Rather, he had underestimated the *lag time* between the two.

Standing on tiptoe, Henry heaved both of their suitcases off the luggage rack and, with one in each hand, somehow managed to coax the professor out onto the platform.

As they stepped onto the platform and were jostled from all angles by the surging crowd, Professor Stratford came awake at last.

"Good heavens, Henry, you can't be carrying both suitcases? I'm awake. Here, hand me my bag."

Hefting his book-filled suitcase, Professor Stratford wove his way in the direction of a sign that helpfully read WAY OUT and depicted a pointing hand.

This sign led them into the station proper, which bustled with travelers. Henry and the professor threaded through the crowded, tunnel-shaped building, all the while following posted arrows that finally deposited them at a vast set of doors.

Outside, a line of hansom cabs stood at the curb.

"Where to, guv'nor?" a cabdriver asked Professor Stratford, politely doffing his cap to give a brief glimpse of his shiny bald head.

The professor gave an address and slid into the carriage, leaving his luggage on the curb. Sighing, Henry heaved the professor's bag into the back of the cab along with his own.

It was only when Henry climbed onto the cool bench seat next to Professor Stratford that he realized the cab-driver had been expected to handle their bags.

Reddening slightly, Henry stared out the window as the horse and driver jostled their way down the road. He'd never been in a carriage before, but that experience paled when compared with what he saw on the other side of the window.

Skinny town houses crowded together on opposite sides of narrow alleyways, their chimney tops nearly touching. And along the sidewalks: carts selling everything you could imagine, from wind-up toys to books so tiny they would fit in the palm of your hand to exotic-looking fruits and newspaper cones of fresh-roasted chestnuts. Carved wooden signs shaped like animals marked the entrances to darkened taverns, and ragged children played in the streets.

All too soon, the cab came to a stop. Henry looked around. They were in front of a pleasant four-story brick building with cheery red shutters and a dusty shop on the ground floor bearing a hand-lettered sign that read ALABASTER & SONS, PURVEYORS OF RARE BOOKS SINCE 1782.

"Where are we?" Henry asked.

"A shot in the dark, actually," Professor Stratford admitted, climbing out of the taxi. "After university, I rented a small flat above this bookshop for a summer. I was hoping it might be available."

Professor Stratford paid the driver and, with his suitcase banging purposefully against his leg, pushed open the door to the shop.

Mrs. Alabaster, the widow who ran the bookshop, did indeed have a set of rooms available on the third story that she'd be delighted to let out. Before Henry knew it, he'd been hired for the summer to help out in the shop and was unpacking his bags into a small wardrobe in his new room.

His room. For the first time, Henry had a room all to himself. It was an undreamt-of luxury. Between them, Henry and the professor shared a small washroom, two bedrooms, and a cramped sort of parlor. Never mind that the carpets smelled slightly of cats or that the wallpaper had begun to peel in the corners, to Henry, it was the finest flat he had ever seen.

And before he knew it, Henry came to think of the flat as his home. He and Professor Stratford settled into a routine: steaming mugs of tea together in the mornings during brief tutoring sessions, which always seemed to focus on history these days, and then Henry would spend his afternoons downstairs in the shop, cataloging, mending torn spines, helping customers, and often curling up in a threadbare armchair with any book he pleased. Professor Stratford found work tutoring a young woman who had just moved from abroad and had apparently learned everything backward and all wrong—she spoke of measurements in inches instead of centimeters and didn't understand Celsius at all.

In the evenings, Henry got to know the City: He learned the footpaths and alleyways, the hour at which the gaslights came on, and the moment when the baker down the road put fresh pastries on the counter. He learned the smell of the wharf and the sound of the bridge rising to let tall ships pass beneath, which parks were good for sitting and thinking, and which parks were good for losing one's wallet. He learned which alleyways led to the slums, and which to the darkened pubs where you could hire men to do anything for a price. He learned how to avert his eyes when ragged women begged for change in the streets, or the rouged ladies in low-cut gowns leered and called him "young master." He learned that the factories, more often than not, employed boys half his age for wages that oftentimes made petty theft their only option for survival. And he learned that fearful whispers about the Nordlands were not limited to the Midsummer School kitchen, and had their place among other dark legends—of knife-happy burglars and deranged murderers—in the city taverns.

But I would be a very bad narrator indeed if I led you to believe that the quiet life Henry and the professor shared in the City was without a very surprising interruption.

Curses, as you surely remember, are meant to be broken. And once they break, unlike satchel straps or pairs of spectacles, they do not need to be fixed. However, to break something has consequences, and curses are no exception.

The twelve trustees of Knightley Academy sat around a battered circular table, staring distastefully at their chipped teacups. Lord Winter was late, and until he arrived, the trustees couldn't start yelling at him. It is very difficult, you see, to yell at someone who isn't present.

Lord Winter hadn't meant to be late. In fact, he'd planned to be early, but that was before his daughter had shown up on the doorstep, kicked out of finishing school for the second time in three years.

"What was the problem *this* time, Francesca?" Lord Winter asked, frowning at his angelic-looking daughter.

"I'd rather not say."

Frankie grinned and, without waiting for a servant to help with her things, dragged her trunk along the once-grand carpet in the entryway.

"Careful!" her father warned.

"Of what?" Frankie snorted. "This ratty old rug? Be honest, Father, everything in this place is falling apart and worthless."

She abandoned her trunk in the middle of the foyer and swaggered into the parlor.

"It's like a furnace in here," Frankie complained, pushing up the sleeves of her traveling dress and collapsing into a wingback chair.

"Your mother loved this house," Lord Winter said forlornly, his voice scarcely more than a whisper.

Frankie sighed. It had been six years since her mother died of influenza. Six years since Lord Winter had become ill as well—with grief that turned into a permanent depression.

Frankie remembered many days during her childhood when her father did not stir from his bed and would not so much as lift a cup of tea to his lips. She remembered other days when he would seem to be perfectly fine, and then suddenly he wouldn't be. Lord Winter cried at the opera and the theater, and sometimes, he cried at the sight of cherry tarts, his wife's favorite. The tears collected in his ginger beard, and when Frankie hugged him, she used to think her father smelled of salt, like the sea.

During his depression, Lord Winter had badly managed his accounts, and their once lovely home fell into disrepair. While Frankie was off at various schools, learning how to curtsy and embroider, leaks sprang and were rarely patched, the garden became a snarl and soon a tangle, and as if in response, the manor slowly began to tilt, until Lord Winter's neighbors referred to the place as "that lopsided old manor house" behind the backs of their hands.

But these days, Lord Winter seemed depressed less and less frequently. In fact, he had applied for the headmastership of Knightley Academy when their grand chevalier announced he would be retiring just after his eighty-second birthday.

And now Lord Winter had made a mess of being headmaster barely two weeks into the summer. When Sir Frederick had sent a telegram with the scores from that beastly Midsummer School, Lord Winter had agreed to let him admit the servant boy with the startlingly high marks. After all, with a new headmaster, why shouldn't Knightley undergo some changes?

And then Lord Winter had started thinking. That servant, Harold or Henry or What-have-you, had been the first commoner allowed to take the exam. Perhaps there were more boys who would have scored just as high if they'd only had the chance to try.

There was no rule against letting common-born boys take the exam. Not expressly. It wasn't like he was over-throwing the monarchy by giving them the chance to try. After all, the academy reserved three places each year to admit late students, and after taking on the military history master's nephew, two late places still remained unfilled. But the trustees were in the other room, waiting to convey their dour disapproval.

The trustees! In all the excitement of his daughter's return, Lord Winter had forgotten the hour.

"Wait here," he instructed Frankie. "I'm late to meet with the Knightley trustees, and they'll likely hand me my head on a platter, but you and I aren't finished with this discussion."

"We aren't?" Frankie queried, raising an eyebrow.

"Because I can continue this talk on my own, thanks. 'Oh, Francesca, you're such a disappointment. Oh, Francesca, you're running out of schools to be kicked out of.' Believe me, Father, I've heard it all before."

Lord Winter resisted a very strong urge to sigh. "Just wait here," he instructed, striding purposefully toward the dining room and pushing open the vast carved doors.

"Terribly sorry, gentlemen, but something unexpected came up," Lord Winter said, taking his place in the only empty chair at the large round table.

"That's quite all right, Anthony," Sir Frederick said merrily, helping himself to another cup of tea.

But the others didn't share Sir Frederick's outlook. In fact, the looks on their faces were quite sour indeed.

"Come now, Lord Winter, *what* is the meaning of all this?" A particularly wizened old man asked, slamming a newspaper onto the table so forcefully that his teacup rattled in its saucer, sloshing cold tea over the side.

"Really, Lord Winter, *what* were you thinking?" another ancient gentleman asked, banging the table with his fist so that *his* teacup trembled in *its* saucer.

"I was thinking," Lord Winter said, raising a hand

for silence, "that the times are changing, and if we're not careful, Knightley could very well become a relic of the past. Look how few countries have held on to their history of training knights."

"Or held on to the notion of polite society at all," the man with the newspaper muttered to the gentleman on his left.

"This isn't about other countries," Sir Frederick put in. "It's about progress. You can't stand in the way of progress, gentlemen. I fully support Anthony's decision to admit a few common students. In fact, I've thought for some years now that Knightley could do with widening its applicant pool. Diversifying and all that."

"Next thing, he'll suggest we abolish the aristocracy, like Mors did in the Nordlands," muttered the man with the newspaper again to the gentleman on his left.

"This isn't about the *Nordlands*, Lord Ewing," Lord Winter said sharply. "Truly, it *isn't*. You greatly throw off the proportions of what we're trying to accomplish. I'm not saying that we do away with our class system, but merely that you allow this one opportunity for a few worthy commoners to better the lot they've been cast. Surely even *you* can't see any harm in that."

"You'd understand where Anthony is coming from

if you'd met the boy from Midsummer," Sir Frederick put in.

"Ah, yes, that ghastly servant we've taken as a pupil," Lord Ewing said, drumming his fingers on the newspaper.

"He speaks five languages with remarkable fluency, and they kept him in the kitchen washing dishes," Sir Frederick said. "What a waste of talent! He'd be there still if I hadn't let him take the exam. And that 'ghastly servant,' as you call him, managed to earn the highest score that we've seen in five years."

A few of the men seated around the table exchanged glances; they'd heard that some servant had passed the exam, but they'd never dreamed that the boy had beaten every other student at Knightley.

But still, one could always be counted as a fluke. What would people think if they let *more* commoners into the academy?

"Everyone is so sensitive toward change these days," Lord Winter pointed out. "But have you ever stopped to think that this might give people hope that the turn of the century is nothing to fear? That it may, in fact, bring more good than harm?"

"I still don't like this," Lord Ewing conceded. "But

so long as these common boys score well on our exam, I propose we see what happens when they actually *attend* Knightley. If they succeed, then perhaps you men might be right about letting anyone take the exam next year. But if they fail, this year's 'progress,' as you put it, is an experiment we won't be repeating in my lifetime. If they *fail*, Lord Winter, you'd better not become too comfortable with your new job."

After Henry and Professor Stratford had been in the city for two weeks, there was a most curious edition of the evening post.

As Henry walked back toward the bookshop after delivering a parcel of encyclopedias, he ran into a newsboy selling penny posts with the cry of "Extra! Extra! Knightley Academy now admitting commoners!"

Henry bought a paper and unfolded it where he stood, scanning the article in disbelief.

The newsboy hadn't lied. In the wake of admitting their first common student, "a member of the serving staff at a local boys' school who had been allowed to sit the exam along with the school's pupils," Knightley Academy was administering their exam to any fourteen-year-old boys who wished to take it, regardless of social standing. In three days, all desiring applicants would report to the Royal Museum for the examination, and the two boys with the highest scores would be admitted.

According to Lord Anthony Winter, the newly appointed grand chevalier of Knightley Academy, "Perhaps this adaptation of centuries-old tradition is precisely the 'common' denominator that Knightley needs in these changing times. Here's to new tradition, and to progress!"

Henry tucked the newspaper under his arm and turned down one of the shortcut alleyways that led from the high street to his flat, his cheeks burning in embarrassment. People all over the country would be reading about him in their newspapers, and true, they wouldn't know his name, but there he was, immortalized in print— *a member of the serving staff.*

None of the other boys who had passed the Knightley Exam that year was mentioned in the article. No, it had just been him. Already singled out. Already different.

Henry sighed, walking the familiar cobblestones

that led back to the bookshop. At least he wouldn't be the only commoner at Knightley—that was good news. There would be two others with whom he could share the experience, with whom he could become friends if the other boys were as haughty as he feared. It was a relief, and yet, it also held the capacity to go terribly, horribly wrong.

Perhaps the two boys would become fast friends when they took the exam together, and then Henry would spend the next four years as a permanent outsider, unable to gain the most crucial acceptance of all—that of potential friends. Henry hadn't wanted to be the only boy with his background at Knightley, but then again, he hadn't expected *not* to be either. Now he didn't know *what* to expect.

When Henry arrived back at the flat, he found Professor Stratford curled in his favorite chair, peering at an article in a gossip magazine. A copy of the evening post lay open on the nearby credenza, rumpled and probably read cover to cover, per usual.

"Back already?" Professor Stratford murmured, frowning at the magazine. He glanced up at Henry, then grinned.

"No, actually, I'm not here at all. You're merely imagining my presence," Henry joked.

"Am I? Pity. My imagination could be put to *such* better use."

"Oh, very funny." Henry rolled his eyes.

The professor mock scowled, and then grinned. "It's a good thing you're home early. I've just received some exciting news."

Henry sank into the plush armchair across from Professor Stratford, wondering if this was going to be another of the professor's inane jokes.

"Well?" Henry urged.

"I've accepted a new job. A more permanent one."

Henry's face fell. This was no joke at all—in fact, it was horribly serious. Henry knew what this meant; Professor Stratford was leaving. Soon. They'd say good-bye and promise to write, and before Henry knew it, he would be alone in the City, living by himself in this drafty old flat for the rest of the summer, with no one to quell his nerves or assure him that everything would turn out all right at Knightley.

"Congratulations." Henry's mouth was so dry that he nearly choked on the word.

"Thanks, awfully," the professor said, ignoring Henry's dejection. "Sir Frederick just sent a telegram.

You remember him—the Knightley examiner? Apparently Lord Winter's daughter will be staying at home and will require a tutor this year, and Sir Frederick put in a few good words on my behalf."

Henry shook his head slightly, trying to clear it. Surely he'd misunderstood . . .

"Wait, so that means you'll be—"

"—putting my diplomas to good use teaching a fifteen-year-old girl how to conjugate French verbs and recite poetry?"

"—coming with me to Knightley?"

"Oh, that? Unfortunately." The professor rolled his eyes and shrugged, but a telltale corner of his lip twitched as he held back a smile. "Isn't it quite the tragedy? I knew you'd be disappointed."

Henry couldn't help grinning. Professor Stratford was going to be there, at Knightley. Henry wouldn't be alone after all. Everything would turn out all right.

And as if the professor could read Henry's mind, he said, "It's a curious thing, change. You never get used to it, and you're never sure where it comes from, but you better learn to expect it."

"I don't recognize the quotation." Henry frowned, trying to place it.

"That's because it isn't one. It is simply advice, and advice you'd be well advised to take, especially now."

"So that means you've heard? About Knightley admitting two more common students?" Henry asked.

"Oh, that." The professor was suddenly fascinated by his dented old pocket watch. "I seem to recall reading something about that in today's paper. Terribly boring article, wouldn't you say? Absolutely nothing at all to do with the two of us."

"I could barely force myself to skim it," Henry said, playing along.

"Bet you're glad they didn't mention your name, though," the professor said, suddenly serious.

Henry sighed, flopping back in his chair. "Because then it would have been *more* embarrassing, you mean? Why did they single me out like that?"

"Rags-to-riches stories, my boy. That's what everyone wants to read. It gives them hope."

"If you ask me, it's no better than those silly gossip magazines, planting seeds of ideas in people's heads that sprout into awful rumors."

"Better to know where the rumors start than believe those who tell them to you," the professor said with a wink, holding up his magazine. "But as to your new-found fame"—the professor smiled as Henry pulled a face—"at least now everything's out in the open. The other students at Knightley know your background. There's nothing to hide. And you'll have two other boys in a similar situation. Not a bad bargain."

"Everything's a bad bargain if you never meant to gamble in the first place," Henry mock grumbled, and then he rolled his eyes. "Oh, Lord. Now you have me doing it too."

But the professor was right. Henry wouldn't have to pretend or explain himself to the other students at Knightley. Everything did seem to be working out for the best, which was a new sensation for Henry.

But for reasons he couldn't explain, the back of his neck still prickled when he thought of the whispers he sometimes overheard during his walks through the City. Perhaps, even though he did not recognize it, he knew, deep down, that a man as learned as Professor Strat-ford could not be reading those inane gossip magazines purely for amusement, and that it was no error how his lessons now centered on history, particularly that of the last hundred years. No, everyone was hungry for news, and not of the rags-to-riches variety. But in that moment, news of Knightley's new policy was all they had, and it would have to suffice.

6

THE CODE OF
CHIVALRY

I t is a truth universally acknowledged that the problem
with new shoes is that they are never as comfortable
as the ones they are meant to replace. But Henry
hadn't known this. After all, he'd never had a pair of
new shoes before.

Trying not to wince as the backs of his new boots
chafed against his open blisters, Henry hobbled through
Hammersmith Cross Station. His new suitcase banged
against the leg of his new trousers, and his new haircut
felt too short, leaving the back of his neck exposed.

Professor Stratford had left three days earlier to
get settled in with his latest pupil, and so Henry had
locked up their flat, returned the key, and found his

own way to the station on a crowded omnibus.

"Look at you!" old Mrs. Alabaster had clucked over Henry not fifteen minutes earlier. She'd exclaimed over his pressed gray trousers with the first-year yellow piping down the sides, his crisp white shirt, his yellow-and-white-striped tie, and his navy blue formal jacket, done in a military cut, with brass buttons, a white braid at the left shoulder, and the school crest sewn over the right breast pocket, bearing the silhouette of an old-fashioned knight with a lance, seated upon a prancing horse. Henry carried the boxy, stiff-brimmed ceremonial school cap under one arm, as it was possibly the most unflattering piece of clothing he'd ever owned—and that was saying something.

When Henry looked in the mirror that morning, he'd hardly recognized himself. As per the admittance letter Sir Frederick had given him, Henry was to arrive at Hammersmith Cross Station on the fifteenth of August to take the ten o'clock train to Knightley Academy, and to arrive in formal school uniform (which could be purchased, along with a regulation blazer and scarf, from a specialty shop on Bond Street), unless he desired to arrange private transportation to the school, in which case he should telegram in advance.

And so, there he was, at a quarter to ten, receiving the strangest looks from the other people in the station who scurried past, some of their faces downright fearful—no doubt they had all read that week's *Tattleteller*.

But because of his new uniform, the crowds parted for Henry—almost respectfully, he thought—and a little boy holding his mother's hand had paused for a moment to stare. Oddest of all, when Henry stopped to ask a police knight where he might find platform three, he was met with a salute.

"Oh, er," Henry said, raising his left hand to his eyebrow in an awkward approximation.

The police knight chuckled. "Yellow tie, of course! You'll be a first year, then, am I right?"

"Yes, sir," Henry said.

"Well, good luck. You'll want the platform just past that newsstand there." The police knight pointed. "Perhaps best to buy something to eat on the train. Nerves always made me hungry when I was your age."

"Thank you, sir. I think I will."

"And next time I see you, you'd better have learned a proper salute," the police knight called after him.

With the dregs of his money, Henry bought a few apples from the newsstand and couldn't help glancing at the *Tattleteller*'s headline. Only yesterday, the gossip rag had taunted the city with another unconfirmed rumor: CHANCELLOR MORS DECLARES EDUCATION "FOR MALES ONLY!" Of course it couldn't be true. Girls had to be allowed in schools. How else would they learn the skills they needed to attract prospects for marriage, or how to manage households once they had married? Henry didn't believe it, and he stared sourly at the front-page headline as he took his change from the vendor. As Henry searched for a place to stow his apples (eventually using his hat as a basket), he noticed that a lot of the shabbier passengers in the station, the ones who looked so jittery and fearful, carried copies of the tabloid tucked under their arms.

For pity's sake! Henry thought, clutching his hatful of apples. Some people will believe *anything.* Finally, at five minutes until ten, Henry took a deep breath, tightened his grip on his suitcase, and walked through the archway that led to platform three.

"All aboard," the conductor yelled, clanging a handbell. "Ten o'clock express to Knightley Academy, Avel-on-t'Hems."

The platform bustled with students and their families, all saying stiff, last-minute good-byes. Henry hurried past the happy families and bland butlers (none of whom carried that silly magazine, he noticed), pretending he didn't care that he was on his own, as always. Finally, Henry found an open door and presented himself to the conductor.

"Yellows're in the last two cars," the conductor grumbled, jerking his thumb in the proper direction.

Henry nodded and ducked into the last car, hoping for an empty compartment. He stuck his head into one just as the whistle blew and the train lurched out of the station.

"Hello," Henry said, as there were two boys already seated inside.

"Hallo there," the tall blond boy said, grinning amiably. "I daresay we're a bit full already, but nonetheless, a pleasure to make your acquaintance."

The blond boy stuck out his hand, which glinted with the delicate gold of a signet ring.

"I'm Henry Grim," Henry said, giving the boy's hand a firm shake.

"Theobold Archer IV." Theobold pompously returned Henry's handshake. "You've got an interesting surname there. Any relation to the Brothers Grimm?"

"I'm not really sure," Henry said truthfully, surveying the overhead rack only to find it already crammed with both boys' bags. Stowing his suitcase at his feet, Henry sat down next to the other boy.

"Edmund Merrill," the boy mumbled without looking up from the magazine he was reading.

"His brother's in third year with mine," Theobold said, as though storklike Edmund needed explaining. "So, Grim, you must tell me, I'm terribly interested to know, what school are you coming from?"

"Er, Midsummer," Henry said. "But—"

"Midsummer? But that's brilliant! You lot *never* make it into the academy. Or, at least, that's what I've heard." Theobold leaned in and lowered his voice to a conspiratorial whisper. "So, Grim, what do you make of the school letting in commoners this year? I gather it's some sort of stunt from the new headmaster, but no matter; we should be able to spot them easily, eh?"

"How do you figure that?" Henry asked, watching the outer reaches of the city fly past outside the large window. It was just his luck to have picked this compartment, he thought glumly.

"'Ent you never 'eard a com'nor talk?" Theobold mocked. "Or something like that. At least, that's how the staff at the Easton School sounded."

Easton. Henry was impressed in spite of himself. And he hardly needed more clues to piece together Theobold's background. The family ring, the toff accent, the brother already at Knightley, and now Easton School; Theobold was practically royalty.

At that moment, a knock sounded on the compartment door.

"Come in," Henry called, thankful for the interruption.

The door opened to reveal a boy with a thin, pale face topped by a cloud of brown curls.

"Oh, great, even here's full," the boy complained, offering an apologetic grin.

"Listen, chap, the rear compartments are bound to be empty," Theobold said, his gaze lingering on an unusual necklace charm that glittered beneath the boy's tie.

"What a party for me, an empty compartment," the boy said, his smile wavering.

"I say, what's that on your head?" Theobold asked, narrowing his eyes.

The boy clapped his hand to the top of his head as if embarrassed.

Henry stood up.

"There's no room for my suitcase in this compartment anyway. I'll join you in the rear," Henry said.

"Really, Grim, you should stay," Theobold said. "There's no need to keep Mr.—I'm sorry, I've not caught your name—company."

"Beckerman," the boy said, sliding his hand back down to his side.

Theobold's eyes narrowed into even smaller slits.

"Right guv'nor, I'll be takin' my leave 'bout now," Henry said in his best impression of a city cabdriver. Hefting his suitcase, Henry followed the boy called Beckerman out into the narrow hallway.

"What was that about?" the boy asked.

"I'll tell you later. I'm Henry, by the way. Henry Grim."

"Adam Beckerman. Do you really think it's empty in the back?"

"Possibly," Henry said, following Adam, who had some kind of small, flat circular hat on top of his head.

"Well, that wasn't the most polite greeting I've ever received," Adam said wryly, stumbling a little as the train lurched forward.

"Unfortunately, he took to me quite well." Henry rolled his eyes. "Probably would've booted me from the compartment once he realized I was one of those 'ghastly common students,'" he finished, performing an impression of Theobold's uppity accent.

Adam chuckled. "That's not bad, Grim. So you're the servant boy from the newspaper?"

"That would be me."

"I'm, well, obviously I'm one of the students who were admitted late. The other boy looked a decent sort as well. Indian bloke."

They reached the back of the car, and Adam flung open the door to the right rear compartment.

"Ahh, glorious space," Adam said, heaving his two bags inside and onto the luggage rack. "Here, Grim, hand me yours. . . . Cripes it's heavy."

"Books," Henry admitted sheepishly.

"No kidding? Which ones?"

"Mostly classics, but a few detective stories. I worked in a bookshop all summer."

Adam hauled Henry's bag onto the rack, and then collapsed onto the bench. "Your summer sounds loads better than mine," he said. "I had to do accounting for my father."

Henry looked up in surprise. "Your father's a banker?"

Adam smiled. "Of course. What'd you think, I come from a family of costermongers down at the wharf?"

"I hadn't really thought about it at all, to tell the truth," Henry admitted. "I don't actually know anyone who's . . ."

"Jewish?" Adam supplied.

Henry reddened. Was he so obvious?

"Don't worry about it," Adam said with a chuckle. "You're not from the City, I take it."

Henry shook his head. "The Midl'lands. Midsummer."

"I've heard of it. They have that awful school there, the one full of snobbish boys who never get into Knightley."

"That's where I worked."

"Didn't you go to school?"

"Not really, no," Henry said, grabbing two apples out of his hat and tossing one to Adam.

Adam smiled his thanks, shined the apple on his sleeve, and then took a bite. "But you passed the exam." *Crunch.* "Whatcha mean, 'no'?"

And so Henry explained. He told Adam about his life at the orphanage, the job at the Midsummer School, Professor Stratford, the exam, and getting fired. While Henry talked, the boys polished off an apple apiece. Then it was Adam's turn. He told Henry about his father and brother being bankers, and how he'd secretly switched his extra math lesson at school for the fencing elective. Adam hated mathematics. He hated numbers and ledgers and everything about banking. He'd taken the Knightley Exam without telling his parents, and when he got in, they'd had no choice but to let him go.

"The way I see it, Grim," Adam said cheerfully, "is that *you're* at Knightley to find your life, and *I'm* here to run away from mine."

Henry didn't deny it. And when the train pulled into the Avel-on-t'Hems station an hour later, the boys had become fast friends.

Knightley Academy didn't look like an elite school for young aristocrats. In fact, it rather reminded Henry of a ramshackle country estate built by a slightly eccentric duke. The buildings were a mishmash of styles: flying buttresses topped with thatch, turrets on innocent-looking wooden cottages, mansard roofs, and ivy-covered brick, all connected by a series of cobblestone paths that threaded through a grassy quadrangle complete with an absurd hedge maze that came only waist high.

Henry and the other first years were crowded together in an echoing, tapestry-hung chamber outside the doors to the Great Hall. Servants wearing Knightley school livery had met them at the station and taken their bags, and Henry had felt disoriented playing the role of the student for the first time in his life. The disorientation, Henry noted, staring nervously at a bleak battle scene depicted on one of the centuries-old tapestries, still hadn't fully left.

"Hey, Grim," Adam said, nudging Henry in the side. "What do you think is going on?"

"Haven't a clue," Henry whispered nervously, and at that moment, the vast carved doors were flung open.

A tall, pallid gentleman in an impeccable tweed suit surveyed Henry and the other first years, his enormously bushy eyebrows knitted together in a frown. The man wore a master's cap and gown, and his jaw was peppered with dark stubble. This was a man, Henry thought, who wouldn't be caught dead believing anything printed in a tabloid magazine.

"I am Lord Havelock," the man barked, his voice stern and deep, as if daring any of the boys to whisper. "I am master of military history, and head of your year. If there are any problems, you will be dealing with me. I trust you boys won't be *too* much trouble, but then again, I am often accused of being an overly optimistic man."

Lord Havelock clasped his hands behind his back and once again glowered at the first years in what Henry was already starting to think of as the Havelook of Doom.

"Now," Lord Havelock continued, "I am about to ask you to step into the Great Hall and sign the school's Code of Chivalry. This is a code of honor that you must not break without expecting to suffer great consequences. If you do not wish to sign, simply hand me your pen and you will be sent home on the next train. If you *do* wish to sign, your signature is a solemn vow to live your life here at Knightley according to the Code. Stealing, lying, cheating, wandering the corridors after curfew, and dishonoring schoolmasters are grounds for instant expulsion. As first years, you are also restricted from having female visitors other than members of your direct family, especially in your rooms. Do not test me, gentlemen. I have *excellent* powers of deduction."

With a final Havelook of Doom, Lord Havelock snapped for the boys to follow, and turned on his heel, gown billowing behind him as he strode away.

Henry shuffled along with the crowd of students, his stomach a reservoir of nerves. Lord Havelock was not a man whose bad side Henry ever wanted to see. And yet, something told him it was inevitable.

But Henry's misery was quickly forgotten once he got a look at the Great Hall. The hall was incredible, at least twice the size of the Great Hall back at the Midsummer School. The walls, made of thick wooden paneling, held flickering gaslight sconces and ancient shields that bore the liveries of legendary noble lineages. An immense fireplace almost as large as the doorway loomed at the far end of the hall, with two jousting lances crossed above the mantle. And carved into the mantelpiece was the inscription: *A true knight is fuller of bravery in the midst, than in the beginning, of danger.*

The quotation sounded like something Professor Stratford would have said, and the thought of him so close by, settling into his rooms in the headmaster's manor house, lessened Henry's anxiety.

"Hey, Grim," Adam whispered. "Spot your family's crest on the wall yet?"

Henry rolled his eyes. "No, but I've spotted *yours*, I think: that water stain in the corner, there?"

Adam snorted.

"When I call your name," Lord Havelock barked, startling the boys into attention, "step forward and take the pen. Read the code and sign your name upon the scroll if you intend to become a knight."

Lord Havelock stood next to the High Table, having just removed an old-fashioned quill and inkpot from a fold in his master's gown.

"Theobold Archer IV," Lord Havelock called, and Theobold strode pompously forward, received the quill and ink with a slight bow, and stepped to the table, where he skimmed and promptly signed the Code of Chivalry.

"Adam Beckerman," Lord Havelock called, and a fair amount of boys nudged one another and whispered as Adam stepped forward with his chin held high and his small circular hat (he'd told Henry on the train that this was called a yarmulke) clearly visible.

After Adam, a number of other boys were called forward without event. Lord Havelock deliberately wasn't using courtesy titles, no doubt to move the process along faster, and Henry was grateful. He didn't think he could take it if he had to listen to every boy's proper station, a constant reminder of his own lowly status and how undeserving he was to be here alongside these young aristocrats.

Henry's mouth went dry when Lord Havelock called his name, but no one took any special notice of him. Heart pounding, Henry took the quill and ink, smiling his thanks. Yet when he looked up, Lord Havelock's face was contorted into an expression of sheer loathing.

Trying to convince himself that he had imagined the look on Lord Havelock's face, or at least that it hadn't been directed toward himself, Henry approached the High Table. Unrolled on the table was a thick sheet of parchment paper bearing the inscription:

Hear Ye, All Who Would Become Men of Honor,
Sons of Chivalry:
The path you boys intend to take,
Is rewarding, yes, but with much at stake:
For if your honor durst to stray,
In any moment of any day,
Then of this warning, please take heed,
Or else suffer consequences unpleasant indeed.
A knight is a peer to honor bound
Whose fears dare not to make a sound.
With words suffused in honesty
And deeds steeped long with chivalry,
A knight defends those in need
Whether of common or noble breed.
And on this day an oath I swear
This Code of Chivalry henceforth I bear.

Taking a deep breath, Henry touched his quill to the parchment and signed his name.

Henry couldn't help but grin as he rejoined the crowd of boys. Suddenly, Lord Havelock's imposing manner did not seem nearly as frightening, nor the recent tabloid headlines anything more than preposterous. After all, look where he, Henry, had wound up. At Knightley Academy, in the finest set of clothing he had ever owned, a proper student bound to a code of chivalry and on his way to becoming a knight.

Henry glanced toward Adam, who stood, hands in his pockets, watching the next boy approach the parchment.

When Lord Havelock called "Rohan Mehta" and a proud boy with brown skin and dark flashing eyes stepped forward to regally receive the quill and ink, Adam grinned.

"Like I said, Indian bloke."

Henry nodded, curious as to Rohan's story. In fact, he was so lost in supposing that he almost missed Lord Havelock call the final student's name.

"Fergus Valmont," Lord Havelock said with an indulgent smile.

Henry couldn't believe it. But sure enough, he would

recognize that swagger anywhere. Valmont, Henry's tormentor from the Midsummer School who had failed the exam despite boasting of his family's connections, snatched the quill from Lord Havelock. And with a nasty sneer in Henry's direction, Valmont signed his name to the parchment without even bothering to read the message.

7

SERVANTS AND SCHOLARS

The ink had scarcely dried on the *Code of Chivalry* before Lord Havelock hurried the boys off to their new lodgings. The First Year Corridor, with its adjoining common room, was just a short ways from the Great Hall. Henry and the other first years squeezed through the narrow hallway, which was made even slimmer by the antique suits of armor that stood at attention between every flickering sconce.

"Your lodgings have already been assigned," Lord Havelock barked, and although he had not turned around, his voice echoed off the polished armor and filled the hallway. "There will be no room changes, not even trading among yourselves. As first years, your doors do not lock. Curfew is ten o'clock, lights at a quarter past."

Lord Havelock came to a halt with no warning, then turned on his heel to glare at the lot of them, and the boys at the front of the crowd nearly jumped backward to avoid a collision. Behind Lord Havelock was a shabby sort of corridor lined with brass-knobbed doors. Each door bore a plaque engraved with the names of its occupants.

"You may not, under any circumstances," Lord Havelock said, as though suspecting that they already had, "decorate your doors, rearrange the furniture, disrespect the housekeeping staff, make excessive noise, or neglect to keep your property clean and neat. My own chambers are at the end of the corridor, next to the bath. Bear in mind that I sleep—"

"In a coffin," Adam murmured, and Henry, despite his worries about Valmont, had to stifle a laugh.

"—lightly, and do not appreciate being disturbed or woken for any reason short of an emergency," Lord Havelock continued. "The bells will ring half an hour before the evening meal. Supper is formal, and tardiness, for whatever reason—"

"Short of an emergency," Adam whispered, and again, Henry bit his tongue.

"—will not be tolerated. That is all, gentlemen."

Lord Havelock—his gown billowing behind him in a way that, now that Henry thought about it, did make one wonder if he slept in a coffin—marched toward an elaborately carved doorway at the end of the corridor. The door slammed behind him, the lock clicking into place.

Collectively, the boys relaxed. And then they all raced down the corridor, looking at the names on the doors.

Henry stayed back by the archway that led to the threadbare common room, watching the others find their rooms. He was so overwhelmed that he could scarcely think. And yet, the one thought that surfaced was a desperate, last-minute wish: *Please let my roommate be anyone besides Fergus Valmont, anyone besides Valmont . . .*

"You coming, Grim?" Adam asked. "Got to figure out which room we'll be sharing."

"How do you reckon, sharing?" Henry asked.

"Well, it's obvious they've put us together. I mean, do you honestly think Theobold Archer IV would share a room with *me*?"

Henry sighed in relief. Of course Adam was right.

But there was just one problem: out of the fourteen

rooms, many had plaques that bore the name of a single student, and a good number bore two names, but not one of them said "Henry Grim" or "Adam Beckerman."

The corridor was emptying now as the other boys disappeared into their rooms, shaking hands with a new roommate or checking to make sure all of their bags had arrived safely.

"Do you think they've forgotten us?" someone asked, and Henry and Adam turned.

Rohan Mehta stood, arms crossed, in the center of the hallway.

"I expect so," Henry said miserably.

This was even worse than rooming with Valmont. Henry's mind churned with possibilities of what was going to happen next: they'd have to live in the servants' quarters or on a corridor with bullying fourth years or be sent home because there wasn't enough space.

"Well, this certainly won't do," Rohan said, and with his chin in the air, he strode confidently toward Lord Havelock's door and knocked sharply.

The door clicked open.

"My, my, emergencies *do* happen quickly." Lord Havelock glared. "*Who* has died?"

Rohan went pale, but he swallowed and bravely said,

"No one, sir. However, the three of us have not been assigned rooms. I trust there is a good reason."

Henry and Adam exchanged a look of shock. Rohan's accent was unbelievably upper-crust, but even more surprising was how he faced Lord Havelock without fear.

Lord Havelock also seemed taken aback, but he reached into a fold of his master's gown and produced a small, grubby plaque.

"I'm afraid your nameplate was ordered late, and arrived only this morning," Lord Havelock said, brushing past them. "And here we are, *gentlemen*. Your chambers."

Lord Havelock stopped at a shabby wooden door across from the common room. It was not a grand door—the wood had gone warped in places, and the doorknob was made of unfinished wood rather than shining brass. Henry would have thought it was a broom cupboard if he had noticed it, but it was not a very noticeable sort of door.

Lord Havelock tacked the plaque—rather crookedly, in fact—to the door and, with a cold smile, turned on his heel and returned to his chambers.

"Shall we?" Adam asked, hand on the doorknob.

It wasn't so bad. This was Henry's first thought as he surveyed the room. Certainly it was a bit cramped with three beds, desks, and chairs—none of which matched. But the far wall held a lovely large latticed window that looked out onto an expanse of lawn and, in the distance, the limestone walls of the headmaster's house. Unfinished wooden beams sloped overhead, angling to the right, where a battered wardrobe had been wedged, rather exactly, into the space between the floor and the ceiling.

"The bed on the right is mine," Adam called, flopping onto the down-filled coverlet nearest to the window.

Henry and Rohan stared at each other with polite smiles until Henry motioned toward the two remaining beds and asked, "Which would you prefer?"

"I'll take the one on the left, thank you," Rohan said, but remained standing. "It's frankly a disgrace the way they're treating the three of us, and I have a mind to write home about it. If you've noticed, our things have yet to arrive."

And then, as if in answer to Rohan's complaint, there was a timid knock on the door.

"Come in," Rohan called imperiously.

A serving boy of about their age ducked his head respectfully and said, "I've brought yer bags, if you'd please t'let me bring 'em inside?"

"Of course," Rohan said. "You can set my trunk at the foot of my bed and my valise next to the wardrobe."

"Ver' good, sir," the boy said, and then looked to Henry and Adam.

"Oh, er, anywhere's fine," Henry said, his cheeks flushing. He didn't think he'd ever get used to giving orders. "And, uh, sorry it's so heavy."

"'S quite alrigh', sir," the boy said, struggling with Rohan's trunk.

Adam swung his feet over the side of his bed.

"I can get my own," he said, disappearing for a moment into the hallway and returning with his suitcase.

The serving boy grunted with the effort of dragging Rohan's trunk along the floor beams.

Rohan, arms still folded, merely stood and watched.

"Here, let me help," Henry said, grabbing one end of the trunk. The serving boy stared at Henry in shock.

"Ugh, this is even heavier than mine," Henry said, shoving the trunk into place.

As the serving boy tackled Rohan's valise, Henry retrieved his own bag from the hallway and tossed it onto his bed.

"That will be all, thank you," Rohan told the serving

boy, reaching into his pocket and flipping him a coin.

"Yessir," the boy said with a grin, giving a proper bow this time as he closed the door.

Henry opened his suitcase and hung his spare uniform, blazer, and scarf in the wardrobe. He was so curious about Rohan that he could hardly stand it. The other "common" student didn't seem common at all. And the way Rohan had tipped the boy for bringing his bags, as though he had always done that sort of thing, as though he had the sort of pocket money that never ran short at the end of the week . . .

"You from the City, mate?" Adam asked.

"No, but we keep a house there for the Season," Rohan said, staring at his trunk as though he expected it to unpack itself.

Henry met Adam's glance and shrugged, as if to say, I dunno either.

"Yeah, so, don't take this the wrong way or anything," Adam said cheerfully, folding together two mismatched socks from his luggage, "but I was sort of wondering about the accent and the, uh, 'house for the Season' and all that."

Rohan, with an audible sigh, unzipped his valise and extracted a small set of leather-bound books.

"Well, I was adopted after my mother died," Rohan said, placing his books on the least battered of the desks. "She'd been the housekeeper for an English couple, and they had no children of their own. I was just a baby, so they couldn't very well pack me off to an orphanage."

No, Henry thought, somewhat bitterly, *of course they couldn't.* As soon as he'd thought it, Henry was ashamed. It was just that . . . he wasn't sure he liked Rohan all that much. It was clear that Rohan felt he was being treated far beneath his station.

"So did they send you off to Easton and all that?" Adam asked.

Rohan's cheeks flushed dark, and Henry realized that all of Rohan's confidence and pride had been a mask, which had just slipped.

"No, actually. My father, er, thought it best for me to have private tutors because . . ."

Because no respectable school would take an Indian boy, no matter who had raised him, Henry said to himself. At least, that had been true until now, until anyone was allowed to take the Knightley Exam.

Well, that explained everything. Rohan had never been away to school before, or been around other boys his age. He'd thought they would treat him according to his father's status, and it had been a bit of a nasty shock when they hadn't done. Henry was almost sympathetic toward his regal new roommate.

"Blimey!" Adam exclaimed. He'd wandered over to have a look at Rohan's books and was pointing at the gold-leaf library crest on the front cover. "Your father's the duke of Holchester?"

Rohan ducked his head but didn't deny it.

Well, Henry thought, *at least I let him choose beds first.*

When the bells rang, signaling a half hour until supper, Henry's stomach lurched—not out of hunger but habit. At the Midsummer School for Boys, this was when he'd dash down to help Cook in the kitchens, staggering under the hot, heavy serving platters, eating only when everyone else had finished and long after the food had gone cold.

Now, for the first time, the half-hour bells meant something different: comb your hair, straighten your tie, and for God's sake, don't embarrass yourself. Because Henry's place was no longer in the kitchen, it was at the table.

There were four long tables in the Great Hall, one for each year of students, and a High Table for the professors and headmaster.

The first years, terrified by Lord Havelock's warning that tardiness would not be tolerated, had arrived early. Gradually, the older students trickled in, laughing and horsing around, yelling across the room to say hello to friends they hadn't seen over the summer.

The scene was so similar to the one Henry had watched during his first week working at the Midsummer School that it gave him chills. A little voice in the back of his head that he didn't know how to switch off kept shrilling, *Everyone knows you don't belong! Everyone knows!* He tried his best to ignore it.

Henry, Adam, and Rohan sat in the middle of the long table, suddenly glad that they had one another to talk to. Many of the boys who had been assigned single rooms sat silently, afraid to start or even join a conversation.

Nervously, Henry and his roommates examined the professors who took their seats at the High Table. That one looked kind, that one looked ancient, there was Sir Frederick, and there! Henry couldn't stop his face from breaking into a wide grin. There was Professor Stratford in his rumpled tweed, seated next to his pupil.

Henry hadn't been around a lot of girls. The ones at the orphanage had gotten by because they acted like the boys, with rough clothes and even rougher manners, and the few scullery maids at Midsummer had been timid little things, always getting fired for stealing something they hadn't actually stolen.

This girl, in her sweet lace dress with its modest collar, looked to be around Henry's age. She reminded Henry of a doll, with her blond curls and wide eyes and fair, pale skin.

"Who's the girl?" Rohan asked.

"The new headmaster's daughter," Henry said, pleased he knew something—anything—the others didn't.

And just then a hidden door beside the vast fireplace swung open and Headmaster Winter stepped into the Great Hall, out of breath and still fastening his cravat.

Everyone quieted.

The headmaster finished with his cravat and turned his attention toward his left cuff link as he made his way to the center seat at the High Table.

Everyone waited.

The headmaster nervously cleared his throat, slumped his hands into his trouser pockets, and gave an apologetic grin. Even in the soft candlelight at the High Table, Headmaster Winter looked every one of his forty years, his ginger beard gone patchy with gray, his skin pale and drawn as though he were recovering from a recent illness.

"Wel–welcome to the new term," he said, gaining confidence now that the worst of it—the beginning— had already passed. "I shan't trouble you with long-winded introductions. It's been a tiring day for us all, and there is a warm supper waiting to be served. But we *do* need to go over some preliminaries, to refresh ourselves on the rules and all that rot."

Some of the older boys laughed, and Headmaster Winter grinned sheepishly.

"You may laugh, but rules *do* molder with time and need to be tossed out or reformed on occasion. This is *not* one of those times. There shall be no bullying on my watch, and I hold no tolerance for boys found tormenting any of the first years. Class attendance is not optional, and sleep is to be done in your rooms, not at your desks or in the chapel pews."

Again, some laughter.

"I'm sure your heads of year have already covered the rest. Do I hear some grumbles of disagreement, or is that just my stomach wanting its supper?"

Even the first years couldn't help laughing this time.

"Well, that's all I can bring to mind at the moment.

Welcome, welcome to Knightley Academy! I know this shall be the best term yet," Headmaster Winter said, taking his seat to enthusiastic applause.

"*What* was that?" Rohan asked.

"Headmaster Winter," Adam said with a shrug. "Bit of an eccentric bloke, but what d'you expect—he *did* decide to open the exam to commoners for the sake of 'progress.'"

"It's all the better for us," Henry said as the doors to the kitchen swung open and servants in school livery staggered out with platters of food. "I mean, could you imagine *two* Lord Havelocks?"

Adam shuddered, and even Rohan made a face at the thought.

Piping hot baskets of bread arrived at the table, and suddenly every boy remembered how very hungry he was.

"Can you pass the butter, please?" Rohan asked the blond-haired boy across from him.

The boy looked as though he wanted to say something quite horrible, but then he remembered his manners and stiffly pushed the butter dish toward Rohan without comment. Rohan pretended not to notice, but Henry saw that when Rohan took a second roll, he ate it dry.

When the main course of roast duck was served, Henry chanced to look up and find more than a few boys staring in his direction.

"It's terribly surprising," Adam said, just a bit too loudly, "when us commonfolk don't eat with our hands like savages, isn't it?"

Henry elbowed him under the table.

"What?" Adam protested. "That's why they're watching. Not because I'm such a terribly handsome fellow or because you happen to have a gigantic spot on your face."

Henry tried to ignore it. He told himself that the boys would realize there was nothing to see and eventually lose interest, but even so, he felt as though he and his roommates were having their supper on a stage.

Finally, the meal ended and, full of cakes and tarts, the boys streamed out of the Great Hall.

Henry suddenly felt a sharp shove from behind. He lost his footing and stumbled forward, only narrowly avoiding a collision with a suit of armor as he slammed painfully into the wood-paneled wall.

"Hello, servant boy," a familiar voice drawled.

Henry sighed and picked himself up. He'd been expecting this.

"Hallo, Valmont," Henry said, facing the tormentor he thought he'd left behind at the Midsummer School. "I was ever so surprised to see you here, since you failed the entrance exam."

Valmont's eyes narrowed. "I could hardly be expected to concentrate, what with the stench of an unwashed servant filling the exam room."

Henry felt his cheeks go pink. Of course it was a lie, but lies often sting—or stink, as the case may be—worse than the truth.

"So I take it your family connections came through in the end?" Henry said. "Pity you didn't make it in on merit, like the rest of us."

"Fergus, you coming?" Theobold Archer IV clapped his hand onto Valmont's shoulder, and then shot Henry a horrible smile.

"He'll be along in a minute," Henry answered. "We're just catching up, since we're such old *friends*."

"I didn't ask *you*, Grim," Theobold said, all traces of his earlier friendliness gone. "It was a good thing you left our compartment on the train ride over. The carriage *was* a bit cramped, and of course, we hadn't been properly introduced."

"Seemed proper enough to me," Henry said coolly.

"I was so surprised to see you finally learned to use a knife and fork at supper," Valmont said.

Henry resisted the urge to roll his eyes. Valmont's insults were many things, but clever and original were not among them.

"You'll be even more surprised when I come out on top in lessons, I'd expect," Henry said. "If you gentlemen will excuse me, I've still some things to unpack."

"Have fun sorting your rags," Valmont snickered, falling into step with Theobold.

Henry watched them go. Only when Valmont was out of sight around the corner did he dare to rub the sore patch on his elbow from where he had fallen.

8

CHALKBOARDS
AND SWORDS

By the time the half-hour bells rang for chapel the following morning, Henry had already washed, dressed, and made his bed. Despite staying up late the night before to swap stories with his new roommates, he had woken at dawn on the unfamiliar mattress, his head thrumming with too much excitement to roll over and go back to sleep.

Instead, he had listened to his roommates' quiet breathing (or snoring, in Adam's case), waited until the sun rose over the roof of the headmaster's house, and then quietly slipped out of bed.

This was it: the first day that he was expected to learn from—rather than scrub—the blackboards. The thought carried Henry through morning chapel, where the other boys stared when Adam sat silently in his seat as everyone else rose for prayer. It carried Henry until breakfast, where he was too nervous to eat anything besides a piece of dry toast.

"Bacon?" Valmont simpered, pushing the plate across to Henry.

"No, thank you." Henry shook his head, while Valmont shook with laughter.

"Didn't I *tell* you?" Valmont hooted to Theobold, who sat by his side. "None of them will eat bacon. The other two are religious about it, but you know why the servant boy won't?"

"Why?" Theobold asked, and Henry felt himself wondering the same thing.

"Because," Valmont crowed, gasping for breath through his hysterics, "because he used to sleep in the *barn* with the *pigs*. Feels *sorry* for them."

Theobold smiled nastily at this news.

"You know that isn't true, Valmont," Henry said, his cheeks burning.

"Now, now, Grim, there's no need to be *ashamed*," Valmont drawled, as though there were a very great need to be ashamed indeed. "You needn't be *embarrassed* that you came to think of that old potbelly sow as your mother, seeing as how you haven't got any parents."

Henry banged his teacup down onto the table—hard. Despite the cup being mostly dregs, liquid poured over the side, soaking the tablecloth.

"Manners, manners, Grim," Theobold said, "or we'll send you back to the barn."

"Blast!" Rohan said. He'd just upset the pitcher that sat between himself and Theobold, sending a tidal wave of pulpy orange juice onto Theobold's half-full plate.

"You oaf!" Theobold sneered.

"Frightfully sorry," Rohan said, calmly forking up a bite of eggs. "I'm just not used to having to serve myself at meals."

At this, Adam snorted so loudly that Valmont asked if he were actually *related* to pigs, at which point a proper food fight might have broken out if the second-year monitor hadn't come over to see what was the matter.

By first lesson, Henry was in a foul mood. Valmont and Theobold had nicknamed Henry and his roommates the Three Little Pigs, and sat in the row of desks behind them, alternately oinking and snickering.

Henry could hardly enjoy the sensation of sitting at the handsome wooden desk, or the way the latticed windows bounced sunlight onto the strange instruments that sat on the master's table. ,

The other students whispered to one another:

"Do you think we'll just use textbooks or also do practical lessons?"

"I heard they broke a boy's leg last year for a demonstration."

"I heard that too. Except it was his arm."

"Rubbish. We're going to learn to brew poisons."

"That's rot. Where do you think we are, magic school?"

"Yeah, I guess not poisons. But maybe antidotes."

Suddenly, it dawned on Henry that his first lesson was medicine—with Sir Frederick! A sense of relief washed over him, and he was finally able to ignore Valmont and Theobold's mocking.

"We've got Sir Frederick!" Henry told Adam.

"All right, of course we have. It's on the schedule," Adam said.

"No." Henry shook his head, realizing that Adam and Rohan sat the exam with hundreds of others and hadn't met the chief examiner as he had. "Well, I know.

I mean, he's brilliant. *He's* the one who let me sit the exam even though—"

The room quieted as Sir Frederick burst through the door, carrying an armload of bedsheets.

"Good morning, boys," Sir Frederick said kindly, his master's gown swishing neatly behind him. The boys stared as their teacher made his way up the center aisle, deposited the bundle of sheets onto his lectern, and turned to face them, hands clasped behind his back.

"I am Sir Frederick, and welcome to Beginner's Medicine. You might recognize me as chief examiner from last May, but as some of you know, I am also medicine master here and head of second year. So you'd best try to get on my good side, since the lot of you will be stuck with me for a long while."

Sir Frederick began to pace, jumping right into that day's lesson.

"Now. The Code of Chivalry requires you to 'defend those in need.' In this course, we will study science, and we will do so practically. I will lecture, and then you will roll up your sleeves and learn by doing."

"Told you it was practical," Henry overheard a boy whisper.

"Medicine concerns the assessment of and defense

against disease and pain," Sir Frederick continued. "Hundreds of years ago, the Knights Templar watched their brothers fall in battle, with no one to tend their wounds. Cuts became infected. Limbs were amputated. Disease brought swift and welcome death. A knight who *fell* in battle *died* in battle."

The boys stared, pens hovering above blank sheets of paper, entranced.

"But the Knights Templar learned to defend, and as many of you may not know, they invented mouth-to-mouth resuscitation.

"You may be thinking, 'We no longer fight wars and battles,' or 'We have surgeons to repair us when we are hurt.' You may be wondering when you will ever use a practical discipline like medicine."

Sir Frederick surveyed his pupils, as though suspecting each and every one of them of entertaining these very thoughts.

"How many of you have considered becoming police knights?"

A few hands went up.

"You are called to the scene of a robbery. A shop-keeper is injured and bleeding. The Code of Chivalry obligates you to help—to bandage his wounds, to assess his injuries and decide whether to send immediately for a doctor or to take a testimony of the crime. Now, how many of you have considered the knight detectives?"

More hands.

"How would you know if a man had died of natural causes or been murdered? How could you tell from a man's demeanor if he told the truth or lied?"

Sir Frederick went on to give more examples: What if a colleague was injured protecting a member of the royal family? What if you could recognize the symptoms of smallpox and noticed an infected child during a street patrol? Would you be able to aid a person who was choking? To determine whether a prisoner was truly ill or faking?

Sir Frederick was a wonderful lecturer, he could make anything sound fascinating, could interest even the most disinterested student. By the time he had demonstrated on shy Edmund Merrill how to correctly bandage a wound, the students were itching to give it a go themselves.

"Partner up," Sir Frederick called, tearing a bedsheet into strips with a *rrrrripppppp*ing sound. "Grab some bandages and take turns. Raise your hand for me to examine the work once you are satisfied."

A tap on Henry's shoulder. He turned.

"We'll be partners," Valmont announced, his lips curved into a nasty smile.

Henry felt as though his stomach had rolled over and was playing dead. He glanced over at Adam and Rohan, who had already partnered together.

With his mouth dryer than the toast he'd eaten for breakfast, Henry collected a handful of bandages from the front table.

"I'll do you first," Valmont said, snapping the bandage like a whip. "Give me your arm."

Mournfully, Henry rolled up his right sleeve.

All around him, other boys did the same.

Maybe, Henry thought wildly, maybe nothing bad would happen, and Valmont would wrap the bandage the way Sir Frederick had demonstrated.

Right, and maybe Lord Havelock would knit them all matching scarves as a surprise.

"Here, hold this," Valmont said, putting the bandage roll in Henry's fist just as Sir Frederick had taught them.

Henry watched Adam sloppily roll the bandage while Rohan looked on and sighed.

Suddenly, Henry's arm began to burn as if it were

being poked with hundreds of sewing needles. Valmont, his jaw clenched with the effort, was rolling the bandage as tight as it would go.

"Is it too loose?" Valmont asked, faking concern.

"I am going to *destroy* you for this," Henry muttered.

"Tighter, then," Valmont said, as though taking part in an entirely different conversation.

Henry's arm throbbed. Black spots danced in the corners of his vision. He felt dizzy, and so he closed his eyes.

"*What* are you doing?" Sir Frederick thundered, rushing over to Valmont and Henry. "Are you trying to *hurt* him? Take that bandage off *now!*"

Valmont scowled and, as slowly as he dared, unwound the strip of bedsheet from Henry's forearm.

The dizziness faded. Henry flexed his arm as it flooded with warmth. The bandage had left angry red creases that spiraled upward toward his elbow.

Sir Frederick slammed a ruler inches from Valmont's fingers. Valmont flinched.

"Are you *stupid*, boy?" Sir Frederick hissed, his voice dangerously low. "I don't *ever* want to see *anything* like this asinine, immature, *dangerous* display of idiocy in my classroom again, do you understand me?"

Valmont nodded.

Sir Frederick raised his ruler again but did not strike.

Valmont flinched.

"From now on, you are my little helper. *Every* demonstration, for the rest of the month, you will practice *only* on me, until you learn proper respect for what I am teaching. Is that clear?"

Meekly, Valmont inclined his head.

"I *said*, is that clear?"

"Yes, sir. It's clear, sir," Valmont mumbled.

Adam snorted, and Rohan somehow managed a straight face as he offered up his monogrammed handkerchief to muffle Adam's enormous grin.

Military history with Lord Havelock was next, to everyone's terror—except for Valmont's. When Henry, Adam, and Rohan entered Lord Havelock's austere and windowless tower classroom, they were surprised to find Valmont and Theobold seated in the center of the front row, grinning hugely.

"They're mad," Adam murmured, claiming a seat in the second to last row. "Couldn't pay *me* to cozy up to Havelock."

Henry shrugged and took out his notebook, enormously glad that Professor Stratford had tutored him so thoroughly in military history. They were to receive their textbooks at the end of the lesson, but Henry was fairly certain that his strong background in the past hundred years of military history would impress even Lord Havelock.

Valmont reclined in his chair, pillowing his hands behind his head as he chattered with Theobold, but he snapped to attention when Lord Havelock swept into the room.

"We meet again, first years. I trust that you are not deficient of memory, that neither I nor my subject require reintroduction."

With a Havelook of Doom, Lord Havelock yanked a map down from the ceiling and removed a pointer from a fold in his master's gown.

He smacked the pointer across the map.

"Examinations," he began, "will be given whenever the mood strikes, so you must always be prepared. For instance, I wonder how many of you are prepared . . . now."

With a wicked grin, Lord Havelock struck the pointer against his palm.

Henry half expected it to draw blood, but Lord Havelock didn't even wince as he asked, "What was the name of the revolutionary party which Yurick Mors headed to overthrow the Nordlandic monarchy?"

Henry nearly sighed with relief; he knew this.

"Rohan Mehta?"

"The Draconians, if I remember correctly, sir," Rohan answered.

"*If* you remember correctly?" Lord Havelock simpered. "Is there something *wrong* with your memory?"

"No, sir. The correct answer is the Draconians, sir," Rohan said.

"Obviously," Lord Havelock said, unimpressed. "And in what year did the Sassons divide the Isles into four distinct territories?"

Henry bit his lip. It was ancient history. Were they truly expected to know the exact year?

"Adam Beckerman?"

"Somewhere around fourteen-something, I'd expect," Adam said cheerfully.

"You may leave the room, Mr. Beckerman," Lord Havelock said. "The correct response when one does not know an answer is, 'I don't know, sir. I am unprepared.' Cheek is *never* acceptable."

"Yes, sir," Adam said, going red.

"Pack your things," Lord Havelock said. "I shall not ask you again."

With every eye on him, Adam picked up his notebook and disappeared into the hallway.

"Now," Lord Havelock said, pressing the tips of his fingers together so tightly that his knuckles went white, "who can tell me the name of the knight after whom our peace treaty is called?"

Henry almost laughed. A child's question!

"Fergus Valmont?"

"Sir Arthur Longsword," Valmont answered promptly.

"Excellent. Someone here knows his history." Lord Havelock smiled.

Is he mad? Henry scrawled in his notebook, tilting it toward Rohan. *That question was so simple!*

Rohan shrugged.

"Now, who can tell me what was the fate of a nobleman captured in battle, and how did it differ from the fate of a commoner?" Lord Havelock asked, and without even pausing to consider, said, "Henry Grim."

Henry gulped. This wasn't a date or a name; it was a proper essay. And even if he *had* known the answer, how could he have given it without saying either too much or too little for Lord Havelock's satisfaction?

No, Henry thought wryly, this wasn't an interrogation, it was an execution. Lord Havelock intended to break him, to kill his confidence. Humility was his only chance.

"I don't know, sir," Henry said, as Lord Havelock had instructed. "I am unprepared, sir."

"Pity," Lord Havelock said. "And I had harbored *such* high hopes for you, Mr. Grim."

Henry was certain Lord Havelock had done no such thing. The question was impossible.

"A nobleman captured in battle," Lord Havelock intoned as the boys all scribbled in their notebooks, "had the right to be ransomed, and as such, was treated in a manner befitting his station. A commoner, however, had no such right. Commoners who were not killed outright were thrown into dungeons called *oubliettes*, where they faced starvation and, often, torture."

Five pages of detailed notes later, Lord Havelock dismissed the class.

"How are we going to manage to read three chapters by tomorrow?" Rohan complained, flipping through a copy of their new textbook.

"We'll do it together," Henry said. "A study group. You, me, and Adam."

"I suppose," Rohan said doubtfully, "although Adam still has to copy the notes he missed."

"Isn't Uncle a brilliant lecturer?" Valmont boomed. "It's a pity your friend had to miss it."

Henry and Rohan turned.

"Uncle?" Henry asked, hoping he'd misheard.

"Yes, my dear Uncle Havelock. Absolutely illuminating lesson, wouldn't you agree? I mean, imagine if we still went to war . . . why, if we were captured, *I'd* sleep on a pillow mattress while my family paid for my release. But you lot, well, *you'd* be tortured in a dungeon."

"My *father* is—," Rohan began.

"Dead, and such a pity," Valmont simpered as Rohan clenched his hands into fists.

"You *deserve* to be captured in battle," Henry said. "And if you're anything as horrible toward your family as you are toward my friends, they'd refuse to pay your ransom and leave you to rot."

"Easy, Grim," Valmont said. "I was only *supposing*. Temper, temper. I wonder if I should tell my uncle how much his class upsets you?"

"If you have a last wish," Henry retorted.

"Oh, I do," Valmont assured Henry. "But I wouldn't want to keep you up at night with terror, so I'll spare you the specifics."

As Valmont left, Rohan shook his head.

"I don't understand why he's so horrible," Rohan said.

"Neither do I," Henry admitted. "But I wouldn't waste my time thinking about it."

Their schedules blocked the next hour as free before supper. Suddenly, the enormity of the day seemed like a pressing weight upon Henry's shoulders. He felt exhausted.

"Coming back to the room?" Rohan asked.

"In a while," Henry said.

Through a window outside Lord Havelock's classroom, Henry could see sunlight streaming across the quadrangle, beckoning him outdoors.

The sunlight was as warm and inviting as it looked. Henry tilted his face upward as he traipsed through the grass, his mind a mess of that day's classes, of Valmont's taunts and Rohan's shy friendliness and Adam's inability to keep his mouth shut, even in front of the terrifying Lord Havelock.

At the other end of the quadrangle, beyond the rather pathetic hedge maze, was a stone bench dappled with sunshine. Henry sprawled gratefully onto the bench, closing his eyes.

After being continuously surrounded by other students for the past twenty-four hours, it was immensely satisfying to be alone, with no one staring at him curiously, no constant pressure to prove himself.

"Sir Henry Grim," Henry murmured, reassuring himself. It was all worth it for that.

And then someone giggled.

Henry opened one eye.

The headmaster's daughter leaned against the nearest tree, a book under her arm, laughing at him. Her white frock was covered with bits of twigs, and the bow in her hair had come untied.

"Oh, er, hello," Henry said, surging to his feet. You were always to stand in the presence of a lady, he knew.

"So who's Sir Henry Grim?" the girl asked.

Henry reddened.

"Um, no one. I mean, just me. Well, not yet, but—"

"I'm Frankie," she said, calmly picking a bramble off her skirts. "*Don't* call me Francesca. It's a perfectly horrible name. I like yours, though, rather a lot. It doesn't sound nearly as formidable as it should for a Knightley student."

That, Henry thought miserably, *is the problem.* He sighed.

"What are you doing?" Frankie pressed.

"Thinking," Henry said. "What are you reading?"

Frankie hid the book behind her dress. "Nothing."

"Well, sorry for asking," Henry said, nettled.

Frankie stared at Henry a moment, considering him. Finally, she said, "Promise not to tell?"

"I promise."

"Do you *swear*?"

"I already gave you my word. Code of Chivalry and all that. Either tell me or don't. I've only got an hour free and I don't want to waste it."

Frankie showed him the cover. It was an ordinary Latin textbook.

"So?" Henry said. "It's just a textbook. I had the same one last year."

"Are you dense?" Frankie snorted. "Do you think girls learn the same things as boys?"

"Well, of course not. You learn embroidery and painting and poetry. Those sorts of—" Henry stopped midsentence, realization dawning. "You *stole* that?"

Frankie shrugged. "I'm going to return it. Besides, no one will miss it. I just swiped it from an empty class-room."

Henry couldn't stop a broad smile from creeping across his face.

"What's funny?" Frankie asked.

"I used to do the same thing," Henry said, realizing that textbook stealing seemed to be a habit among Professor Stratford's pupils of late. "And anyway, if you want to learn Latin, just ask Professor Stratford. He won't mind."

"How do *you* know my tutor's name?" Frankie accused, taking a few curious steps toward Henry.

"He used to be *my* tutor," Henry said. "After he caught *me* stealing textbooks. Although mine was Milton, not a Latin primer."

Henry made a face at the thought.

"He'd really teach me? And other things too? Like history and . . . classics?"

Henry shrugged. "I don't see why not." And then he told Frankie about Professor Stratford and the Midsummer School, the only interruption being when Frankie delightedly shrieked, "He *does* fall asleep at breakfast!"

"So how about you?" Henry asked, tucking his feet onto the bench and clasping his hands around his knees. "I mean, it's not the best luck to be stuck at a boys' school for the year."

"Nowhere would have me," Frankie said proudly. "I've been kicked out of three finishing schools already."

"What for?"

Frankie grinned. "See, that's the problem with people. Everyone's always too polite to ask what I've done. But anyway, Headmistress Hardwicke at the Maiden Manor School for Young Ladies dismissed me over embroidery."

"Embroidery?" Henry didn't think he'd heard correctly.

"Madame *did* say we could embroider the cushions

with whatever words we wished. How was I to know she didn't mean it?"

"What did you write?" Henry asked.

Frankie told him.

Henry choked. "You're joking."

"Not at all. And it looked so lovely displayed on a chair in the school parlor."

"You didn't!" Henry laughed.

"Well, it worked, didn't it? No more of those prissy, proper girls who talk only about the weather and their suitors, as if I could care."

Before they knew it, the sunlight was slanting toward the hedge maze, leaving the bench to cool in the shadows. The sound of the chapel bells ringing startled them both.

"Blast," Henry cried, standing up and brushing off his uniform. "Did you know the time?"

"Maybe," Frankie said, grinning evilly. "Loosen up, Grim. Be tardy. Who cares?"

"Have you *met* Lord Havelock?" Henry asked, gathering his books.

"You mean Count Dracula?"

"He's head of my year."

Frankie swore.

"Go! Run like breaking wind," she called.

"I thought it was 'Run like *the* wind.'"

"It's funnier my way," she said cheerfully.

And if Henry hadn't already been sprinting back toward his room, he would have agreed.

9

THE QUEST FOR STRAWBERRY TARTS

Girls are rubbish," Adam said over supper, dismissing Henry's story about the headmaster's daughter. "Trust me, I've got two sisters."

"All they talk about are their gowns and the weather," Rohan agreed, forking up a mound of mashed potatoes. "And they giggle at everything you say, even if it's not funny."

"Well, *Frankie* didn't," Henry protested. "I don't know. She's lonely. We should visit her during free hour."

Rohan dropped his fork.

"Are you *mad?*" Rohan asked. "You can't just visit girls. It's not proper. It's not *done.*"

"Yeah, mate," Adam said. "You need chaperones,

and her family has to approve of yours and all that rubbish."

"Just to visit?"

"You can't visit girls," Rohan hissed.

"Fine. I get it," Henry said crossly, letting the subject drop.

After a late night spent studying military history, no one was in a very good mood the next morning.

Henry swayed sleepily as he bent over his prayer register an hour after sunrise, his eyes red and scratchy. His brain begged for another hour's sleep, and the lull of the pipe organ made it hard not to give in.

Beside him in the pew, Adam gave a small snort. Henry elbowed him.

"Wake up," Henry murmured.

"Just resting my eyes," Adam muttered, slumping lower.

Rohan stepped on Adam's foot, jolting him awake.

"Thanks, mate," Adam said, straightening his shoulders.

That morning's sermon went on for ages. Henry's stomach, the only part of him that was fully awake, grumbled.

And then, up front, the chapel echoed with a sneeze.

"God bless you, my child," the priest said, and then returned to his sermon.

Another sneeze. And another.

Everyone looked around, trying to see who was dying of a cold.

Another sneeze.

The sermon had stopped.

Henry, now wide awake, began to grin.

"What's funny?" Adam asked as the priest resumed his sermon, only to be interrupted once more by a bellowing sneeze.

"Frankie," Henry said.

Adam and Rohan followed his gaze. Sure enough, with an apologetic grin, Frankie had wrapped herself in a shawl, as though cold. But she wasn't fooling Henry. He rather suspected that, before embroidery, Frankie had been kicked out of finishing school for sneezing.

Later that morning, in languages, Professor Lingua, a small round man with small round glasses and fingers like fat sausages, frowned at his bookshelf.

"I could have sworn I had twenty-five copies of *Novice Latin*, not twenty-four," he murmured. "In any case, we'll begin with French. I'm sure many of you have already studied Latin and Greek, the backbone of a gentleman's education, but French—before girls learned it to sound pretty—was the language of politics. And it is still the preferred language by many of our neighboring nations for diplomatic discussions."

Professor Lingua strutted across the front of the classroom, his sizable stomach swelling beneath his waistcoat.

"Bet you he pops a button before class is over," Adam whispered.

"I wouldn't be surprised," Henry murmured.

"Gentlemen!" Professor Lingua called, frowning at Adam and Henry. "Is there something you wish to share? In *French* perhaps?"

"Pardon, mais non, Monsieur Lingua," Henry apologized.

"Tu parles français, garçon?" Professor Lingua demanded, an accusing finger directing all attention toward Henry.

Henry gulped. "Un peu, monsieur."

"More than 'a little,' from the sound of it," Professor Lingua said.

Henry turned red.

"Yes, sir."

"And Latin?" Professor Lingua asked.

Henry nodded.

"Greek? Italian?"

Henry nodded again.

"Both or just the one?"

"Both, sir," Henry said.

"I see," Professor Lingua said coolly, as though he did not see at all. He picked up his class register. "Name, please."

"Henry Grim, sir."

"Well, Mr. Grim, I'll make a note to expect flawless work from you. One wrong answer or improperly conjugated verb in any language I teach and you'll redo the entire assignment during your free hour, understood?"

"Yes, sir."

Henry slumped his forehead into his palm, wishing he'd kept his mouth shut.

"Anyone else speak French?" Professor Lingua demanded.

Silence.

"As I thought. Repeat after me: *'Bonjour, monsieur.'*"

"*Bonjour, monsieur,*" the class chanted.

"*Bonjour, madame,*" the professor prompted.

* * *

"Bad luck," Adam said after class let out.

"It was *your* fault," Henry accused.

"Well, I was right though, he *did* pop a button during '*mare-see bo-koop*.'"

"You don't pronounce the *p* at the end," Henry said irritably.

"Bloody French," Adam muttered. "It sounds like a donkey blowing its nose."

Henry laughed. "That's just Professor Lingua's accent," he said. "Oh, *hello*, Valmont. Eavesdropping *again*?"

Valmont scowled. "You think you're so special, don't you, Grim?"

"Not at all," Henry said airily. "But *you* are, aren't you? Sir Frederick's little helper. I *do* hope he shows us all how to do a full body cast today."

Adam snorted. "Yeah, you're not afraid of needles, are you, Valmont?"

Valmont paled.

"Poke, poke," Adam said.

"Stop!" Valmont didn't look nearly so confident now.

"Poke, poke, poke," Adam threatened, his finger extended menacingly.

"Oh, grow up," Valmont snarled, "and it's ethics this afternoon, not medicine." And with that, Valmont stalked off toward Theobold.

The week progressed, as weeks tend to do. Henry and his roommates lived for medicine, where they delighted in Valmont's humiliating punishment to serve as the professor's demonstration dummy. They studied late into the night for military history, puzzled through parables for ethics, and Henry checked everyone's homework for languages.

More than once, some boys in their year caught Henry's eye during meals, or seemed to linger outside the door to his room, but they always pretended it had been an accident.

Probably they wanted help with French, Henry thought. But Theobold, with his signet ring, mocking drawl, and older brother as third-year monitor, had fast become the king of their year—with Valmont as his ever-eager second in command. They lorded over the common room, with its battered chess sets and checkerboards, as though it was their own personal sitting room. And of course, under the reign of Theobold the Great, speaking to Henry and his roommates was forbidden.

Even though some boys may have been desperate for help with French, they didn't quite dare to ask. And so long as they let Theobold control them like that, Henry wasn't offering.

"I'm starving," Adam complained one evening, while they reviewed the credit and banking system of the Knights Templar. "Can't we take a break?"

Adam was hunched over his desk, chewing his pen as though he hoped it held some nutritious value. Henry and Rohan sat side by side on the floor, making a chart. They looked up.

"Have you gotten to chapter seven yet?" Henry asked.

"I've glanced at it," Adam said. "Sort of. Why, how far are you lot?"

"We're doing a chart of names and dates," Rohan said with a frustrated sigh. "*We've* already finished the reading."

"Well it's not *my* fault I got bogged down with the French," Adam accused. "If you'd only have—"

"I'm not doing it for you," Henry said, frowning at his and Rohan's chart. "You have to *learn* this stuff. What happens when you meet a foreign dignitary and the only thing you know how to say is *'Bonjour, madame'*?"

"I reckon he'll ask if I need glasses."

Henry snorted.

"I could use a break too," Rohan admitted. "Think we could pay off someone in the kitchens to give us a snack?"

This was how, three hours after supper, Henry, Adam, and Rohan found themselves sneaking down the corridor that led to the kitchens. Rohan's pockets jingled with each step, and Henry wished his friend would stop paying people to do things for him. Good manners went just as far as good money, in any case.

"I hope they have some leftover strawberry tarts. Those were excellent," Adam said.

"I hope we don't get detentions," Henry muttered.

And then they heard voices. The three friends stopped.

"You don' go believin' that the evenin' curfew in the Nordlands is fer everyone's own good, do ye?"

"Y'mean it isn't?"

"'Course it isn't, Mary, you dunner. Chancellor Mors has a reason fer keepin' people off the streets. A *secret* reason."

It was two servants gossiping just around the corner, Henry saw, peeking around the bend. Two kitchen maids, and from the looks of them, they knew exactly where the strawberry tarts were kept.

"Er, excuse me——," Henry began politely.

The younger of the two maids stared at him in horror, wringing her apron in her hands.

"Oh! Forgive us fer gossipin', sir. We don' mean no harm and we wasn't s'posed to be doin' anythin' else. Honest."

Henry almost laughed. At the Midsummer School, he'd been bossed around and piled with extra work from the kitchen staff, and now they were terrified of him.

He looked down at his uniform—the sleeves of his shirt rolled, his tie loose and flapping. It didn't matter if his uniform was in tatters; it still bore the crest of Knightley Academy and the stripes that showed how many years away he was from earning his knighthood.

"I believe you," Henry said, enjoying the new sensation of being treated as though he were respectable. "Really. My friends and I were just wondering, if it isn't any trouble, if there might be some of those tarts left from supper."

"The *strawberry* ones," Adam called from around the corner. "The peach are rubbish."

"I thought the peach were quite nice," Rohan protested.

Henry resisted the urge to roll his eyes. It figured that his friends, who had been the ones to drag him to the kitchens, were shy of the servants.

Well, fine, Henry thought, and anyway, he was actually enjoying this. The kitchen maids' eyes widened at the sound of Rohan's posh accent.

"Please?" Henry asked. "If it isn't any trouble."

"Well bless 'is soul, Mary. You ever heard one o' these boys ask fer sumthin' so polite?"

Mary, still in shock, shook her head.

"O' course there's some tarts left fer the likes o' *you*. Tell yer friends to stop hidin' an' follow me."

"Thank you," Henry said with feeling, hoping Rohan would learn a thing or two.

Adam and Rohan emerged sheepishly from around the corner.

"Haven't got any cream for the strawberry tarts, have you?" Adam asked brightly as Rohan elbowed him. "Owww, what'd you do *that* for?"

Henry smiled reassuringly at the kitchen maid. "I'm Henry, and these are Adam and Rohan."

"Well, pleased t'make yer acquaintance. I'm Liza."

Henry shot his friends a look.

"How do you do, Liza?" they mumbled.

"Not bad," she cackled, having a grand old time. "Not bad atall. Now yeh wanted what kind o' tarts? Raspberry?"

"*Strawberry,*" Adam whimpered.

"Jus' jokin'," Liza said, clearly pleased with herself. "Follow me."

It was strange, Henry thought, as he sat at a stool in the kitchen between his two friends, drinking milk and munching tarts. There was a whole separate world going on at Knightley, parallel to his own. A world of cooking and cleaning and gossiping to pass the time, so similar to what he had known as a servant boy.

And how quickly he had forgotten all of it now that he had a set of textbooks to call his own. Henry wondered after the boy his own age who had helped with Rohan's trunk on their first afternoon. Did that boy wish he were a knight? Had *he* sat the exam in the City with Adam and Rohan, his score high but not high enough?

Until he had startled Liza and Mary in the hallway, Henry hadn't realized that he was homesick—that he had anything to be homesick *about*. But he was, and he did.

He missed being able to be invisible, and his favorite windowsill where he read books in the dappled sunlight, and the way, after a late-night tutoring session, Professor Stratford would clap a hand on his shoulder and say, "Well, g'night, my boy."

Henry sighed into his tart.

"Aww, poor little deary," Liza said thickly, as she had also treated herself to a few tarts. "Wha's the matter?"

Henry reddened.

"Nothing," he muttered. "Just thinking."

"Abou' the Nordlands, am I right?" Liza crowed.

Henry nodded. He didn't dare admit in front of his friends that he was *homesick*.

"See!" Liza said triumphantly. "I was tellin' Mary 'bout that earlier. Bet you're studying it in yer classes?"

"Not really, no," Henry said.

"What're they *teachin'* you boys, then?" Liza asked, scandalized.

"About *banks*," Adam said mournfully. "I left home so I wouldn't have to go into banking, and now I find out that it was the Knights Templar who *invented* the bloody profession in the first place."

"Well I don't know nuthin' 'bout no Knights Templar," Liza said, "but I was just tellin' Mary how the Nordlands got to be hidin' somethin' bad."

Henry resisted the urge to groan. The Nordlands—again. He thought he'd left that rubbish behind to rot in the grubby public houses in the City.

"You don't say," Rohan said politely.

"Don't I just!" Liza crowed. "Women can't go to school, Chancellor Mors says, and I says, well wot's happenin' to those who get caught doin' it anyway? Not a warning, no sirree. I hear stories that would make yer head spin' round yer neck 'bout the consequences fer breakin' laws in the Nordlands."

As Liza spoke, her eyes took on a faraway look, as though she had seen, rather than heard, the "truth" about the Nordlands.

"We should be getting back to our homework," Henry said, standing up. He didn't know how much more talk of rumors and rubbish he could bear. And worse, it just made him even more homesick for Professor Stratford.

Maybe, Henry thought suddenly, he could visit the professor after their lessons tomorrow. The thought cheered him so visibly that when Liza bade them good night and slipped Adam an extra strawberry tart with a wink, she said, "There now, you just let ol' Liza do all the worryin' for ya. There's a good lad."

❧ 10 ❧

THE HEADMASTER'S DAUGHTER

Friday morning dawned wet and dreary. Henry stared out the window at the pudgy gray clouds and sloshy grass while he fastened his tie.

Adam moaned sleepily and curled up into a tighter ball beneath his down quilt. His military history textbook was splayed across the floor by his bed, pages down.

Rohan joined Henry at the window.

"Will it be strawberry tarts for breakfast?" Rohan joked, and Henry smiled in appreciation.

"I don't *ever* want to see another strawberry tart," Henry said, making a face. "Whose bad idea was that?"

"Mine," Rohan admitted, straightening his cuffs.

"Although I have to say, that kitchen girl was rather entertaining. I can't think why I rarely asked Father's staff for their opinions on politics."

Henry bit his lip and shoved his military history book into his satchel. He'd learned that the best response when Rohan went all posh like that was no response at all.

"Oh, get up," Henry said, yanking at Adam's blanket. "We've got fencing first lesson. That should cheer you." Adam was always going on about his talents with a sword.

"Have we really?" Adam asked, brightening. "Have I mentioned how talented I am with a sword?"

"Oh, once or twice," Henry said.

"More like once or twice *an hour*," Rohan put in, straightening his tie. "I'm not answering to Lord Havelock for tardiness. I'll see you at chapel."

Henry looked at Rohan, and then back at Adam.

"Go," Adam said. "If there's anyone who can get away with being late to chapel, it's me."

That was true enough, Henry thought.

"Rohan, wait a moment, I'm coming," Henry said, looking once more out the window and wishing he owned an umbrella.

Adam made it to chapel on time, but only just. His smugness on the matter carried on through breakfast until Rohan stood up and said crossly, "*Do* put a lid on it, Adam. I'd rather wait outside the armory than listen to you gloat about your good fortune that the back door to the chapel hadn't been locked."

Henry rather felt the same way.

"Coming, Grim?" Rohan asked.

Caught in the middle, *again*, Henry thought glumly.

"All right, I'm *sorry*," Adam said. "I won't mention it again. See? Not mentioning it."

Henry watched as Luther Leicester and Edmund Merrill gathered their things and left breakfast early.

"I bet they're going to the armory," Henry said.

Rohan consulted his gold pocket watch. "Hmmm, we've still got ten minutes. But it is the first lesson and we might get lost on the way . . ."

They didn't get lost. In fact, they arrived early, joining seven other students who had turned up early out of excitement, forming a crowd around the half-open door.

"Why's no one going in?" Henry asked, unable to see past everyone's backs.

"There's a private lesson on," Edmund said, turning

around. "Whoever he is, he's rather advanced."

"Like you can even see from all the way in the back," a familiar voice scoffed.

"Well, not everyone is rude enough to shove his way to the front, Valmont," Edmund said crossly.

"I say, stop crowding me. We might as well wait inside the armory," Theobold drawled. And because Theobold said it, everyone did it.

Henry and his friends followed Edmund into the armory, which was a converted ballroom and absolutely cavernous.

Sure enough, the fencing master was engaged in a bout with a student, the two of them blurs of white jacket padding and silver masks across the piste.

Henry, who knew nothing about fencing, turned to Adam for an explanation.

"They're fencing foil," Adam said knowingly. "You can tell from the strike zone and the swords. Only the torso is fair game for a touch."

"I bet he's a third year," Henry overheard bespectacled Luther whisper to one of his friends.

"Well, he's rather small for a third year," Adam said, and then let out a low whistle. "*Brilliant* footwork, though."

So swiftly that Henry barely knew what he was watching, the student took a huge lunge and scored a touch on the fencing master.

"Touché!" The fencing master called and removed his mask for a handshake.

The first years leaned forward eagerly to see who the student was.

The student reached up and unfastened his mask.

But it wasn't a he.

It was Frankie, her hair tangled and her face red and sweating in a rather unladylike manner. She grinned as she stowed the mask under her arm and shook hands with the fencing master.

The crowd of first years began to whisper:

"A girl!"

"The headmaster's daughter, I heard."

"Still, a girl!"

"She wasn't *that* good, actually. My mistake."

"*I* could have done the same my first time with a sword."

Henry could hardly believe how ready the other students were to write off Frankie's skill once they realized she was a girl. One moment they had been watching in awe, and the next moment she was utterly unremarkable.

"*I* still think she was brilliant," Henry muttered, nettled.

"Well, Theobold doesn't," Rohan said with a small smile.

The fencing master finished talking with Frankie and turned to the boys.

"Being early will earn you no points with me," he said, and then paused. "Get it? Points? As in, fencing?"

A few boys smiled politely.

"Right," the fencing master said. "Anyone here left-handed?"

With a sinking feeling, Henry raised his hand.

"I'll have to fetch a left-hander foil and glove from the storeroom, then," the fencing master said, half muttering to himself as he disappeared through a doorway.

Frankie stood there calmly removing her glove, regarding the crowd of boys as though she knew a particularly hilarious joke that she had no intention of sharing.

"Girls should stick to sewing and piano, in my opinion," Theobold said loudly.

"Yes," Valmont agreed with a sneer in Frankie's direction. "I rather support the Nordlands' banning women from schools. An educated woman is the same as a ruined woman, in my opinion."

"That's enough," Henry said sharply, whirling to face Valmont.

Everyone quieted.

"Look at that, you've gone and upset the servant," Theobold said. "How sweet, he's going to defend her honor. Have at it, then, Grim, we haven't got all day."

"I can defend my own honor, thanks," Frankie said with a derisive snort.

Before Valmont could react, Frankie had crossed the piste, slapped him across the face with her glove, and told him exactly what she'd embroidered on her pincushion.

The boys gasped.

Valmont stood there, rubbing his cheek.

"Why aren't you hitting back?" Frankie asked, casually twirling the glove around a finger. "Or are you afraid to hit a lady?"

Valmont's fists clenched.

"Code . . . of . . . Chivalry," he managed to growl.

"Pity," Frankie said. "I was *so* hoping to discover that you hit like a girl."

Things might have gotten very sticky indeed if the fencing master hadn't chosen that moment to walk back into the room, his arms full of fencing gear.

"Francesca, is there a reason you're still here?" he asked.

"None at all, maestro," she said with a curtsy that, judging from the look of surprise on the fencing master's face, was purely for show. "Thank you for the lesson."

With a wink in Henry's direction, Frankie held her chin high and strutted from the room.

"Well, line up," the fencing master commanded. "Two rows, face the mirrors. We'll start with a review of footwork and then split the beginners from the intermediates."

Henry, who had never fenced before, fumbled with the advance-retreat for a bit, but managed to get it right after watching what the others did. Valmont, to Henry's dismay, could do the exercise with his eyes shut—and, not surprisingly, so could Adam. Rohan was excellent as well.

Theobold, however, was another story.

"Archer, you're too heavy-footed," the fencing master said, coming around to Theobold's side and demonstrating. "You must step like a feather, on the balls of your feet."

Theobold sneered and went again, making no adjustment.

"Think of feathers, boy! Feathers!" the fencing master shrilled, as the rest of the class dissolved into snorts and giggles.

Theobold, red in the face, rushed through the move, just as thundering as ever.

"No, no, *no*!" the fencing master cried.

"What's the difference anyway?" Theobold retorted. "Footwork doesn't matter if you lose."

"With form like that, I would be shocked if you won," the fencing master said. "Beckerman, come here and demonstrate. As I call it: advance . . . retreat . . . advance . . . retreat . . . advance . . . lunge."

Adam did as the fencing master said, trying not to grin at Theobold's humiliation.

"Do you see?" the fencing master said, now addressing not just Theobold but the entire class. "*Exactly* like that."

Adam couldn't have wiped the grin off his face if he tried.

And when the fencing master divided the class into beginners and intermediates, he hesitated so long over Theobold that Henry was rather disappointed when Theobold was finally sent over to the intermediates.

While they put away the equipment, sweating and

exhausted, Henry reminded his friends that they had an hour free after Havelock's class.

"Yeah? Well, we've always got an hour free after second lesson," Adam said.

"I'm going to visit Professor Stratford," Henry said. "Want to come?"

"To the headmaster's house? No, thanks," Rohan said.

"Will Francesca be there?" Adam said, a very strange look on his face.

"She's called Frankie," Henry said. "And I'd expect so, but then, why does it matter, since *we're not allowed to visit girls*?"

Adam turned crimson. "Just wondering," he muttered.

"Do get over it," Rohan said, rolling his eyes at Adam.

"Over what?" Henry wondered aloud, and then he understood. "Oh."

"I'm coming with you," Adam mumbled.

"Isn't she fantastic?" Adam asked Henry as they crossed the quadrangle toward the headmaster's house during their hour free. "When she struck Valmont with her glove and told him to—"

"I was *there*, Adam."

"Oh. Right."

Not a moment too soon, they reached the head-master's front door.

Henry rang the bell, and a maid opened the door and stared at them.

Henry thought that the headmaster probably didn't have many students turn up at his front door.

"Er, hello," Henry said. "We're here to see Professor Stratford."

The maid frowned. "Wot's yer names?"

"Henry Grim and Adam Beckerman," Henry said.

"Wait here," the maid said, shutting the door with them still outside.

A moment later, the door opened.

"Professor Stratford will see you in his study," she said, as if she rather wished the professor had declined to receive them. "This way."

Henry and Adam followed the maid through a hand-some sitting room with bright imported carpets and a merrily flickering fireplace. They followed her up a car-peted stair, through a wallpapered hallway, and into a book-strewn room where Professor Stratford promptly crushed Henry in a massive hug.

"Henry, m'boy!" the professor said. "It's been ages!"

"Mmm ytmm," Henry said, his face squashed against Professor Stratford's waistcoat.

The professor let go.

"I said, 'I missed you too,'" Henry said, straightening his uniform. "And it's barely been a week."

"A week too long, if you ask me," Professor Stratford said. "Who's your friend?"

"Adam Beckerman, sir," Adam said shyly.

"Well, sit down, the both of you, and tell me *everything*," the professor said with a grin.

"Did you know Valmont is here?" Henry blurted.

Professor Stratford suddenly went serious. "I did. Is he giving you trouble?"

"Nothing I can't handle," Henry said.

"Well, be sure you don't get kicked out for 'handling' things," Professor Stratford advised.

Henry smiled, relaxing. It was wonderful to see Professor Stratford again, and the remainder of their free hour wasn't nearly enough time. Henry was sorry to say good-bye, but he promised to come back soon and to try and bring Rohan along.

"He's a nice bloke, your Professor Stratford," Adam said as they walked toward the dining hall in the darkening twilight. "Pity we didn't get to see Frankie, though."

"Oh, get over it, Adam," Henry said.

"Yes, Rohan," Adam said, grinning.

But Adam didn't get over it. He stared longingly toward the High Table at supper, sighing.

"Fair Francesca," Adam murmured over a forkful of peas, "the maiden of my heart."

Henry and Rohan laughed, as Adam had just tipped the peas into his lap.

That night, Adam was even slower with his reading than usual.

"What's the point?" he asked, throwing down his military history book in disgust. "It's the weekend, anyhow."

Through their door, Henry could hear the other boys horsing around in the common room.

The point, Henry knew, was to make it hurt less that the other boys kept away from them. With a sigh, he returned to his chart, though he'd memorized it long ago.

The noise outside their door grew louder.

Rohan poked his head out to see what was going on.

"Well?" Adam prompted.

"They're fencing," Rohan said disapprovingly, "in the common room. With rolls of paper as weapons."

"That sounds fun," Adam said, his voice small.

"Well, we're not invited," Henry said.

And then there was a knock at their window, and Adam nearly toppled off his chair.

Outside the window stood a ghostly figure in white, its hand groping blindly against the glass.

Henry laughed. "It's Frankie," he said, crossing to open the window.

"Hello," Frankie said, grinning. "Or should I say 'Boo'?"

"Very funny," Adam muttered.

"Can I come in? I brought lemon cake."

"It's against the rules," Rohan said haughtily.

"Blast the rules," Frankie said. "Did I mention the cake has meringue on top?"

"Against the rules," Rohan repeated.

"Then go study in the library," Henry said.

"No, I'll stay," Rohan said in a long-suffering sort of tone, and then turned to Frankie. "I'm Rohan, by the way."

"I know," Frankie said, still poised on the windowsill.

"And that's Adam. Henry's told me all about you."

"Do you need a leg up, fair damsel?" Adam asked, a silly grin on his face as he gallantly extended a hand.

"Oh, save it for someone who cares," Frankie said, boosting herself onto the window ledge. There was a muffled rip. "Petticoats *again*," she moaned.

"There is a girl in our room," Rohan announced to no one in particular, "with ripped petticoats."

"Must be your lucky day," Frankie said, landing with a thud. "So who was the boy I smacked with my glove?"

"Fergus Valmont," the boys chorused.

"What a name." Frankie made a face. "He even *sounds* horrible."

"He's Lord Havelock's nephew," Henry said.

"That would explain the resemblance," she said, unwrapping a large piece of cake.

Adam stared at it longingly.

"Would you like a slice?" Frankie asked patiently.

"Yes, please," Adam said.

"Well, you'll have to win it," Frankie said, pulling out a deck of cards. "Anyone for poker?"

Rohan put his face in his hands.

"There is a girl in our room . . . ," he began again.

"Yes, yes, with ripped petticoats and gambling," Frankie said dismissively. "So you've said. Now you can sit down here on the nice floor and play a civilized game of cards, or you can go out there and whack around a paper stick like a barbarian."

Rohan sat.

"I shouldn't warn you," he said, "but I'm rather good at cards."

"I'd be disappointed if you weren't," Frankie said, shuffling the deck with an expert *snap!*

"I have a different bet," Adam said.

Everyone stared at him.

"If I win this hand," he told Frankie, "you and I fence a match tomorrow after chapel."

Frankie grinned. "Think you're up to it, suitor boy?"

Adam didn't flinch at Frankie's mocking nickname. "Absolutely."

"We'll fence foil," Frankie said decisively. "Easier to limit the strike zone."

"Done. Now deal," Adam said.

Frankie dealt.

And she lost. Badly.

"Ha!" Adam crowed. "I win! Foil. Tomorrow morning."

"Of course," Frankie said calmly, shuffling the deck. "Why do you think I threw the hand?"

"You lost on purpose?" Rohan asked.

"That's what I said." Frankie smiled. "It was a good bet to lose. I wanted to fence you tomorrow morning."

After the bet was won—or lost, in Frankie's case—they settled in to properly play cards, and it was a good time all around. Frankie wasn't half bad, nor Adam. Rohan was rather good, and Henry held his own, as Sander had often bullied him to play when he first started working at the Midsummer School.

They played for hours, munching on the cake rather than betting on it, and suddenly their slope-ceilinged room was quite cozy. The noise from the common room, rather than serving as a reminder that they weren't allowed to join in, made Henry, Adam, and Rohan very smug indeed. They were breaking the rules. They had a secret. And—there was no question of it now—they had best friends to share it with.

11

THE FORBIDDEN
FENCING MATCH

The next morning, Adam was the first one awake and dressed for chapel.

"Get up!" he yelled, pouncing on Henry's bed.

"Aaahhh!" Henry shouted, bolting upright, his heart pounding frantically. "Don't *do* that."

"Sorry," Adam said contritely. "But guess what today is?"

"Bloody *Saturday*," Rohan groaned. "So let me sleep."

"The moment of truth!" Adam said. "The greatest fencing match of them all."

Adam kept this up all through chapel, where he bounced in his seat so vigorously that Edmund leaned over from the pew behind theirs and asked him if he needed to use the toilet.

Frankie caught up with Henry after chapel. She carried a large sewing basket and wore a satin ribbon in her hair.

Henry tried and failed to suppress a smile.

"Lovely day for embroidery," he commented, only to be whacked rather hard with the sewing basket.

"I've hidden my fencing kit inside," Frankie whispered. "Now tell your friends to meet me in the armory in ten minutes."

"What about breakfast?" Adam asked stubbornly when Henry related the message.

"I'd expect," Rohan said, "that breakfast is the time you're least likely to be caught."

"You mean *we*," Henry said.

"I most certainly don't." Rohan gave Henry and Adam a severe look and dropped his voice to a whisper. "Girls in the room at night. Fencing girls on school grounds. I'll be in the library, studying the *passé composé*. You'll let me know the outcome, I expect?"

"*Rohannnnn*," Adam whined. "Forget the *passé composé*. Come on. We're not forbidden from going into the armory. We're not forbidden from seeing Frankie during the weekend, in a classroom."

"The Code of Chivalry," Rohan said stiffly, folding his arms across his chest. "You can't fight girls."

"I gave my word," Adam said. "You all heard me last night. It was a wager. Only a coward like Valmont would break his word to a lady."

Rohan sighed. "I'll keep lookout," he announced.

"*Thank* you," Adam said.

"Come on, we'd better go," Henry said.

Frankie had already changed into her fencing gear when they arrived. She handed Adam a foil and asked with a frown, "Where's Rohan?"

"Keeping lookout," Henry said with a warning glance at Adam.

Adam, for once, kept his mouth shut about Rohan's refusal to take part in their illicit fencing match.

"Well, Henry can referee," Frankie said.

"Wait, I hardly know anything about fencing," Henry protested.

"A hit is valid anywhere on the torso," Frankie said, "and you'll know about right of way?"

"Er, a little."

"If a hit is scored without a riposte, arm signal,

or forward step, it doesn't count," she said. "That's it. Adam, you ready?"

"No," Adam complained, holding up the gear that Frankie had brought. "This is huge on me."

Frankie bit her lip. "It's my father's. I thought it best not to borrow school equipment. Can you go without?"

Adam pushed up his sleeves. "Why not? After all, I'm fencing a girl."

Frankie's eyes gleamed.

"Take that back," she demanded, striking an "on guard" position. She was left-handed, Henry suddenly realized.

"Make me, fair damsel." Adam grinned.

"First to five hits?" she asked.

Frankie, in her full fencing gear, and Adam, in his glove, mask, and shirtsleeves, readied themselves on opposite ends of the piste. They saluted each other with their swords, and then turned and saluted Henry.

"Ready?" Henry called from the midpoint. "And fence."

Frankie sprang forward, her sword extended. Adam met her sword with his, and they parried so rapidly that all Henry saw was a blur of metal dancing forward and backward across the piste.

Suddenly, Frankie's back arm went down to signal an attack and she lunged forward, leading with her blunt-tipped sword straight into Adam's stomach.

"Hit!" she called, looking to Henry for confirmation. He nodded.

"One-zero, Winter," Henry called. "And fence!"

Again, their swords clashed, and again, the point went to Frankie.

Adam managed a swift hit, and then Frankie retaliated.

"Three-one, Winter," Henry called. "And fence!"

Adam shot forward, and so did Frankie. Their swords met, and Frankie riposted, freeing her sword to the outside. Even though he didn't have the right of way, Adam struck out, and Frankie, surprised by Adam's move, did as well.

Her sword struck Adam's exposed arm.

The point was blunted for practice, but it had been the edge that caught Adam just above the elbow.

An angry red welt sprang there, trickling blood into the crook of his arm.

Frankie stared in shock, her hand to her mouth. "I'm so sorry!" she cried.

"It's fine," Adam said stiffly.

But it wasn't fine. It wouldn't stop bleeding, even when Henry bound Frankie's ribbon around it the way Sir Frederick had shown them.

Rohan poked his head into the armory.

"It's awful quiet in here," he said, and then saw Henry rewrapping the blood-spotted ribbon around Adam's arm. "Oh. Er, that looks bad."

"It's fine," Adam said crossly. "Just a scratch. Can we get back to the match?"

Henry nearly laughed.

"The match is over," Henry said. "It's a draw."

He shot Frankie a look daring her to argue otherwise.

"We should take him to the sick matron," Rohan said.

"And say what?" Henry asked. "Sorry, we were fencing without proper padding and with no supervision, please don't tell Lord Havelock?"

"I'm fine," Adam insisted, and then he looked down at his arm and winced. "That's a lot of blood," he said weakly.

"Sir Frederick!" Henry said. "We'll take him to Sir Frederick. He's medicine master, he'll know what to do. And he wouldn't tell Lord Havelock."

"Let's go," Frankie said.

"Frankie," Adam said. "Can I lean on you for support since I'm dying of blood loss?"

Frankie rolled her eyes. "Is he always like this?"

"Always," Rohan said.

"Never speak ill of the dying," Adam complained.

"You're not dying." Henry did a final sweep of the armory to make sure everything had been put back into place. "Come on, to see Sir Frederick."

Sir Frederick kept his office in the thatch-castle thing, on the first-floor corridor. By the time Henry wearily raised his fist to knock on Sir Frederick's door, Adam's dramatics had tripled.

"Is this an angel I see?" Adam marveled, staring at Frankie. "I must not be long for this world."

"Only because I'm going to finish what I started," Frankie muttered.

Sir Frederick opened his door a crack, surveyed the scene, and then burst out laughing.

"I'm sorry," he said, "but you'd better come inside. I'd hate to have it on my conscience if Mr. Beckerman perished in the corridor."

Sir Frederick's office was rather larger than Henry had expected, and it was wonderfully strange.

Brass-knobbed objects cluttered the shelves—

well, the shelves that weren't already filled with pre-served specimens in cases, laboratory beakers stained with brightly colored residue, thick medical books, or daguerreotype photographs of old men in white coats.

With a severe look at the four of them, Sir Frederick opened a drawer in his paper-piled desk and took out some antiseptic and bandages.

"Give me your arm, Mr. Beckerman," Sir Frederick said.

Meekly, Adam obliged.

"Was there rust on the sword?" questioned Sir Frederick.

"How did you know we were fencing?" Adam asked in surprise.

Sir Frederick merely raised an eyebrow. Frankie was still in her fencing gear. And carrying a large basket filled with knitting. No wonder Sir Frederick had laughed, Henry thought.

"No rust," she said, looking at the floor. "It was an accident."

"Well, of course it was an accident," Sir Frederick said. "Do you think I entertained the possibility, even for a moment, that you purposefully impaled Mr.

Beckerman with a sword and then came to me to con-fess your crime?"

Sir Frederick finished fixing up Adam's arm and dusted off his hands.

"You're not going to tell my father, are you?" Frankie asked.

"Nor Lord Havelock," Henry, Adam, and Rohan put in.

"That depends on one thing," Sir Frederick said.

Henry forced himself to exhale. "What's that, sir?"

"Whether or not you'll stay for tea and biscuits." Sir Frederick smiled.

"Well, I am dying of hunger," Adam said.

"You're not dying of anything," Rohan said crossly.

"We'd be delighted," said Frankie, with a stern look at the boys.

Sir Frederick rang a bell on a thick cord behind his desk and, when an out-of-breath maid appeared, asked for a pot of tea. With a calm smile, he took a tin of bis-cuits out of his desk.

"Which one of you bandaged Mr. Beckerman's arm with that ribbon?" he asked, prying the lid off the tin.

Henry felt his cheeks flush. "I did, sir."

"Not bad at all," Sir Frederick said, proffering the biscuits.

"What kind are they?" Rohan asked, peering into the tin.

"Longbread biscuits, imported specially from the Nordlands," Sir Frederick said. "Try one."

Henry warily bit into his, as he wasn't certain what a biscuit with "bread" in the name would taste like. A rich, buttery flavor filled his mouth, with just a hint of cinnamon.

"This is brilliant," Henry enthused.

Encouraged by this, Adam, Rohan, and Frankie nibbled at their own biscuits.

When the tea came, Sir Frederick began to talk. He told them of his work as a young man in a hospital in the Nordlands, and of the strange foods the Nordlandic people ate: animal jellies and purple soups and raw fish. He asked the boys how their classes were going, and even inquired of Frankie how her lessons were getting on with Professor Stratford.

"I am on the edge of triumph," she said, her mouth twisting into a wry smile. "I feel certain I'm about to master the art of not dribbling paint onto my smock when I watercolor fruit."

Everyone, even Sir Frederick, laughed.

When a second-year student in his green and white tie knocked on Sir Frederick's door and reported that he definitely smelled pipe smoke coming from someone called Jasper Hallworth's room, the four friends were sorry to leave. Sir Frederick had treated them as though they were worth something—as though they were adults and not first-year students whom the other boys would not befriend, or a girl who wasn't very good at being one.

"Come and visit me anytime," Sir Frederick said with a little wave, and then followed the second-year boy down the hallway in the opposite direction, muttering about wooden beams and stray sparks.

"That was lucky," Adam said as they returned to the main building, passing a group of first years playing cricket in the patchy sunlight.

"I know. I can't believe he's not going to tell Lord Havelock," Henry said.

"I meant that Sir Frederick fed us, since we missed breakfast," Adam replied. "Owww, don't *shove* me, Frankie."

"Sorry, I slipped."

Rohan snorted. "Pity I missed the fencing," he said.

"It would have been immensely gratifying to see Adam run through with a sword."

One of the boys playing cricket had put down his gear and was heading toward them. Because of the slant of the sunlight, Henry couldn't tell who it was; it could have been anyone—not that anyone talked to them—but Henry had a sinking feeling.

Too late to turn and walk the other direction, they realized who it was: Valmont.

"Nice trousers," Valmont said to Frankie with a disapproving frown. "It's a shame you weren't raised to behave decently. Haven't you a mother who cares?"

"My mother's dead," Frankie said, clenching her fists, "as you soon will be."

Valmont threw his head back and laughed.

"As if you could hurt a fly without sobbing into your little embroidered handkerchief about it," he said, and then his eyes narrowed as he spotted the bandage on Adam's arm.

Adam pushed his sleeve down over the bandage, but it was too late.

"You've been fencing," Valmont accused, and then he put two and two together and his eyes widened.

"You've been fencing a *girl*. And she *hurt* you. Oh, this is precious."

"Keep your mouth shut, Valmont," Henry said, at the same time Rohan said, "Sir Frederick was giving us an extra lesson in medicine. Adam isn't hurt; he just forgot to take the bandage off."

"Is that so?" Valmont asked, and then, without warning, his hand shot out and squeezed Adam's bandage, hard.

"Ahhhhhhh!" Adam yelled. "I'm dying!"

"Don't you dare touch him," Henry said.

"I won't have to," Valmont said. "I was just on my way to see Uncle Havelock. I wonder what he'll think when I tell him you've broken into the armory?"

"It's rather warm these days, isn't it?" Frankie said suddenly.

Henry shot her a questioning glance, but Frankie merely smiled.

"So?" Valmont asked.

"Warm enough that you'd sleep with the windows open?"

"Maybe," Valmont acknowledged warily.

"Well," Frankie said. "Maybe I'm taking a walk

around the quadrangle early one morning, and I see a wide open window at just the right height for me to wriggle inside and do terrible, terrible things to whomever I find there, fast asleep."

Valmont gulped.

"But the window doesn't need to be open," Frankie continued with a grin. "I just wiggle my hairpin in that old lock and no one would ever know I'd been there until they woke."

"You'd get . . . ," Valmont began, and then stopped.

"What?" Frankie laughed. "In *trouble*? Why do you think I'm *here*, Valmont? Because I'm so much trouble that no school will have me. So think of the worst things that the worst boys ever did back at your baby secondary school, and know that I've done those things, and that I could do them to you, and there's nothing anyone can do to punish me that I haven't already had done to me a thousand times."

Valmont glared. "You're just a silly little girl," he muttered.

"Even worse for you, then, because you're scared of me," Frankie said.

"I'm not scared," Valmont said fiercely. "I'm just waiting until I can prove it. But I know you lot are up to something illicit, and when I have proof, you'll be sorry."

"And you'll be sleeping in your own pee," Frankie said with a snort. "All it takes is for me to put your hand into a cup of warm water when you're asleep."

"You are a horrible, filthy girl!" Valmont shouted.

The boys playing cricket looked up from their game to see what was going on.

"And *your* name on the Code of Chivalry is nothing more than an unwelcome stain, Fergus Valmont," Henry spat. "Let's go."

12

A FRIEND IN THE LIBRARY

I f Henry thought his first protocol lesson had been horrible, it was nothing compared to the second. On Tuesday afternoon, Professor Turveydrop made them stand in a long line and practice bowing to men of different stations.

"His Grace, the Duke," Professor Turveydrop called, and the boys bowed as they would to a duke.

"Good, Mr. Mehta," Professor Turveydrop cried. "And his lordship, Lord Someone-or-other."

The boys bowed again, differently.

"Henry Grim!" Professor Turveydrop cried. "Is there a reason you're bowing like that?"

Henry straightened, feeling his cheeks color.

"Like what, sir?"

"Like a servant bringing in the tea," Professor Turveydrop said with a dismissive wave of his hand.

The class died with laughter. Only Rohan, Adam, and quiet Edmund managed to keep their faces straight.

"Is something funny?" Professor Turveydrop asked severely.

No, Henry thought. The truth is often uncomfortable, but rarely funny.

"I didn't realize I was doing it, sir," Henry said.

"Yes, well, try to practice. You are a knight in training, not a common houseboy. Mr. Valmont, why are you smirking like that?"

"No reason, sir," Valmont said.

"And now, Sir So-and-so," Professor Turveydrop prompted.

The boys frowned.

"When faced with another man who has taken the Oath of Chivalry," Professor Turveydrop explained, "you salute. Watch me."

Henry floated through the rest of the lesson in an embarrassed sort of trance.

The professor's word echoed through his head: *Why*

are you bowing like a servant bringing in the tea? followed by the raucous laughter of his classmates.

Henry and the other first years spent that evening in the library, writing an essay for Lord Havelock. Every so often, Theobold would catch Henry's eye and bow elaborately, pantomiming holding out a serving tray.

With a sigh, Henry began building a little fortress of books around his place at the table, walling himself into his misery.

The library, like everything at Knightley Academy, was far grander than its counterpart at the Midsummer School. The books stretched upward for two stories, requiring both ladders and a wrap-around balcony for access. The ceiling, painted in fresco, was a dome depicting the celestial sphere and the myths of the constellations. Between every three seats at the long tables sat a green reading lamp, and the chairs, although worn from centuries of use, were comfortable.

The silence of the library was punctuated only by the occasional sigh or flipping of a page. The first years bent over their papers, scratching out their essays in careful, neat script.

Suddenly a group of second years, their green-striped

ties loosened around their necks, pushed open the library door, joking and talking loudly.

"You're not serious, Jas," a big, bespectacled boy said, clapping a hand on his friend's shoulder.

"Certainly I'm serious," the boy called Jas boomed. "That's what they call it."

"In your dreams," a shorter, stouter boy said, laughing.

"Not in mine!" Jas winked.

The older boys were seemingly unaware that they'd interrupted the first years, or that there was anyone else in the library at all. They passed by the end of the table where Henry, Adam, and Rohan sat, and the boy called Jas, explaining something with big, sweeping gestures, knocked part of Henry's book fortress to the floor.

Suddenly the silence seemed to widen. All of the first years stared.

With a sigh, Henry got to his knees and began picking up books.

"Frightfully sorry, there," the older boy said, stooping down and gathering up two of the books he'd upset. "I got a bit carried away."

"Not a problem," Henry said, surprised and pleased that he wasn't being treated like an outcast first year.

"Anyway, I'm Jasper Hallworth," the older boy said.

"Henry Grim," Henry said, and then, before he could help himself, "you're the one with the pipe."

"Well," Jasper said, straightening. "I'm not going to ask how you know about that, except to hope that my celebrity has reached even you titchy first years."

"I'm not titchy," Henry protested, drawing himself up to his full height. The top of his head reached Jasper's chin.

"You are; you're an armrest."

"And you're a chimney," Henry said, "or at least you smoke like one."

At this, Jasper threw his head back and laughed so loudly that the librarian came over and shushed him.

"You're all right, Henry Grim," Jasper said, ruffling Henry's hair and then taking the spiral stair up to the second level of books.

The other first years went back to their work, as though the conversation between Henry and Jasper had never happened.

But it had, and Henry returned to his essay with a small, secret smile and just a little bit less dread.

* * *

"Is this going to happen every night?" Rohan asked with a sigh as Frankie tumbled through the window a few hours later.

"I just came to see how Adam's arm is doing." Frankie pouted.

"Really, my fair damsel?" Adam asked, grinning over the top of his protocol notes.

"No," Frankie said, snorting.

"So guess what?" Henry said. He was rereading his essay for Lord Havelock, lying stomach-down on his bed. "Another student spoke to me tonight."

"You should have seen it," Adam enthused. "This bloody huge second year toppled Henry's books and then *helped pick them up.*"

Frankie shook her head. "You can't be serious. Come on, Rohan, was it *truly* that exciting?"

Rohan pressed his lips together and said nothing.

"Rohannnnn," Frankie whined. "Are you angry with me?"

"I am ignoring you," Rohan said, "in hopes that you will go away and Lord Havelock won't expel us."

"So this is you ignoring me, then?" Frankie queried.

"Yes, it is," Rohan said, primly picking up a novel from his desk and hiding his amused expression behind it.

"Well, I just came by to see if someone could help with my French."

"Let's see it," Henry said, scooting over on his bed to make room for Frankie.

"You're joking!" Adam cried. "You never help *me* with French and I *always* ask."

"I never help you precisely because you want me to do it *for* you," Henry said. "And besides, Professor Lingua would know. You're terrible at French."

"He wouldn't know I was terrible if you'd done my homework for me from the beginning," Adam protested.

"Believe me, he would," Rohan said, turning a page in his book. "And by the way, Henry, if you're planning for Frankie to stay, she should use Adam's desk, rather than sit on your bed."

"But *I'm* using my desk!" Adam protested.

"So use your bed," Rohan said, flipping another page in the novel he obviously wasn't reading.

"Fine," Adam said sulkily.

Frankie laid an exercise book on Adam's desk, and Henry scooted his chair and craned his neck to see.

"That," Frankie said, pointing. "What the devil is that?"

"It's a tense," Henry said.

"Why does it look like that?"

"Like what?" Henry asked patiently.

"Like something evil."

Henry tried not to laugh. "Because the verbs are irregular. Here, like this." Henry penciled the verb stems and their meanings into the margin of her notebook.

"That's it?" Frankie asked, wrinkling her nose.

"Well, no, there's more of them. Just memorize the verb stems, write them on cards or something, and then you won't think they're evil."

"They'll still be evil," Frankie grumbled, collecting her things.

"You're leaving?" Rohan asked cheerfully.

"Er," Henry said, ignoring the glare Rohan gave him. "Frankie? Could we swap tutoring?"

"Ask Adam to help you with fencing," she said.

"No . . . I meant protocol," Henry said, his face reddening.

"What, Rohan wouldn't do it?"

Rohan gave up the pretense of reading. "You never asked," he accused Henry.

"Because I thought you'd say no," Henry mumbled.

"I wouldn't have done," Rohan said, putting down

his book. "Frankie and I will help you together. After all, we can't have a repeat of this morning."

"What happened this morning?" Frankie asked. "And I haven't agreed to tutor you."

"This morning," Henry said, willing himself not to sound bitter about it, "Professor Turveydrop asked why I was bowing like a servant bringing in the tea."

"Oh, dear," Frankie said with a giggle. "When's the funeral?"

"Sorry?" Henry asked.

"Didn't you murder him for that?"

"He didn't mean anything by it. It was just an unfortunate choice of words."

"Well, stand up," Frankie said. "Let's see it."

Henry stood up.

"Whom am I addressing?" he asked.

"Lady Winter," Frankie said grandly, and then giggled as Henry bowed. "Oh, Lord, it *is* like you're bringing in the tea."

"Well, how do I fix it?" Henry asked, annoyed.

"First," Rohan said, "don't bow so low. You aren't meant to truly be humble; after all, you're a knight yourself. Just show respect, not obedience."

Henry tried again.

"Better," Frankie said. "Maybe try it a bit slower."

Henry went again.

"That's loads better!" Frankie said.

Henry sighed with relief.

"Yeah, now you bow like a serving *woman* bringing in the *newspaper*," Adam joked.

Henry picked up his pillow and threw it at Adam.

"Hey! I'm injured, so watch it!" Adam protested.

13

THE MYSTERIOUS
LETTERS

Over the next few weeks, Frankie regularly climbed through the boys' window. Her French improved, and Professor Turveydrop stopped singling out Henry in protocol. Occasionally, Edmund Merrill sat near Henry, Adam, and Rohan's end of the breakfast table and smiled shyly. All would have been going very well indeed if not for the letters Henry and his friends began to receive.

The first letter, addressed to Henry, arrived five days after the fuss in the library with Jasper and the books. Upon first glance, the envelope did not appear ominous. In fact, it appeared perfectly ordinary, a plain white rectangle, just another piece of post from the stack that

Luther, the first-year monitor, handed out at the beginning of breakfast.

"Who's that from?" Adam asked, leaning over Henry's shoulder for a better look.

"Dunno," Henry said, shrugging. He couldn't think of anyone who would send him a letter. Maybe Professor Stratford, but that seemed unlikely. Or perhaps it was one of Frankie's jokes.

In any case, there were no clues on the envelope. Just his name and *Knightley Academy, Avel-on-t'Hems*, for address. Henry ripped open the envelope.

It was empty.

Or so he thought at first.

At least, there was no letter inside.

But there, stuck to the side, was a tiny, grubby newspaper clipping, small enough to fit in the palm of his hand.

Henry removed the clipping, smoothed it onto his napkin, and frowned.

"What?" Adam asked petulantly. "What's it say?"

"Rubbish," Henry said, crumpling the scrap of newspaper and stuffing it into his jacket pocket.

"I want to read it," Adam whined.

"Trust me, you don't," Henry said.

During that afternoon's hour free, Henry went into

the most out-of-the-way toilets—the one in the tower by Lord Havelock's classroom—and reread the article scrap:

> in that tiny Nordlandic prefecture, he found two dozen women and children living in squalor in a tiny basement room of an old schoolhouse, without heat or running water. According to High Inspector Dimit Yascherov of the Nordlandic Policing Agency, and head of Partisan School, the women and children were half frozen, and nearly all suffered from terrible dysentery, and preparations were immediately made for transport to a nearby hospital. Despite the inspector's claims, the hospital holds no records of treating any women or children who match the description. It has been nine days since the inspector uncovered the illegally operating girls' school from an anonymous tip, and as of yet, no bodies have been found. In the Nordlands, it is an offense punishable by three years' hard labor to

Henry shredded the scrap of newspaper into the toilet. Who would send him this? And *why*?

But then, there was no reason to be upset, Henry reasoned. It was just a joke, a scrap from some gossip magazine whose articles were more serious than most. Or maybe it was from that kitchen maid Liza, who was so keen on conspiracy theories that she hadn't realized how creepy it would feel to receive it.

Henry had never paid much attention to the post, although he knew sort of hazily that Rohan was always getting letters from home, and once or twice, Adam had received a letter from his sisters that their mother had obviously forced them to write. But when the next morning's post was distributed, a letter came for Adam.

"My mum is always forcing them to write . . . ," Adam complained, tearing open the envelope. "Oi! There's nothing in here but a scrap of newsprint."

"Don't read it," Henry said darkly. "I'd expect it's the same as what I got yesterday."

"Oh, you mean if I read this, I'll know exactly what was in that mysterious letter you've been refusing to talk about?" Adam asked.

"Well, now I'm feeling left out," Rohan said.

"Trust me, you shouldn't," Henry said, quickly telling his friends about the oddly chilling news scrap he'd received.

"That's awful, mate," Adam said, smoothing out his piece of newspaper. "Maybe there was a nice wart removal cream advertisement on the back of yours, offering a discount, and that's what someone meant to send."

"Right, because my warts are ever so painful these days," Henry said dryly.

And then, as if through some unspoken agreement, the three friends bent their heads over Adam's piece of newspaper.

It was a different article, about shops in the Nordlands being forced to close if owners didn't display portraits of Chancellor Mors in their windows, and about shop looting and vandalism in the dead of night—crimes targeting shops owned by immigrants and those outside the religious majority.

Adam gave his friends a shaky grin once they'd finished reading the scrap of article. He turned it over.

On the back was an innocent advertisement for collapsible top hats.

And written in black ink across the advert: WISH YOU WERE HERE.

"Well, that's odd," Adam said, pulling a face. "Who'd wish I were inside of a collapsible top hat advert?"

But Henry and Rohan could see that, despite Adam's joking manner, he too had found the article disturbing.

"I'll bet it's Valmont," Henry whispered the next morning, on their way to chapel.

"I wouldn't be surprised, after what Frankie threatened to do to him," replied Rohan.

But at breakfast, no letters arrived. And none came the following day or the day after that.

"Definitely Valmont," Henry whispered to his friends when Professor Lingua's back was turned. "Two letters? I mean, it's a bit pathetic to send just the two and then forget about it, but that's Valmont."

The next morning, a letter arrived for Rohan.

"He probably overheard us in languages," Rohan commented, calmly slitting the envelope with his butter knife. "In any case . . ." Rohan trailed off and went quite pale.

"What is it?" Adam asked, leaning across the table and trying to make a grab for the letter.

But Rohan wouldn't show them until they were in private, so the classes that morning and afternoon seemed to go on for an age.

"Let me see it," Adam said the moment they'd escaped back to their room during the hour free.

Wordlessly, Rohan slammed the piece of paper onto his desk.

It wasn't newsprint. Henry could see that right away.

No, it was worse.

It was a scrap of paper torn from a book. There was an illustration, a gross caricature, really, of turbaned men with long, curved swords and evil grins of triumph, holding up the bloody, severed heads of their enemies by the scalp.

Written across the picture in thick black letters: GET OUT BEFORE WE MAKE YOU.

"If you'll excuse me," Rohan said stiffly, exiting the room.

Henry and Adam looked at each other, and then back down at the cartoon.

"He's gone too far," Henry said, "which means that we haven't gone far enough. I say we retaliate."

"How?" Adam asked.

"Frankie would know."

"I suppose," Adam said. "So, do you think we should go after Rohan?"

Henry shook his head. He was fairly certain that Rohan just wanted to be alone.

When Frankie climbed through their window that night, Rohan grinned.

"Oh, hello, Frankie. Glad you could make it," he said.

Frankie raised an eyebrow. "Who are you and what have you done with Rohan?"

"How terribly funny," Rohan said. "Isn't she funny, Adam?"

"Who are you and what have you done with Rohan?" Adam asked.

Henry quickly filled Frankie in on the letters.

"So you think it's Valmont?" she asked, wrinkling her nose.

"You don't?" Henry asked.

"No, I do. I was just hoping you hadn't made any other enemies that I didn't know about."

"It's either Valmont or Lord Havelock," Adam said. "Which do you think is the most likely?"

"Point taken," Frankie said. "Now, how badly would you like to get him back for this? We can humiliate him, get him in trouble, scare him, or hurt him. I'd recommend the first."

"All four isn't an option, then?" Rohan said, smiling ruefully.

"I think I like evil Rohan," Frankie said, and Rohan bristled.

"I agree, humiliation seems the way to go," Henry said, rescuing Rohan from Frankie's inevitable teasing.

"Then listen carefully . . ." With a wicked smile, Frankie told them exactly what she had in mind.

Come Monday morning, they were all exhausted. Henry nearly nodded off into his toast at breakfast—just like Professor Stratford used to.

"Long night?" Edmund asked, looking up from the book he was reading.

Henry yawned and shrugged. "Longer day ahead," he said, as they had medicine, then military history, then extra fencing.

"Did you know about the reading room on the second level of the library?" Edmund asked.

"No, why?"

"My brother told me that it's really good for quiet studying," Edmund said, topping off his tea. "Since *some people* seem to feel that they own the main library and can be as loud as they wish."

Henry smiled sympathetically. He knew exactly what Edmund was talking about. Theobold and Valmont had styled themselves after the older students, joking around in the library and ignoring the librarian when he told them off, much to the annoyance of everyone who was actually trying to study.

"Thanks," Henry said. "I'll take a look."

Even though medicine was his favorite class, it seemed to Henry that the clock's minute hand had lost all will to move. Finally, *finally*, it was time for military history, and Henry, Adam, and Rohan tried very hard not to look guilty as they took their seats.

Valmont, as usual, swaggered to the front row, alongside Theobold.

Henry's heart thundered when Lord Havelock swept into the room.

"Textbooks out," Lord Havelock snapped. "Turn to chapter twelve, on the crusades, and answer the end-of-chapter questions, the odds . . ." Everyone sighed. Lord Havelock smiled nastily. ". . . as well as the evens. This is individual work. You may begin."

Henry removed his textbook, notebook, and pen from his satchel, trying very hard not to look at Valmont. He opened to chapter twelve, on the crusades, and wrote at the top of a fresh notebook page *Chapter Twelve Questions*, also trying very hard not to look at Valmont.

But Henry couldn't help it—he looked.

Valmont, rather red in the face, was staring down at his closed textbook, hands on his lap.

"Mr. Valmont, is there a *problem*?" Lord Havelock asked.

Valmont looked up at their professor as though he could hardly believe what was happening. He shook his head.

"I said, is there a problem?" Lord Havelock asked, his voice lowering to a dangerous hiss.

"No, sir," Valmont said.

The classroom had gone eerily quiet. Lord Havelock was a teacher who played favorites, and everyone knew that he often indulged Theobold and, especially, Valmont.

"Then why are you sitting there *like an imbecile*?" Lord Havelock roared.

Valmont clenched his fists at his sides. "I can't open my textbook, sir," he whispered.

"Show me." Lord Havelock folded his arms and, in his billowing black master's gown, rather resembled a bat staring down at Valmont as though poised to attack.

Valmont handed Lord Havelock the book.

Lord Havelock tried to open it, failed, and then examined the book closely.

"This has been plastered shut," Lord Havelock announced, and although the class was too terrified to laugh, they all exchanged amused glances.

Someone had plastered Valmont's textbook shut!

Henry wished Frankie were there to see the results of Adam's expedition into the common room to borrow the textbook, Rohan's foray into the kitchen for the ingredients, and his own replacement of the pilfered text into Valmont's unsuspecting satchel.

"I suppose you'll have to share with Mr. Archer," Lord Havelock said, and Theobold shrugged indifferently. "You can do the odds while he does the evens."

This time a murmur rose up from the class. It wasn't fair! Valmont's and Theobold's assignments had been halved.

Henry exchanged a horrified look with Adam and Rohan, then bent over his notebook and scratched out the answers for the next ninety minutes, wondering why the perfect plan had backfired.

* * *

"Thanks, Grim," Valmont said after class.

"I haven't a clue what you're talking about," Henry said.

Theobold caught up with them and flexed his hand.

"Yes, I'm awfully in your debt, Grim," Theobold said. "I can't imagine how cramped *your* hand must be after having to write out the whole assignment."

Theobold and Valmont drifted ahead, laughing.

"That was horrible," Adam said, shuddering. "Bloody horrible. It didn't work!"

"Really?" Rohan said. "Because I thought it *definitely* worked. To the *opposite* effect."

Collectively, they groaned.

"Was it you?" Edmund whispered to Henry as they practiced parry-riposte exercises in fencing that afternoon.

Henry grinned.

"I knew it!" Edmund said, missing a beat with his riposte so Henry's sword landed a hit. "Sorry, let's go again. I wasn't ready. But anyhow, Luther said he thought it was some second years putting Valmont in his place for the business with the library, but I knew it was you and Adam."

"Shhh," Henry said, parrying again. Edmund's riposte connected and they switched roles, Edmund parrying this time. "It wasn't just the two of us."

"Not *Rohan*?" Edmund whispered, with a parry so anemic that Henry nearly lost his balance on the riposte.

"And Frankie," Henry admitted.

Edmund's grip went slack.

"The girl?"

"It was *her* idea."

"No!"

"Mr. Grim! Mr. Merrill! Have you perfected the move already?" the fencing master snapped.

"No, sir," Henry said.

"Sorry, sir," Edmund said fearfully. "It just takes some getting used to, fencing a left-hander."

Good save, thought Henry.

"Then watch me," the fencing master said, taking Edmund's place opposite Henry.

Not so good save, thought Henry with a gulp.

Henry adjusted his stance and saluted the fencing master.

"No need for formalities," the fencing master said. "And riposte!"

Without warning, the fencing master's sword shot out, and Henry deflected the blow, then came back to center and struck, the master turning away Henry's sword.

"Good," the fencing master grunted at Henry, moving on to the next pair of beginners. The intermediates were in the corner, doing lunges in full gear. It looked horribly painful.

14

LOCKED IN THE LIBRARY

The textbook incident should have been the end of it. Henry, Adam, Rohan, and Frankie should have shrugged, chalked it up to bad luck, and gone on with their evenings as usual—playing cards, helping with one another's homework, telling jokes, and generally pretending that they had never declared war on Valmont in the first place. There should have been a stalemate.

But that isn't how it happened.

The letters, although not specifically addressed to Henry, Adam, and Rohan, continued to arrive in the morning post.

For "the occupants of the triple room, first-floor corridor, Knightley Academy," there came an envelope containing a note quite possibly written in human blood. The message: YOUR TIME HERE IS FINISHED.

Henry flushed it down the toilet, but the next morning, another letter arrived, stuffed under the door to their room: YOU'RE GOING TO FAIL.

Henry, Adam, and Rohan tried their best to ignore it. After all, what else *could* they do? Reignite a prank war that could get them all in trouble? And anyway, it was just silly messages—it wasn't as though Valmont had done anything to back up the threats . . .

Two days later, Lord Havelock kept Henry after lessons.

Henry gave his friends a brave look and waved them ahead as he approached Lord Havelock's desk at the front of the room.

"Can you tell me," Lord Havelock began, and Henry nearly forgot how to breathe, "on what topic you chose to write your quarter-term essay?"

"On the plague, sir," Henry said, puzzled.

"Just on '*the plague*'?" Lord Havelock asked with a threatening smile.

Up close, Henry could see the graying stubble on Lord Havelock's cheeks, could smell a sinister, spicy pipe tobacco clinging to the professor's tweeds.

"No, sir," Henry said. "Specifically, I wrote about how Eastern and Western military conquest led to the opening of trade routes, which, in turn, brought the plague to the West and thus killed so much of the population that anyone left over was no longer restricted by the rigid class system, because there was no competition for land or resources."

Lord Havelock frowned. "I received no such essay from you."

Henry was horrified. What had happened to the essay? He'd worked so hard on it, staying in the library even long after Adam had left, and Adam always took forever because he pooled ink when he was nervous.

"Well, I turned it in, sir, yesterday, along with everyone else."

Henry tilted his chin up, eyes meeting Lord Havelock's, willing the professor to believe him.

"I received no such essay from you," Lord Havelock said again, and Henry hung his head.

He wouldn't be kicked out of Knightley Academy—he'd flunk out. Just like the letters had warned. Just like Valmont wanted.

"But there has been some tomfoolery as of late," Lord Havelock continued, and Henry glanced up, hardly daring to hope, "and from your description, I have no choice but to conclude that you did indeed complete the assignment and hand it in on time."

"Thank you, sir," Henry said, feeling a rush of gratitude toward Lord Havelock.

"However," Lord Havelock said with that dangerous smile, "as I have nothing to grade, you must do the assignment again. And I'll want a different topic. Whatever happened to your essay, I'm sure its disappearance was provoked, and this will teach you not to let it happen again."

"Yes, sir," Henry said, relieved and yet exhausted at the thought of redoing the essay. "When shall I rewrite the paper?"

"Tonight," Lord Havelock said. "I shall inform our librarian that you are to stay as late as you'd like past curfew."

"Yes, sir," Henry said.

And then Henry spent a far from delightful free hour in the library, going through the books to find a new topic for his essay.

At supper, Rohan asked Henry where he'd been.

"The *library*," Henry said with a sigh, indicating the pile of books at his side.

"I'm guessing this has something to do with Lord Havelock?" Rohan asked.

"And *Valmont*," Henry said darkly, stabbing violently at his pork tenderloin until it was full of little holes from the fork tines. "It seems my quarter-term essay was *misplaced*, so I'll have to do it over, on a different topic."

"That's really awful, mate," Adam said. "If I had to do mine over, I'd die."

"I worked so *hard*," Henry said. "It isn't right. It isn't as though he got in trouble for the textbook either. I mean, he said it himself: we did him a favor. So he does me this nasty turn in response?"

Henry shook his head, upset and disgusted at Valmont. The letters he could take. The letters were nothing, really. But this? He could have been *expelled*.

"At least Lord Havelock didn't give you a zero," Edmund said, sliding closer on the bench so that he joined Henry and his friends.

"True," Henry said. "But that isn't the *point*. Just look at him over there, drinking his cider like he hasn't a care in the world."

They all looked.

"He's only a bully," Edmund said, shaking his head.

"Theobold's by far the worse of the two. I promise you."

"How do you mean?" Rohan asked, but Edmund just shook his head.

Henry wrote his essay in the study room off the second level of the library, the one Edmund had told him about. It was a small room, the size of his dormitory, with an oval table and squashy upholstered chairs going bald in the seats. There was one small window near the ceiling, heavy wooden paneling, and a wall of bookshelves nearly bare save for a few dictionaries and a decaying book of maps.

Hours passed, and Henry fell into the rhythm of his paper, not noticing that the cup of tea he'd brought had gone cold hours before, not noticing that a moth fluttered in the corner by the dictionaries, not noticing that the side of his hand had become gray with ink stain.

Finally, Henry capped his pen and read over his essay.

It was good. Possibly even better than the first. And he was exhausted.

If Henry owned a pocket watch, he would have checked the hour. Instead, he gathered his things, stretched his stiff legs, and turned the doorknob.

The door was locked.

Oh no, thought Henry.

He tried the knob again, but it was no use. He'd been forgotten, and worse, locked in for the night.

"Hello!" Henry called, pounding on the door.

No answer.

For a good ten minutes, he pounded and yelled. But no one came.

And no one was going to come, he knew, so he better make himself comfortable for the night.

With a sigh, Henry pushed two of the squashy armchairs together into a makeshift bed and climbed in, covering himself with his coat. From that angle, the small study room looked spooky, with its dark walls cast in shadow. Henry closed his eyes, wondering what time the door would be unlocked the next morning, and if Adam and Rohan would wake up and realize he hadn't been back to the room.

Henry woke to the sound of a muffled click, a soft creak, and then the rather louder sound of a maid shrieking.

Henry bolted upright.

It was Liza, from the kitchens, a thick ring of keys attached to her belt.

"Hello, Liza," Henry said, stretching and running a hand through his sleep-rumpled hair. "Could you tell me what time it is?"

"Quarter past six," she said. "Whatchoo doin' sleepin' in the library, Master Henry?"

"Got locked in," Henry said, picking up his satchel.

"Not overnight?" she asked, horrified.

"Overnight," Henry said. "So thank you for coming along to unlock the door."

"I only come because Mary said she 'eard rattlin' and howlin' las' night and the library was prob'ly haunted."

"That was me," Henry said, and then, with a sinking feeling, asked, "so what time is this door usually unlocked, then?"

"Jus' before lunch," Liza said.

"I have to wash up before chapel," Henry said. "You can tell Mary the library isn't haunted."

And before his expression could betray him, he slipped out the door and back to the first-year corridor.

When Henry got back to his room, Adam was fastening his tie while Rohan looked on and tapped his foot impatiently.

"Where *were* you?" Adam asked.

"The library."

"All night?" Rohan asked, raising an eyebrow.

"I was locked in overnight," Henry said miserably, changing into his spare uniform with no time to wash up.

Rohan shot Henry a tortured look.

"Chapel's in five minutes, and you tell us this *now*?"

"Sorry," Henry said. "Go on ahead. I'll tell you about it at breakfast."

Adam and Rohan exchanged a look.

"Go," Henry said.

At breakfast, Rohan was horrified.

"We should have waited up for you," he said. "We should have *known* something was wrong."

"Well, we *did* think it was strange when you weren't there in the morning," Adam amended. "But you wake up so early sometimes, I figured you'd gone back to the library to finish your essay."

"It's fine, honestly," Henry said.

It was touching that his friends were so concerned, but the worst that could have happened hadn't—he hadn't missed Lord Havelock's class and lost his chance to hand in the new essay.

And anyway, Henry hadn't mentioned his suspicion that he'd been locked in on purpose, thanks to one

Fergus Valmont. It sounded silly, and besides, he didn't want to put ideas into Adam's head, since Adam was so prone to dramatics.

"Frankie's upset with you, did I mention?" Adam said.

"Why?" Henry asked, gulping coffee.

"She had to memorize some awful poem in French last night and wanted you to correct her pronunciation."

"I'll tell her I'm sorry that I was too busy being locked inside the library overnight," Henry muttered, and Rohan began to cough.

"You all right?" Adam asked.

Rohan shook his head.

Henry put down his coffee, and even Edmund looked up from his copy of the morning news.

Henry grabbed for the pitcher of water and hastily poured Rohan a glass, splashing water onto the tablecloth. Rohan gulped at the water, but his face had turned purple.

"Nuts," he wheezed.

"Nuts?" Adam asked, raising an eyebrow.

Rohan drew in a tortured breath and indicated the muffin he'd been eating. It looked like ordinary blueberry—the same thing Rohan always had for breakfast—but sure enough, it was dotted with finely chopped nuts.

"You're allergic to nuts?" Henry asked.

Rohan nodded.

Henry shot Adam a look and they helped Rohan out of his seat.

"Want me to come?" Edmund asked.

"No, thanks," Henry said. "We're just taking him to the sick matron. But could you take my satchel to military history and give Lord Havelock my essay?"

"Of course," Edmund said. "I'll tell him what's happened."

Henry glanced at the High Table. Lord Havelock stared sourly down at them, watching as Henry and Adam dragged Rohan to see the sick matron.

"There's *never* nuts in the blueberry muffins," Henry told Adam after first lesson, as they ran toward the sick bay to check on Rohan before medicine.

"I know. It's really strange," Adam said.

"Strange how?" Henry asked. "Clearly Valmont did this."

"But how?" Adam asked.

"He could have paid off the cook," Henry said, and then affected Valmont's nasty drawl. "'Oh, I do wish there were nuts in the blueberry muffins, like there are in all the best city restaurants.'"

"But how would he have known that Rohan was allergic?" Adam asked. "I mean, we didn't even know. It must have been a coincidence."

But Henry wasn't so sure.

They'd reached the sick bay, and the matron, a severe old woman with a hairy mole on the exact center of her chin, glared at them from beneath her nurse's cap.

"You're supposed to be in class," she said witheringly, hands on her wide hips.

"We know, ma'am," Henry said. "We've only just come to check on our friend."

"He's resting," she said, as though they'd insulted her by asking. "No visitors. Go back to class."

"Yes, ma'am. Sorry," Henry said, backing down the hallway.

"I . . . have . . . an idea," Adam panted as they sprinted toward medicine.

"What?"

"Let's fix up . . . let's fix up Sick Matron with Lord Ha-Havelock."

Henry laughed until his sides hurt.

Most of the time he wanted to give Adam a good smack, but sometimes Adam was the only one who made life at Knightley bearable.

Rohan missed the rest of that day's classes. He showed up for supper, though—a little pale, but smiling.

"Did I miss anything extraordinary?" he asked, pouring himself a glass of cider.

"Just a scintillating lecture on the Reformation," Adam said. "Why didn't you tell us that you're allergic to nuts?"

Rohan shrugged.

"Well, you're all right now," Henry said, even though Rohan didn't look all right at all. There were purplish bruises under his eyes, and his hand trembled as he lifted his cup of cider to take a tiny sip.

"Good as new," Rohan said, nibbling at the edge of a roasted potato.

Rohan kept up the facade of being recovered for the next hour, until he fell asleep directly after supper, fully dressed, on top of his bed.

"Should we wake him?" Adam asked.

Henry shook his head.

"He's really ill, Adam. I bet he lied to the sick matron to release him."

"Well, he *did* look a bit peaky at supper," Adam said.

There was a scratch at their window. Henry pushed it open.

"How's Rohan?" Frankie asked, propping her chin on the windowsill.

"Asleep," Henry whispered. "Meet you in the library?"

Five minutes later, they'd claimed the study room that Henry had been locked inside the night before.

With a small shudder, Henry left the door open a crack.

"Well, what's going on?" Frankie asked. "You two dragged Rohan out of breakfast this morning as though he was dying, and then he shows up at supper looking like death warmed up."

"He's allergic to nuts," Henry said.

"So why did he eat them?" Frankie asked.

"It seems Cook created a new dish this morning: the blueberry and nut muffin."

Frankie winced. "Bad luck," she said. "And speaking of, I made Professor Stratford cringe with my poetry pronunciation this afternoon. Where *were* you last night?"

"Here," Henry said.

"He was locked in," Adam added.

"All night?" Frankie asked.

Henry nodded. "They should do a plaque. 'This room is the historic site where Henry Grim was forced to spend the night,'" he said.

None of them smiled at the joke.

"This is really bad," Frankie said. "The point of plastering Valmont's textbook shut was to put an end to this sort of thing."

"Well, that *was* the point," Henry said, "but *clearly* it didn't work and hasn't for some time. I just want to know how he managed it."

"We could ask Liza," Adam said.

"Good idea," said Frankie.

But it was late, and unless they wanted to break curfew, asking Liza would have to wait.

15

A DANGEROUS SWORD

The next afternoon in fencing, Henry could hardly concentrate on their form exercise of tossing a small, bean-filled bag back and forth, catching it in a lunge position.

He'd partnered with Rohan, who was definitely off form. His movements were sluggish, and one time, when he dropped the bag, he'd rested a moment on the floor when he stooped to retrieve it, as though exhausted by the warm-up.

"Are you certain you're feeling all right?" Henry asked as the bag landed a good meter short of his outstretched hand.

"Fine," Rohan said tensely. "It's just difficult with your being left-handed."

"Mr. Mehta! Mr. Grim! Let's have some energy!" the fencing master cried.

"Yes, sir," Henry said, tossing the bag toward Rohan.

Rohan, teeth gritted, stepped into a spectacular lunge and made the catch.

"Watch that front leg, Mehta," the fencing master said, walking over. "It needs to be in line with your sword arm, not diagonal. Go again, without the bag."

Rohan gamely took his stance and lunged again.

"Good. Again!" the fencing master cried.

Rohan went again. His face was ashen and sweat trickled down his temples.

"Again!" called the fencing master.

"Sir," Henry said, "Rohan isn't well."

"Is that so, Mr. Mehta?" the fencing master asked.

Rohan looked for a moment as though he was going to deny it. But Henry gave him a stern glare and Rohan nodded.

"Yes, sir. Allergic reaction. I spent yesterday in the sick bay."

"Switch into the beginners for today," the fencing

master said. "Grim can take your place in the intermediates until you're recovered, and after that, we'll see.
I was going to promote him soon, anyway."

"Yes, sir," Henry said, flushing with pride.

"Yes, sir," Rohan said weakly, putting his hands on
his knees to catch his breath from the lunges.

Adam shot Henry a questioning glance when the
class divided into skill levels and Henry went off with
the intermediates.

"What's going on?" Adam asked, taking his usual
sword from where they were stowed in the gear cubbies.

"I've been promoted."

"Well, congratulations, mate."

"Thanks," Henry said, turning around so Adam
could help fasten his kit.

"What's this?" Valmont asked, putting on his glove.
"Where's Indian boy?"

"That's rude," Henry said. "And he's ill. I trust *you*
know why."

"Living with *you* would make anyone ill, servant
boy," Valmont said.

"Oh, how terribly clever," Henry retorted.

"Intermediates," the fencing master called. "Partner

up! First to three hits rotates to challenge the winner of the pair two over."

Henry looked at Adam. "Fancy a bout?" he asked.

"I'll beat you with my eyes closed, you know," Adam said cheerfully.

"Better you than Valmont." Henry said darkly. "*He'd* beat me with my back turned."

Adam laughed. "Fair enough."

With their masks on, the intermediates lined up at the far end of the room.

Henry could see the beginners at the other end doing advance-retreat exercises.

You've been promoted, he thought, willing himself to feel happy. But all he felt was nervous.

With a salute, Henry settled into his fencing crouch and hoped Adam wouldn't make him look too horrible.

Adam shot forward, sword outstretched, and Henry approached carefully. He was a cautious fencer, he'd discovered recently, always thinking and strategizing, always looking for an opening rather than taking his chances. Adam was just the opposite.

So fast that Henry could hardly believe it, Adam's sword shot out.

Henry riposted in retreat, and then, sensing an opening, lowered his back arm to signal attack and lunged.

"Off target, mate," Adam called, his voice muffled by the mesh visor.

He was right. Henry had struck Adam at the collarbone.

"Sorry," Henry said, and they resumed the bout.

They finished 3–1 Adam, and the only surprise was that Henry had managed to land a hit at all. Adam was easily one of the top three fencers in their year.

The pair two over was finishing as well. With their gear on, it was difficult to tell their classmates apart, but Henry had no trouble realizing that it was Valmont and Theobold they'd be facing.

"Who won?" Henry asked, walking over.

"Not you, obviously," Valmont said, sounding eerily like his uncle.

"No," Henry said.

"Well, it was three-oh, my victory," Valmont drawled, "but I have a proposal. I'd rather fence you than Jewish boy."

"Would you stop with the names?" Henry asked. "It's *rude.*"

"So what do you say? You and me, Beckerman and Theobold."

"You're on," Henry said, dashing back over to Adam to let him know what was happening.

"You're joking," Adam said.

"You don't want to?" Henry asked.

"No, I do. Theobold's rubbish. I'd love to slaughter him."

It was settled.

Henry took his place across from Valmont, his heart clamoring crazily. He didn't expect to win. But maybe he could land a hit and wipe that awful smirk off Valmont's face, repay him for all those horrible acts of the past week . . .

Valmont flicked his wrist slightly in the most pathetic salute Henry had ever seen. Henry returned the wrist-flick-as-salute and settled his stance.

Their swords clashed, and Henry disengaged to the outside, pressing his left-hander's advantage.

Valmont growled beneath his mask and struck a hit that landed off target. Henry used the outside angle and glanced a small blow off Valmont's chest.

"Hit," he called.

"I didn't feel anything," Valmont said.

"It was a hit," Henry insisted.

"Liar," Valmont hissed.

"You're the liar," Henry retorted. "Fine. It isn't worth the aggravation. Let's go again."

Valmont adjusted his grip, and Henry tried to slow his breathing. It *had* been a hit.

Valmont rushed forward, looking for an opening, the point of his sword circling. Henry focused as well. The world slowed until it was just this bout, just his hand in its suede glove with the blunt-tipped foil, and Valmont's white cotton target zone.

And there! Henry's back arm went down in signal, and he drove the foil forward, scoring an undeniable hit.

"Hit," Henry called tersely. "One-zero."

Valmont said nothing, only took his stance and rushed forward so quickly that Henry could barely react before he'd been struck on the rib cage.

"Hit! One-one," Valmont called.

And then Adam screamed.

Henry turned.

Theobold stood there, his mouth open in horror, the tip of his foil strangely wet.

No, not wet.

Covered with blood.

Adam's hand clutched at his side and then came away. There was a neat hole in his cotton vest, ringed red with blood.

"I'm dying," Adam accused, his voice muffled by the visor.

Everyone had stopped.

Henry threw down his sword and rushed over, helping Adam into a sitting position on the floor. Theobold just stood there, staring down at Adam in shock.

"It wasn't blunted," Theobold mumbled, as though in disbelief.

Henry took off Adam's mask, revealing Adam's face to be ghostly pale, his dark curls sticking to his soaked forehead.

"How deep is it?" Henry asked.

"Not so bad," Adam said weakly, trying to move his hand away to give Henry a look.

"Keep the pressure on," Henry snapped.

The fencing master had reached them. "What's happened?" he asked.

"Theobold's weapon wasn't blunted," Henry said.

"Take him to the sick matron," the fencing master told Henry and Valmont.

Henry stared at Valmont in horror.

Theobold had lost the first bout against Valmont. He hadn't even scored a hit. In all rights, Theobold was supposed to fence *Henry*. But Valmont had switched it. First the letters, then the library, then the nuts in the muffin, and now the unblunted sword. It kept getting worse.

"Yes, sir," Henry told the fencing master a beat too late. He helped Adam to his feet. "You helping or not?" Henry snarled at Valmont.

Valmont shook his head slightly, as though clearing it. "If I have to," he said, hoisting up Adam's other side.

Slowly, they made their way to the sick bay.

"You again!" the matron said, frowning at Henry, but then she saw Adam and her face wrinkled with concern. "Och, you poor dearie! What's happened to you?"

"My number's up," Adam said weakly, wincing as Henry helped him onto a cot.

"Your number's *not* up," Henry said, and then realized Valmont was still there, watching silently.

"We don't need *you* anymore," Henry said. "Go back to fencing."

Without a word, Valmont left.

"That was supposed to be me," Henry whispered

half to himself, sitting down in an armchair by the cot.

The matron was peeling off Adam's fencing gear.

"There now," she clucked when she saw the wound. "Just a flesh wound, my love. Just flesh."

"I'm staying with him," Henry said, daring the sick matron to disagree.

"Better ways to clear one's guilt," she mumbled.

"I didn't do this," Henry protested. "I'm his friend."

And I'm supposed to be there, in his place, Henry thought.

"I can't believe I let him score a hit," Adam said, wincing as the sick matron kneaded the skin near his cut.

"Yeah, what was that?" Henry joked. "Theobold's a worse fencer than I am."

"I know!" Adam said with feeling. Then his face crumpled with pain. "If I weren't so—owww, that *stings!*—confident in my talents with a sword, I'd have quite a complex from this. First Frankie and then Theobold."

The matron finished binding cloth around Adam's middle and brought him a patient's gown.

"Ugh, no!" Adam protested. "I'll wear my shirt."

"Your shirt's got a great bloody hole through the side," Henry reminded him.

"Exactly," Adam said. "It's rather heroic."

Henry helped Adam put on the shirt. It *was* rather heroic, he had to admit.

"You need to rest," the sick matron told Adam. "And your friend needs to leave."

Henry pretended to gather his things, and Adam pulled up the thin sheet and pretended to go to sleep.

Satisfied, the sick matron went into her office and shut the door.

"She's gone," Adam said, opening one eye.

"Finally."

Henry unfastened the neck of his fencing kit and briefly debated whether he should mention that Adam hadn't been meant to fence Theobold.

"Bloody Valmont," Adam said. "Did you see his face when he helped bring me here? He was as white as this scratchy, horrible sheet, and he couldn't say a word for the life of him."

"I noticed," Henry said. "But this is really bad. Even for Valmont. I mean, you could have *died*."

"Have a bit more faith in my fencing talent, Grim," Adam said, and then put a hand to his bandaged side. "Against Valmont, maybe. Against Rohan, perhaps. But Theobold? It was a lucky hit."

"I suppose," Henry said, still wondering why Valmont had insisted they switch fencing partners. Henry wanted so badly to blame Valmont for everything, but it didn't add up. He was missing something.

Adam grimaced.

"What?" Henry asked. "Would you like me to fetch the sick matron?"

"Actually," Adam said, a bit embarrassed, "there's probably sandwiches right now."

Henry glanced at the clock. Trust Adam to always know when it was time to eat. "Want me to get you one?"

"If it isn't any trouble," Adam said. "Turkey and cheese. But *no* tomatoes. And if they have apples, but make sure it isn't *bruised*. And—"

"What?" Henry asked irritably.

"And thank you for staying with me," Adam finished, and Henry felt ashamed.

"You're welcome," Henry said, hand on the doorknob.

"And if there's anything with chocolate, some of that too," Adam said.

Henry sighed.

16

CHECKMATE

Rohan couldn't concentrate on his homework and, for that matter, neither could Henry.

"She's just keeping him overnight," Henry said.

"I know." Rohan twirled a pencil between his fingers, the sheet of paper on his desk still blank.

"He's going to be fine," Henry said.

"I *know*, but—"

"He could have died. Well, he *didn't*. I'd rather not think about it," Henry said. "I'm going to the common room. Want to come?"

"No, thank you."

The common room was full. It was getting colder outside, and a fire blazed in the grate. Games of chess and checkers had been set up on every available surface, and boys who were waiting their turns hovered over the tables, watching those who played.

Henry and his friends rarely ventured into the common room, which was undisputedly Theobold's territory. Valmont and Luther were hunched over a chessboard in the armchairs by the fire, their sleeves pushed up, their attention focused.

Henry glanced at the game. Valmont was winning. Luther played bravely with just his queen, king, two pawns, and a knight remaining. Valmont, missing only three pawns, a castle, and a bishop, was just a few moves away from checkmate. Henry waited on the game, as he wanted to talk to Valmont.

He watched as Valmont, rather than going for the obvious checkmate, drew out the execution of Luther's king, removing first the two pawns, then the knight, and then finally ending it.

"Good game," Luther said chivalrously, standing up.

Valmont yawned. "It was a bore for me," he said. "But then, it's not as though anyone can match my skill."

"Is that so?" Henry asked, with just the hint of a smile.

"This is a *chessboard*, servant boy," Valmont said, as though Henry were quite deaf. "You use it to *play chess*."

"Well, maybe that's how *you* use it. *I* use it to beat you at chess," Henry returned.

"You're on."

Valmont began putting the pieces back in their positions, and Henry helped.

"I'll play white," Valmont declared, and Henry took the seat across from him, in front of the black pieces.

Valmont shot a pawn out two spaces, and Henry calmly considered how he wanted to win. Feign losing and then go in for the unexpected kill? Swiftly and suddenly? Laboriously? Should Valmont believe they were equally matched? There were so many possibilities, because Henry was excellent at chess. He'd learned it as a boy from the orphanage priest, playing games between lessons.

Henry chose the move Valmont would be most likely to expect, blocking his pawn.

"So," Henry said. "Adam's still in the sick bay."

"Really?" Valmont asked, eyes scanning the board. "Is he going to be— I mean, who cares? Your move."

Henry took one of Valmont's pawns.

"He's going to be fine," Henry said.

"Did I ask?" Valmont retorted, a finger on the pawn that Henry wanted him to move.

"You can't hate *all* of us that much," Henry said, capturing the pawn the moment Valmont moved it.

Valmont scowled. "No, I don't," he admitted, "just *you.*"

Henry puzzled over this as they played in silence for a few minutes, glaring down at the black and white spaces. Why would Valmont target Adam and Rohan if he had it in for Henry especially? At first, Henry had been certain that Valmont was the one behind the increasingly more dangerous acts of sabotage, but now he was unconvinced.

Henry forced his attention back to the board. He let Valmont take his castle—in exchange for Valmont's queen.

"I know it was you," Valmont said suddenly.

"What was me?"

"The plaster."

"You deserved it," Henry said.

"Who are *you* to judge what anyone deserves?" Valmont asked.

Henry slammed his bishop down.

"Check," Henry said.

Valmont scowled and again made the move that Henry anticipated.

"You know," Henry continued, "I wanted to ask you why you swapped with Theobold today to fence against me. And it's check again, by the way."

"*You're* the one who swapped with Jewish boy," Valmont said.

"Because *you* wanted to."

"No," Valmont said.

"Check," Henry said disgustedly. "And yes, you *did*. You wanted to have a go against me, and if it weren't for that, *I'd* be the one gutted with Theobold's sword."

"Pity you weren't," Valmont sneered, moving his king back a space. "Are you *accusing* me of something, Grim?"

Not anymore, Henry thought, picking up his queen, fighting to keep his face expressionless.

"Not at all," said Henry. "I am merely thanking you for saving me from the hassle of having a sword run through my side. I'm sorry I couldn't return the favor by sparing your king. Checkmate."

Valmont stared down at the board in shock. "That's impossible."

"We took the same exam, Valmont," Henry said, giving Valmont back his captured pieces. "I scored higher. Why are you so surprised when I beat you at things?"

"Because you're a bloody *servant*!" Valmont roared.

The common room quieted as everyone turned to stare.

"And *you're* a bloody sore *loser*!" Henry retorted, stomping back to his room.

Adam was back the next morning, and woefully unprepared for military history.

"I made sure you had your books when I brought the sandwiches," Henry accused.

Adam shrugged. "I thought Havelock would go easy on me, considering."

"You're joking," Rohan said. "If you'd lost a leg, Lord Havelock would still expect both of your boots to be shined."

Henry laughed.

"What are *you* so cheerful about?" Rohan asked.

Rohan had fallen asleep early the night before, but he was looking a lot better that morning, much to Henry's relief.

"I beat Valmont at chess last night in the common room," Henry said.

"Since when do you spend time in the common room?" Adam asked.

Henry shrugged. And then Valmont passed them in the hall on the way to languages. "Checkmate!" Henry called after him.

Adam chuckled, and then put a hand to his side, wincing.

"Avez-vous vue Frankie?" Henry asked his friends in languages, while they were supposed to be having a conversation about supper.

"What?" Adam asked, and then, receiving a glare from Professor Lingua, said, "I mean, *pardon?*"

Have you seen Frankie around? Henry wrote on a piece of paper.

Rohan shook his head and announced in rather tortured French that he preferred his steaks rare, thank you.

That was strange, Henry thought. Frankie would

have heard about Adam. The whole school had heard. But she hadn't come by the night before. Or caught up with them after chapel.

"*Non, monsieur, j'ai dit que j'aime le mieux les legumes vert,*" Henry said with a sigh.

"Show off," Adam muttered.

"*En français, Monsieur Beckerman!*" Professor Lingua shrilled.

"*Je suis malade!*" Adam protested. "I'm ill!"

"That's the best I've heard you speak French all year," muttered Henry.

Rohan tried very hard not to laugh.

Something itched at the back of Henry's mind throughout languages, a thought that he could not quite reach. And as much as he tried to ignore it, the itch commanded attention, until at last Henry grasped upon what was bothering him: the unblunted sword hadn't been meant for Adam. It had been intended for *him*. And as it was seeming more and more that Valmont *wasn't* the one behind everything, if perhaps the mastermind of these horrible accidents hadn't yet heard that *Adam* had been the one injured yesterday, Adam's intended "accident" could be waiting for him around any corner.

No, the thought was preposterous. Henry tried to dismiss it, but kept coming back to the idea: someone was sabotaging them. Someone who—as much as he hated to admit it—wasn't Valmont. And it wasn't just creepy letters anymore. Who knew what might happen next?

Henry was so shaken by the realization that he mentioned it to his friends after languages.

"I dunno about that, mate," Adam said. "Who would be targeting us?"

"Hmmm, how about Lord Havelock?" Henry asked, realizing how ridiculous it sounded.

"He's certainly horrible and elitist," Rohan said, "not to mention a terrible professor. But I don't think he's capable of doing these things. I mean, you said it yourself yesterday, Adam could have *died*." Rohan paused, and then, as though he didn't want to admit it, said, "*I* could have died, with the nuts."

Henry had rather suspected Rohan's allergy was much worse than he'd been pretending. But that wasn't the point. Rohan was right. There was no reason for Lord Havelock to sabotage them.

"I suppose you're right," Henry admitted.

"If Lord Havelock wanted us kicked out, all he'd

have to do was open our door one night and find Frankie in our room," Rohan said severely.

"Fine," Henry said. "I'll make certain Frankie knows the room is off-limits from now on."

"Thank you," Rohan said.

"Just be careful, all right?" Henry urged Adam.

"But why *me*?" Adam whined. "If anyone's left unscathed, it's *you*."

Henry and Rohan exchanged a look, and Henry realized that Adam still hadn't figured it out.

Wishing he didn't have to speak the words, Henry said, "That sword was meant for me."

"What?" Adam asked, stopping in the middle of the second-floor hallway, beneath the creepy tapestry depicting a unicorn ramming its blood-soaked horn into a dark-helmeted knight.

"Valmont asked to swap," Henry said. "I was supposed to fence against Theobold, but we switched."

"That's right," Adam said, shocked. "I hadn't thought about it, but we *did* swap partners. And, no offense, but Theobold's an equal match for you."

"None taken," Henry said. "Wait, you're not upset?"

"Why would I be upset?" Adam asked. "Blimey, that tapestry is creepy. Anyway, it's not as though anyone *knew* about Theobold's foil. Besides which, he scored a lucky hit on me. He *really* could have killed *you*. No offense."

"None taken," Henry said sourly, and then sighed, raking his fingers through his already mussed hair. "In any case, we're still missing the most important questions: why are these things happening, and who's behind them?"

"Maybe Frankie knows something that we don't," Adam said.

"Maybe," Henry conceded.

They'd begun to walk back to their room, as much to get away from the ghastly tapestry as anything.

"We could go see her," Rohan said as though someone had prodded him with the tip of their pencil to make him say it.

"Good idea," Adam said brightly.

"Seriously, Adam, you'll watch yourself?" Henry pressed.

"Nothing's going to happen," Adam snapped.

And then he opened the door to their room and everyone gasped.

Their room had been ransacked.

Drawers gaped open from the dresser, their contents rifled through and strewn everywhere. Rohan's trunk was tipped on its side, and the three mattresses lay askew, as though someone had searched beneath them for hidden valuables.

Adam cursed.

Rohan, his lips pressed together in a thin, angry line, got to his knees and rummaged through his trunk to see what had been taken.

Henry, who didn't own anything valuable anyway, made a halfhearted inventory of his things. His textbooks, spare clothing, and small amount of coins were all there.

"Anyone missing anything?" Henry asked.

"Nothing," Rohan said, dusting off the knees of his trousers. "And I can't imagine *what* they were looking for. My money's untouched, and my spare pocket watch and father's books are still here."

"Adam?" Henry asked.

Adam sat on his bed, a strange look on his face.

"What?" Henry asked.

Adam shook his head. "It was under the mattress," he mumbled.

"*What* was under the mattress?" Rohan asked.

"I never should have taken it off," Adam wailed. "Stupid, stupid Valmont. I let him get to me, calling me

Jewish boy. And now my father's going to *kill* me."

"Adam!" Henry said sharply. "*What* are you going on about?"

"My necklace," Adam said miserably.

"Right," Henry said, remembering. "I'd nearly forgotten about that. What was it, again?"

"My *chai*," Adam said, and then, noticing his friends' blank looks, explained. "It's a Jewish thing. We become men at thirteen, and my father gave it to me at my bar mitzvah ceremony. It had belonged to his father before him, and his father before him, all the way back to Bohemia or someplace. It's a Star of David with the symbol of life on top. Solid gold on a gold chain. And I *took it off.*"

Adam put his head in his hands.

"I'm really sorry," Henry said, sitting down on the bed beside Adam. "But you're certain it's not here?"

"It was under the mattress," Adam said. "I felt for it every night to make sure."

Henry felt horrible for Adam. He didn't know how Adam did it, walking around with his head held high every day despite wearing the yarmulke that set him apart. Or sitting silently through chapel each morning, watching as everyone else recited the prayers they'd known by heart since they were small. No wonder Adam had taken off his necklace.

"Don't worry," Henry said with more confidence than he felt. "We'll get it back."

"Unless someone's melted it," Adam said with anguish.

"No one's melted it," Henry said with a severe look at Rohan, daring him to say differently.

"We could have another made," Rohan offered. "I'll pay for it."

"That's not the *point*," Adam said, glaring.

"It was just an offer," Rohan said angrily.

"Stop!" Henry said. "Look, we've got to decide what to do. This isn't just about Adam's necklace. Someone's come into our room and gone through our things. That's *really* wrong. We should tell our head of year."

"We're *not* going to Lord Havelock," Adam said. "Absolutely not. He's Valmont's *uncle*, in case you've forgotten."

"We could tell the headmaster," Rohan suggested. "After all, it's a serious offense. Stealing money is one thing, but family heirlooms?"

"That's not a bad thought," Henry said.

"Let's go now," Adam said, standing up. "We've got more than half our hour free left, and we could tell Frankie first. She'd vouch for us."

"Yes, because I'm sure Headmaster Winter would be terribly thrilled to know that we're acquainted with his daughter," Rohan muttered.

"You coming or not?" Adam asked, grabbing his coat.

"*I* am," Henry said.

Rohan knotted his scarf. "Let's go."

A maid opened the door of the headmaster's house and stared at them.

"You'll be wantin' Professor Stratford again?" she asked, holding the door open.

Henry knew he hadn't seen the professor for ages, and so he felt guilty when he said, "Actually, we're here to see—"

"Frankie!" Adam yelled.

Through the foyer, in the small, rose-colored receiving room, Frankie was bent over a tea service. She turned toward them, a look of horror on her face, and shook her head.

"You busy?" Adam called, oblivious as usual.

Rohan winced at the impropriety. "Adam," he said, grabbing hold of his friend's sleeve, "I think she's a bit occupied at the moment."

"It seems you have visitors," a rather severe woman's voice called from inside the receiving room. "Invite them inside, Francesca. I would so enjoy meeting them."

Frankie, looking as though she'd rather do anything but, gave a small curtsy.

"Yes, Grandmother."

Grandmother? Henry, Adam, and Rohan exchanged a look of horror as Frankie stomped toward them.

"Do *not* embarrass me," she hissed. "Now give Ellen your coats and come on."

Shedding their coats into the maid's arms, the boys followed Frankie into the receiving room.

A sterling silver tea set caught the light from a blazing fire, casting a cheery warmth around the lavishly decorated room. It would have been a welcoming little parlor indeed if not for the formidable gray-haired woman who glared at them from a high-backed chair.

"Grandmother Winter," Frankie said meekly, "may I present Adam Beckerman, Henry Grim, and Rohan Mehta."

"Pleased to meet you, Lady Winter," the boys mumbled, bowing.

"You," Grandmother Winter said, addressing Rohan. "How's your father?"

"His grace is very well, madam," Rohan said. "Shall I give him your regards when I see him next?"

"You shall," she said, smoothing her withered hands across the lap of her black lace dress. "Please, sit. Don't let my presence interrupt what is surely a routine visit."

Henry exchanged a horrified look with Rohan. This was extremely bad.

"May I offer you some tea and biscuits?" Frankie asked stiffly.

"No, thank you," Henry said.

"Tea, please," Adam said, and Henry elbowed him.

"Owww!" Adam cried, clapping a hand to his side. "I'm injured, did you forget?"

"Injured?" Frankie asked with a frown.

"Theobold ran me through with a sword yesterday," Adam said casually. "The blunt tip had been removed."

"But that's awful!" Frankie said, putting a hand over her mouth. "I'm so sorry to hear that you're not well, Mr. Beckerman."

Adam's lips twitched, as though he was trying very hard not to smile at Frankie's behavior.

Henry didn't find it funny at all. Now he knew exactly what his friends had meant the first week of school when they'd told him that you couldn't visit girls.

"That's not the half of it," Henry said. "Someone's just broken into our room and taken a family heirloom of Adam's. We were on our way to speak to your father about it."

Frankie again expressed her regret and offered Adam the sugar bowl.

"Mr. . . . Grim, was it?" Grandmother Winter said.

"Yes, ma'am?"

"Can you please explain the reason why you came by the house rather than going to my son's—the headmaster's—office about this matter?"

Henry gulped. "We—I mean, I—well, you see, we wanted to consult Frank— er, Francesca first."

"That's rather modern of you, Mr. Grim," Grandmother Winter said with a cold smile. "I had not realized that men training to become knights were prone to consulting fifteen-year-old girls about their personal affairs."

"Thank you, madam?" he managed. It came out sounding like a question.

"That wasn't a compliment," Grandmother Winter snapped.

"No, ma'am," Henry said.

"Or perhaps I have mistaken modernity for social ignorance," Grandmother Winter continued. "I have often attended galas with the duke of Holchester and his family, yet I cannot fathom having previously met anyone with the surname Grim."

Henry wished—suddenly, vehemently—that they had disturbed Lord Havelock with this matter instead.

"I am orphaned, madam," Henry said.

"So is Mr. Mehta," Grandmother Winter said with an expressive wave of her arm.

"I was never adopted," Henry said.

"I see." Grandmother Winter's lips puckered as though she had just discovered that the lemon tarts had been baked without sugar.

"Mr. Grim has been helping me with my French," Frankie said.

"Is that so?" Grandmother Winter asked.

"Yes, madam. I previously studied under Professor Stratford as well."

"And how much is Francesca paying you for these lessons?" Grandmother Winter asked.

"Nothing, madam," Henry said, his cheeks burning.

"We really ought to be going," Rohan said with an apologetic smile.

"Nonsense, Mr. Mehta," Grandmother Winter said. "I wouldn't dream of your leaving without consulting Francesca about the theft of this *family heirloom*."

"Yes, madam," Rohan replied. "Well, Miss Winter, have you an opinion on the matter?"

Frankie blinked her wide blue eyes as though she hadn't a thought in her head. She giggled and glanced down demurely.

"Perhaps you should consult my father," she said. "He is such a clever man and I know how dear this object must have been to Mr. Beckerman. I do so hope this was all a misunderstanding and there is *another explanation* besides theft."

Henry tried very hard not to register any surprise as Frankie secretly told them what she really thought. "Thank you for your opinion," he said.

Frankie twirled a curl around one finger and blushed sweetly.

"Yes, and thank you for the visit," Grandmother Winter said, standing up.

The boys scrambled to their feet.

"Oh, and Mr. Grim?" Grandmother Winter asked. *"J'espere que vous etes un bon instructeur."*

"Moi aussi, madam, mais le question n'est pas si je suis un bon instructeur mais si Francesca est une bonne etudiante."

Grandmother Winter inclined her head slightly and gave Henry a brief hint of a smile.

"You speak very pretty French, Mr. Grim. That is all."

17

THE CONSEQUENCES OF FAILURE

"Oh, *you speak* such *pretty French,'*" *Adam mocked* as they walked toward the thatch cottage where Headmaster Winter kept his office.

"Do shut up, Adam," Henry snapped.

"Yes, please do," Rohan echoed. "You've caused enough trouble as it is."

"What did *I* do?" Adam pouted.

"'Frankie, you busy?'" Henry mocked.

"Oh, that," Adam said, reddening.

The headmaster's office, when they reached it, was at the end of an imposing corridor lined with portraits of past headmasters. A door twice as tall as could reasonably be expected to fit the space loomed at the end, bearing a shiny plaque: OFFICE OF THE GRAND CHEVALIER LORD ANTHONY WINTER, HEADMASTER OF KNIGHTLEY ACADEMY.

Henry nervously raised a fist and knocked.

"Yes?" a cross voice called from inside.

"Headmaster Winter?" Henry called back. "We'd like to report a theft."

The door opened, and there was Headmaster Winter, his waistcoat covered in biscuit crumbs, wearing a pair of bedroom slippers with his rumpled pin-striped trousers.

"No, don't tell me your names. Let me guess," the headmaster said, surveying the three students. "Adam Beckerman, Henry Grim, and Rohan Mehta. Am I right?"

"Yes, sir," the boys said, surprised that the headmaster knew their names.

"Well, come inside."

Headmaster Winter's office was rather shocking; it had once been grand, that much was clear from the damask wallpaper and marble mantelpiece, but the grandness had been crowded out by rumpled newspapers, a half-eaten tea service long gone cold, a pile of maps, a hat rack hung with a dozen brightly colored umbrellas, and a windowsill jammed with potted plants that looked to be gasping for their last breath.

Thankfully, there was a squashy sofa facing the headmaster's desk, and the boys collapsed into it at Headmaster Winter's invitation.

"A theft, you say?" the headmaster asked with a frown. "And you've consulted your head of year . . . Lord Havelock?"

"Not quite," Henry admitted. "We didn't want to bother him."

"I see," the headmaster said, eyes twinkling as though he guessed that Henry and his friends were terrified of their head of year. "And the theft occurred just minutes ago, I am assuming, after which you rushed straight here?"

"Erm, not exactly," Adam said.

Headmaster Winter stared at them expectantly.

Henry sighed. "We went by your house first and had, er, tea."

Headmaster Winter groaned.

"We didn't mean to," Henry hastily assured him. "The maid let us in thinking we were looking for Professor Stratford . . . and then it was too late."

"Yes, I'd rather suspect it would be," the headmaster said as though enjoying a private joke.

"This is rather serious, sir," Rohan said. "Our room has been burgled."

They told Headmaster Winter all about it. How the drawers had been rifled through and the mattresses moved. How nothing was missing besides Adam's necklace.

"Are you often the target of such misdeeds?" Headmaster Winter asked.

It would have been so easy to tell the headmaster everything. How it had all started with the newspaper clippings in the morning post, how they didn't know why this was happening or who was doing it. How Adam's necklace was just the most recent problem, and far from their only grievance.

But telling is never easy, especially to teachers. And so, through some unspoken agreement, all three boys shook their heads.

"No, sir," said Henry.

"Thank you for alerting me to the problem," the headmaster said. "I shall inform the teachers and staff that we are having an issue with theft, and I shall make it a point to speak out on this matter at chapel in the morning. But hadn't you boys be washing up for supper?"

"Yes, sir," they chorused, struggling to get up from the squashy sofa.

Henry gave Adam a hand, and Adam shot him a grateful look.

"Oh, and boys?" the headmaster called as they were nearly out the door.

"Yes, sir?" Henry said.

"My daughter tells me that the four of you are friends."

Henry, Adam, and Rohan exchanged a look of horror.

"Hopefully you can be a good influence on Francesca, if an unconventional one. But it's best if you keep this information from my mother," Headmaster Winter said with a conspiratorial wink.

"It's too late for that, sir," Henry said miserably.

True to his word, Headmaster Winter addressed the students at chapel the next morning. Theft not only showed that you coveted your neighbor's property, but it went against everything knighthood stood for. "The Code of Chivalry is not used to send scrambled messages," Headmaster Winter concluded, "and as such, there is no reason to break it."

Frankie caught up with the boys after chapel.

"Why, hello, Miss Winter," Rohan said blandly.

"Oh, shove it, Rohan." Frankie scowled. "Ever since my grandmother arrived she's been controlling my life. I can hardly get out of her sight."

"Francesca," Grandmother Winter trilled as she made her way toward the boys' pew. She wore a ridiculous hat covered in plumes, a hat far too grand for morning chapel.

"Ah, there you are, talking to the duke's son," Grandmother Winter said.

Rohan's cheeks colored.

"Hello, madam."

"Yes, hello, ma'am," Henry said, nudging Adam, who had fallen asleep in the pew. Adam snorted but didn't awaken.

"Come, Francesca," Grandmother Winter said. "I have called for tea and biscuits to be sent to my rooms. You may keep me company while you work on your embroidery."

Frankie, making sure that her grandmother wasn't watching, pulled a horrible face. "Yes, Grandmother."

At breakfast, Adam couldn't stop mocking Rohan.

"Oh, it's the duke's son," he said. "What a lovely match for our sweet little Francesca."

"Stow it, Adam," Rohan said sourly, picking at his

scone. He hadn't touched the blueberry muffins all week. "I can't help that she knows my family."

"Maybe if you started courting Frankie, we could see her more often," Adam said.

"Would you stop?" Rohan asked. "I'm not courting anybody. We're *fourteen*."

"And besides," Henry said with a lopsided grin, "we're not allowed to visit girls."

After lessons, Henry, Adam, and Rohan turned up once more at the doorstep of the headmaster's house.

"You *again*," Ellen clucked.

"We're here to see Professor Stratford," Henry said. "Truly, we are."

"I'll jest go an' check with him, shall I?" she asked, shutting the door in their faces.

Minutes later, after Henry had begun to suspect that she might not return, Ellen opened the door and ushered them inside.

"He says he'll see you."

Ellen led the boys through a large and lavish sitting room, which opened onto an orangery where Frankie stood in a white smock, scowling as she watercolored a vase of roses.

Grandmother Winter sat in a wingback chair, watching.

Hurrying the boys past Frankie, the maid led them up a back staircase, through a long hallway, and to the door of Professor Stratford's study.

"Here we are," she said, bobbing a curtsy and scurrying back down the stairs.

Suddenly, Henry realized something. "She took us through the servants' staircase," he said.

Rohan frowned.

"I can't imagine why," said Adam.

Henry, thinking of Frankie's dour grandmother, rather suspected he could venture a guess.

"Is that Henry?" Professor Stratford cried, opening the door to his cozy, book-strewn study with a broad grin. "Good to see you again, Adam! And this must be the infamous Rohan."

"Yes, sir," Rohan said with a slight bow.

"I won't stand for even the smallest whiff of formality," Professor Stratford said with a dismissive wave. "Now get inside and tell me what's going on with this thieving rumor."

"It isn't a rumor," Henry said.

"I didn't think it was," Professor Stratford said seriously, chewing on the corner of his mustache as he settled back into his chair. "And am I also correct in suspecting that this isn't the first thing to happen to the three of you?"

"How'd you know that?" Adam asked with surprise.

"Francesca told me about Henry's being locked into the library overnight."

"Right, that," Henry said. It seemed like ages ago, what with Rohan's allergic reaction, Adam's being stabbed with the sword, and the burglary of their room.

"There isn't more?" Professor Stratford asked, surprised.

With a sigh, Henry began to recount the events of the past two weeks.

"You're right," Professor Stratford said, pressing his fingertips to his temples. "It's not Valmont."

"But if it isn't Valmont," Rohan said, "we can't figure out anyone else with a vendetta against all three of us."

"I take it things are going better for you three socially?" Professor Stratford asked.

Henry nodded. "It's really only Valmont and Theobold who are still bothering us. Everyone else has pretty much dropped it. And Edmund, one of the boys in our year, is quite friendly."

"That's wonderful," the professor said, grinning.

Henry suddenly felt guilty for how infrequently he had visited his former tutor.

"So who do you think is behind everything, then?" asked Adam.

Professor Stratford shrugged. "I'm afraid I don't know, although I'd love to have the answer to this one. But I can certainly guess *why.*"

"*Really,* sir?" Rohan asked curiously.

"I've heard a rumor," Professor Stratford said, putting up a hand to discourage the boys from interrupting, "that your performance in lessons had been declining."

"Lord Havelock," Adam moaned, interrupting anyway.

"Not *just* Lord Havelock," the professor said. "And I wonder if you boys know what is at stake if your marks aren't high?"

Henry frowned. He was doing as well as could be expected in Lord Havelock's class; his marks had greatly improved in protocol; languages, medicine, and ethics were a breeze; and he'd recently been promoted in fencing. Adam, though, was struggling. And Rohan had never been strong in Havelock's class or in languages.

"What do you mean?" Henry asked.

"When Headmaster Winter opened the exam to commoners," Professor Stratford continued, "many of the school trustees were unhappy. They voiced concern that perhaps they had made a mistake in selecting the new headmaster. But they agreed to withhold judgment until they saw how the common students performed once admitted to the academy."

Henry stared at the professor in shock. He hadn't known, but he should have guessed. "And if we perform poorly?" he asked.

"If any of you gives the board of trustees *any* reason for doubt, academic or otherwise, then they may remove Headmaster Winter from his post. The exam would go back to the way it was, and you would no longer be permitted to stay here as students."

The boys exchanged a look of horror.

Not permitted to stay at Knightley? Henry's heart raced at the thought. At the moment, he was doing well at lessons, but Henry couldn't forget how close he had come to failing his quarter-term essay for Lord Havelock—how easily everything could shift toward the worst. What would become of him if he got kicked out?

Certainly no other fancy school would want him—a disgraced orphan, recently given the boot from Knightley as a failed social experiment.

But it wasn't just about what would become of him—the fate of Knightley Academy was at stake. If Henry and his friends failed, no other common boys would have a chance at becoming knights, and it would be their fault—his fault.

Suddenly, Henry felt sick.

Everything that had been happening to them—the threatening letters, the lost essay, being locked in the library, the nuts in the muffin, the unblunted sword, the burglary—was designed to *make them* fail.

It *was* sabotage after all. The warnings in those letters *hadn't* just been empty threats.

"Thank you for telling us," Henry said.

The professor's expression softened. "Oh, Henry," he said, as though they were back at the Midsummer School and once again Cook had refused Henry his supper for no specific offense.

"Really," Henry stubbornly insisted. "We'll do better. We have to. We can't give whoever is doing these things the satisfaction."

"I can call for some tea and biscuits, if you'd like," Professor Stratford said kindly.

"No, thank you," Adam said, and Henry stared at him in surprise. "We should be going."

"Lovely to meet you," Rohan mumbled.

Through an unspoken agreement, they took the servants' staircase down and didn't stop when they passed Frankie on their way out.

18

THE INTER-SCHOOL TOURNAMENT

Henry stayed behind after medicine the next day, telling his friends to save him a sandwich.

"Is there something I can do for you, Mr. Grim?" Sir Frederick asked, frowning as he rolled up his anatomy charts and fastened them shut.

"I was hoping you might have a moment to talk, sir?"

"Of course."

"Well," Henry said, fidgeting with the strap on his satchel, "I was wondering if you knew . . . back when I took the Knightley Exam . . . if you knew what was at stake?"

Sir Frederick finished with a chart and frowned at Henry. "However do you mean?"

"I was wondering if you knew what would happen . . . if I failed."

"What are you failing?" Sir Frederick asked, surprised.

"Nothing. I just mean, back when you fought with Headmaster Hathaway at the Midsummer School to let me come to Knightley, if it had occurred to you that I might fail, say, languages, would you have known what was at stake?"

An odd look crossed Sir Frederick's face.

"An experiment," the medicine master said, "always begins with a prediction of what the results might be. I predicted that you would excel."

"But if you had predicted wrong," Henry pressed.

"Then my hypothesis would be proven false."

Henry sighed.

"I know," Henry said softly, "that Headmaster Winter's job is dependent on mine and my friends' success."

"How do you know that?" Sir Frederick asked, raising an eyebrow.

"The same way I know that if one of us does poorly, the exam might be closed to all common-born boys in the future."

"That's just speculation," Sir Frederick said, picking

up an armload of charts. "And furthermore, in life, unlike in science, whatever happens is usually for the common good."

Henry frowned, but Sir Frederick ruffled Henry's hair and told him not to worry.

"The common *good*, not the common *bad*, prevails. You'll see, my boy. Now run along after your friends. I have to set up for the second years' practical exam."

When Henry joined his friends, the dining hall was echoing with loud, boisterous conversations that all sounded to be about the same thing, from the small bits that Henry overheard.

"—the tournament, I've heard."

"—event are you going to do?"

"—defending champion in history quiz."

"—Partisan always comes out on top in fencing."

"What's going on?" Henry asked, sitting down across from his friends.

"You missed the announcement," Edmund said, sliding over to join them. "They've set the date for the Inter-School Tournament."

"For the what?" Henry asked.

"The annual competition," said Edmund, who always

knew everything because of his older brother, "between Knightley and our rival school, Partisan."

"It's supposed to be some sort of skills contest," Rohan put in. "History quiz teams, fencing bouts, model treaty dispute sessions. But it's mostly for the older students, anyway."

"So when is it?" Henry asked.

"Next weekend," Edmund said. "We're apparently trying to avoid the bad weather expected to hit the Nordlands in November, so they've moved up the date."

"Wait, we're going *there*?" Henry asked, upset that he'd missed the announcement and didn't know any of this. "To the *Nordlands*?"

"Last year they held it here, this year we go there," Edmund said. "So are you looking to participate?"

"Me?" Henry asked, surprised. "I still don't even know what it *is*."

Rohan sighed and explained in full while Henry ate his sandwich. One weekend a year, the students at Knightley had a friendly contest against the students at Partisan, their rival school in the Nordlands. The students competed in all sorts of things—fencing, oratory, composition, model treaty dispute, history quiz team, even choir. First years competed in novice rounds, while second and third years competed in expert. Fourth years were too busy serving apprenticeships in their chosen specialties to be bothered.

While he listened, Henry nodded and smiled, but couldn't help feeling a sense of dread that they were going to the Nordlands—even if the Partisan School was just a few kilometers from the border, at the southern tip of the Great Nordlandic Lakes.

No one went to the Nordlands. The border was closed except to diplomatic parties and natural-born citizens, but then, an envoy from Knightley was certainly considered a diplomatic party. Henry thought—suddenly, unexpectedly—of the sinister newspaper clippings he and Adam had received in the post.

The Nordlands. Well, he'd find out if there was any truth to the rumors soon enough.

They had fencing next lesson, and Adam, despite his recent injury, clamored about how he intended to sign up to fence at the Inter-School Tournament as they made their way to the armory.

"Just you wait, I'm going to slaughter those Partisan students," Adam said.

"Er, right," said Henry, while Rohan bit his lip.

"Mr. Beckerman," the fencing master called the moment they entered the armory, "you'll be sitting out this lesson due to your injuries."

Henry had to stop himself from laughing at the look on Adam's face, which was more injured than his side. But then, it wasn't funny. How could *anything* be funny after Professor Stratford's revelation about their marks at Knightley, about the weight of their actions?

Someone was out to get them, to make sure they failed. This wasn't some dumb prank war or a schoolboy grudge.

It was real, and the stakes were terrifying.

On the fencing master's orders, Henry and Rohan mechanically walked over to the equipment cupboard to pick up their foils with the rest of the class.

But Henry's foil was missing. He stared at the empty cubby, a sense of dread thick in his stomach. Their saboteur had struck again.

"Mr. Grim! Is there a problem?" the fencing master called.

"Yes, sir," Henry said with a sigh. "My foil is missing, and it's the only left-handed sword."

The fencing master frowned.

"It was here this morning, and I've misplaced the

key to the storeroom, so you'll have to make do with one of the right-handed foils today."

Henry opened his mouth to argue, but then closed it. It was just too convenient that the key to the storeroom had gone missing as well.

"Yes, sir."

Henry picked up a spare right-handed foil and tried to grasp it in his left hand. But it was no use—the grip plate was all wrong. Instead of providing grooves for his fingers, the grip dug into them.

He frowned at the sword and tried a few passes, but it felt as though the sword might fly from his hand at any moment. As an experiment, he switched the foil to his right hand, where his fingers easily nestled in the grip. Switching his stance to suit, Henry tried an advance-retreat-lunge and nearly tripped over his own feet.

Rohan caught Henry's eye.

"Bad luck," he said with a sympathetic smile. "Are you going to be able to fence?"

"I'll have to," Henry said through gritted teeth.

The fencing master, apparently satisfied that he had fixed the problem, led the class through a form warm-up.

Henry fumbled along as best he could. It wasn't too hard to do the handwork without the footwork added in.

The fencing master called an end to the drill and divided the class by skill level. Henry and the rest of the intermediates were to partner up and fence to three hits, then rotate.

Henry took his place across from Rohan.

"Go easy on me," Henry said through his visor, his every instinct being to put his left foot forward, as he had learned.

Rohan nodded and gave a broad salute, which Henry returned.

And then Rohan started forward.

Henry fumbled his footwork and, with a useless riposte that missed Rohan's blade by miles, was quickly struck square in his target zone. Rohan did go easy on him, but Henry doubted he could have landed a hit against Lawrence Shipley, the worst of the beginners, so long as he was fencing right-handed.

Henry and Rohan shook hands, and Rohan moved on to fence James St. Fitzroy, the undefeated checkers champion of the common room. But no one wanted to fence Henry.

"Sorry, but you could kill me with that thing."

"I preferred you left-handed, Grim."

"Maybe next time?"

"I've already promised Theobold next bout."

Henry was grateful for the mesh visor that hid his expression as classmate after classmate refused the next bout.

It wasn't as though he blamed them—what was the fun of an easy defeat against an opponent who couldn't put up a fight?—but it still felt awful. As he stood there, his face going hot beneath his mask, Henry had the horrible sensation that he was back at the orphanage in Midsummer, a small, gangly boy who was always picked last for teams, a boy who had learned to prefer the company of books to the company of the bullying, cruel orphans.

"I'll have a go," Valmont said, poking Henry in the back with the tip of his foil to command attention.

Henry nearly refused. "Kick your enemies while they're down, is that the idea?" he asked, walking to position across from Valmont.

"More like watch *you* fall on your arse."

Valmont gave a weak salute, which Henry returned.

"I want a rematch at chess," Valmont said, surging forward and landing an easy hit into Henry's stomach.

"I'll play you again, but it isn't a rematch," Henry replied. "I beat you fairly the first time."

"Hit!" Valmont crowed.

Henry scowled and willed himself to do better. He couldn't let Valmont beat him 3–0.

One hit, Henry thought desperately. *One lucky hit, that's all I need.*

Henry concentrated on his footwork and managed a passable advance. Through some miracle, he was able to disengage his weapon and put his back arm down to signal attack, giving him the priority. Hardly daring to believe it, Henry lunged forward—and tripped.

He sprawled hands-down onto the wooden floor, landing with a theatrical *slap!* Valmont, in the middle of an attempted riposte, lost his balance as well, tripping over Henry.

Henry, his face crimson with embarrassment beneath his mask, climbed to his feet.

"Sorry," he said, offering Valmont a hand up.

Valmont sat on the floor, his sword forgotten at his side, his gloved hand grasping his ankle.

"You filthy servant," Valmont sneered, pushing Henry's hand away.

"I'm sorry," Henry said again, angrily this time, hating that he was apologizing to Valmont for something that wasn't even really his fault. "But are you going to be all right?"

Valmont struggled to his feet.

"Fine," he snapped. But Henry could see that Valmont was favoring his right leg, making no move to put any weight on it.

"Is it sprained?" Henry asked, only now aware of their audience. The other boys had abandoned their bouts, preferring to stare at Henry and Valmont, who were known to be rivals.

"Of course not," Valmont snapped, bending to pick up his sword.

Valmont adjusted his grip and made as though he wanted to continue the bout.

Henry switched the foil to his left hand, deciding to ignore the hindrance of having a right-handed grip plate.

"You're certain you're all right?" Henry asked again.

Valmont grunted and gave a small salute. His weight was still on his left leg, Henry noticed.

Valmont took a step forward, but it was more of a limp.

Henry lowered his foil to his side. "It *is* sprained," he accused.

"Mr. Grim! Mr. Valmont! I saw you take a spill. Is everything sorted?" the fencing master shrilled.

Henry shook his head. "No, sir. Valmont's injured his ankle."

"So many injuries!" the fencing master cried, throwing up his hands in defeat. "Mr. Grim, please take Mr. Valmont to the sick matron for a cold compress."

"Yes, sir," Henry said, and then to Valmont, "come on, let's go."

"I'm perfectly fine, servant boy," Valmont snapped.

"Don't call me that," Henry returned. "And no, you're not. You need to put cold on or else it could swell."

"Look at you, playing nursemaid," Valmont taunted, taking off his mask and glove.

"More like remembering what we've been taught in medicine."

Valmont took a few careful steps, putting as little weight as possible on his right foot. "I can go myself."

"So go, then," Henry snapped.

Valmont hobbled toward the door of the armory. The other students, although feigning that they had resumed their bouts, stared.

Henry felt a knot settle in the pit of his stomach as he watched Valmont limp off toward the sick matron by himself. *It's just Valmont,* he told himself severely.

You hate him. But even so, he looks hurt and . . . alone.

Henry sighed and followed after Valmont.

"What are you doing?" Valmont asked. He'd stopped in the corridor outside the armory and was leaning against the wall.

"I'm helping you to the sick matron," Henry said. "What does it *look* like?"

Henry slung Valmont's arm around his neck, and they made their way to the sick bay in horrible silence.

"You *again*!" the sick matron clucked at Henry.

Henry reddened. It *was* rather starting to seem that way.

"Valmont's hurt his ankle," Henry said, and then turned and marched out of the sick bay.

"Not staying with your friend, dearie?" the sick matron called after Henry.

"He's *not* my friend," Henry muttered.

Valmont hadn't returned by the end of the lesson, so everyone headed to languages without him.

"He's probably faking to get out of lessons," Adam said as they passed beneath the gruesome unicorn tapestry on the way to Professor Lingua's class.

"If he fakes too convincingly, perhaps they'll amputate it," Rohan said with a small smile.

"We can only hope," Adam said. "Oi, Henry. Look alive, mate."

"Sorry," Henry said, shaking his head to clear it. On top of being lost in thought about visiting the Nordlands that weekend, he couldn't forget how Theobold, Valmont's only friend, hadn't cared at all when Valmont limped off to the sick matron.

"Listen, Adam, we should be partners today," Henry said after far too long a silence.

"Really?" Adam asked. "Because I thought you were all about my *learning* French rather than *copying* your work."

"That was before," Henry said.

Before. Already it seemed like ages ago, the days when Frankie would climb through their window with a deck of cards and a sly grin, convincing them to put aside their homework for a game or two. The days when their biggest worry was Valmont's bullying, when Adam's enormous appetite prompted midnight forays to the kitchens.

Professor Lingua waddled into the classroom with an

armload of books, plunking one down between every two seats.

"*Bonjour, classe,*" he called, and waited for a response.

"*Bonjour, Maître Lingua,*" the students called.

"We shall be finishing our unit in French and turning to a review of Latin at the end of next week," he said, his many chins quivering as he tried to catch his breath. "Thus, during the time we have left, we shall make use of the French you have learned."

Henry made a mental note to put aside some time to review Latin.

"Translations," Professor Lingua announced. "From French to English. No dictionaries on the first draft. You'll be working in pairs."

He assigned pages to each pair for translation, and then, with an enormous sigh, heaved himself into his chair.

"Page forty-two," Adam muttered, staring dubiously at the unopened book.

Henry took out a sheet of paper and his pencil, then glanced at the book's spine to see what they would be translating.

"It's Dumas!" Henry cried.

"Who?" Adam asked blankly.

"No, this is good. I've read it before in the original French, so that should help."

Henry turned to page forty-two. A sheet of paper fluttered out of the book and landed on the floor.

"What's that?" Adam asked, reaching down to retrieve it.

"Dunno," Henry said. "In any case, it's not mine."

Adam opened the piece of paper.

"'Full of ideas, he sped off as if on wings toward the Convent des Carmes Descheaux—a building without windows.' What's this? It's like a page of a novel."

Henry grabbed it from Adam.

It couldn't be—but it was. Henry smoothed the paper down on the desk next to their copy of *The Three Musketeers* and compared.

It was a finished translation of page forty-two.

Henry frowned, his eyes scanning back and forth between the documents. He could find no fault with the translation.

"Adam," Henry whispered, placing the open book on top of the paper to hide it. "This is a perfect translation."

"Really?" Adam asked. "Then let's use it. Assignment complete."

Henry shot him a look.

"I'm only joking," Adam said, as though hurt that Henry thought he'd meant it. "I wouldn't really. So, what d'you reckon we should do?"

"Tell Professor Lingua," Henry said, standing up and sliding the paper out from beneath the book.

"He'll think we cheated," Adam said, frantically tugging on Henry's sleeve to make him sit back down.

"No," Henry said, shaking his head. "He'll think we cheated if we *don't* turn it in."

"Cheated?" Theobold called, turning around from two desks in front of theirs. "Who cheated? *You?*"

"What seems to be the problem?" Professor Lingua asked, struggling out of his chair and waddling toward them.

"Grim and Beckerman are cheating," Theobold said, as though commenting on the weather. "Pity."

The other students glanced up curiously from their texts.

"Mr. Grim, Mr. Beckerman, I'll need to see your translation," Professor Lingua said.

Adam shot Henry a horrified look.

"We haven't started, sir," Henry said.

"That's not cheating, Mr. Archer. That's just plain

laziness," Professor Lingua said, and then he caught sight of the piece of paper in Henry's fist. "Or *is* it? Mr. Grim, kindly hand me the paper you're holding."

Henry's heart quickened, and he knew, without a doubt, that he wouldn't be able to talk his way out of it this time. He was finished.

"We found this in the book," Henry said, handing the paper to Professor Lingua.

The professor glanced down at the paper and then at Henry and Adam's book.

"It's a perfect translation of our assigned page," Henry said. "At least, the first few sentences are. I've not had a look at the rest. We didn't know what to do when we found it, which is why we hadn't begun the assignment."

"You found it in the book?" Professor Lingua said, his mouth curled into a deep, disapproving frown.

"Yes, sir," Henry and Adam said.

"I find that hard to believe," said Professor Lingua.

"It's the truth," Henry said simply. "And besides, it's not as though I would need it anyway."

Even though he hated showing off, Henry knew that it was the only way to salvage their situation. So he flipped the page over to forty-three and translated on the spot.

"'Upon my honor I assure you that you hurt me confoundedly. But I will use my left hand, as I usually do under such circumstances. Yet do not imagine that by this means I do you a favor as I fight equally well with either.'"

He made it halfway down the page without an error, reading at a normal pace, as though the text were truly written in English rather than French, before the professor stopped him.

"I'm aware of your skill with languages, Mr. Grim," Professor Lingua said. "And I am also aware that there is no reason *you* would require a cheat page. However, the matter at hand is that you and Mr. Beckerman did not come forward immediately. You've not broken the Code of Chivalry, but you've certainly taken some liberties, and I have no choice but to rebuke you for your actions."

Henry took a deep breath, steeling himself for whatever the punishment might be.

"I hereby forbid the both of you from participating in the Inter-School Tournament," Professor Lingua said. "I shall inform your head of year. And now, if you please, a translation of page one-fifty-eight. And I'll know if Mr. Grim does all the work."

"Yes, sir," the boys said, slumping in their seats.

Adam looked devastated about the tournament.

"That's not fair," he moaned. "I was going to fence foil."

"You're injured," Henry reminded him.

"It's nearly healed," Adam protested.

"I'm sorry about the tournament," Henry whispered, "but at least we're not in worse trouble. Now come on, we have to translate this. How would you start?"

With a sigh, Adam turned his attention to the text.

"Banned! Can you believe it?" Adam wailed during their hour free.

"I was there, Adam," Rohan said, calmly flipping a page in his military history textbook.

"There's always next year," Henry said to make his friend feel better.

But then both boys stared at him, and Henry muttered, "Never mind."

They'd avoided talking about what Professor Stratford had told them since the night before, hinting at things rather than saying what they really thought, as though not speaking the words would make it all untrue. And Henry couldn't stand it.

Through the door to their room, they could hear the

other boys in the common room chattering excitedly about the tournament.

"We need to talk," Henry said, and Rohan sighed.

"It's about time," Rohan said, and Henry was so relieved that he nearly laughed.

"*What* are we going to do?" Henry asked his friends.

"Earn better marks," Rohan said, indicating the textbook he was studying during their hour free.

"No, I mean besides that," Henry said.

"What else *can* we do?" Adam asked.

"We can find out who's behind this and stop them," Henry said.

Adam snorted. "Easier said than accomplished, mate."

"So I suppose you *don't* want your necklace back?" Henry asked.

"I never said that," Adam protested. "I'm just saying that it could be anyone behind this."

"Anyone besides Valmont, you mean," Rohan said.

"Could be," Adam insisted, and then sighed. "Yeah, I know. Not Valmont. By the way, Henry, excellent job tripping him today."

"Thanks," Henry said glumly.

He didn't think it was an excellent job at all. Professor Stratford had made it clear that Valmont wasn't behind any of this, and Henry had already expected as much. They'd plastered Valmont's textbook shut in retaliation for letters Valmont hadn't sent, they'd threatened to make him pee his bed in his sleep, and Henry had taunted him in the hallway about their chess match. No wonder Valmont hated them.

Henry almost felt sorry for Valmont, for the way Theobold hadn't cared when his friend was absent from languages because he was still in the sick bay.

"Hello . . . Henry?" Rohan asked.

"Sorry," Henry said. "I was just thinking that maybe we've been too hard on Valmont."

"Seriously?" Adam snorted.

"Hmmm," Rohan said. "We *were* hasty to react with the textbook incident, but it didn't cause him any harm. Havelock cut his assignment in half."

Henry nodded. "I know."

But he couldn't help replaying in his head all of his past encounters with Valmont.

"You deserved it," Henry had told him about the textbook plaster.

"Who are you to judge what I deserve?" Valmont had responded.

"*I* think it's Lord Havelock," Adam said. "He loathes

us. If anyone wanted to rid the school of commoners, it would be him."

Rohan considered this.

"And you have to admit, he's not particularly keen on the headmaster," Rohan commented.

Henry had to agree that Lord Havelock was the most likely to be behind everything. After all, Lord Havelock had detested Henry on sight. He had singled out Henry and his friends again and again. Havelock certainly could have pretended to lose Henry's term paper and then neglected to tell the librarian that Henry was staying late. He could have swapped the swords and changed the menu at breakfast and gone into their room. He could have done the French translation, a translation of which Valmont certainly wasn't capable. They just needed proof.

But first, Henry needed to do something else.

19

THE CAUSE OF THE CURSE

O h, it's you," *Valmont said sourly when Henry* turned up at the sick bay. "What do *you* want?"

Valmont was slumped in a chair, his ankle wrapped in a bandage and propped on a stack of pillows. In his lap was a thick pile of magazines.

Which means no one has brought 'round his assignments, Henry thought.

"Look," Henry said, "can we talk?"

"Say what you need to say, servant boy."

"When my friends and I plastered your textbook," Henry began, sitting gingerly on the edge of the bed and accidentally jostling Valmont's pillow tower in the process. "Sorry about that. It was because we thought you'd been the one behind something worse. But now we know you weren't the one doing those things, so I wanted to apologize."

"You're *apologizing*?" Valmont asked incredulously. "*You're* apologizing to *me* about the *textbook*?"

"Yeah, I am," Henry said quietly.

Valmont gave a hollow little laugh.

"I don't care about the textbook," he said. "The worst part is that you don't even know what you've done—what you've cost me."

"What are you talking about?" Henry asked.

"You *really* want to know?" Valmont asked angrily. "I was supposed to be the one to pass the Knightley Exam. Not you."

"We're back to that?" Henry groaned. That had been nearly six months ago.

"'We're back to that?'" Valmont mocked. "Yes, we are. Because *I* was supposed to pass the exam."

"*Supposed* to?" Henry asked. "What? It's not like the exam was rigged . . ." Henry stopped, his eyes wide with realization. No one had passed the exam at the Midsummer School for years. Everyone thought the school was cursed. But what if the school hadn't been cursed? What if the exam had been rigged to make the boys fail?

"Maybe it was," Valmont said coolly. "Uncle Havelock used to be the chief examiner, you know. Maybe he made sure that none of the boys at Midsummer passed the exam for just long enough that the next boy who passed would have the glory of restoring honor to the school. So that the next boy who passed became a hero. And then the headmaster up and quit and Sir Frederick was appointed the new chief examiner and instead of *me* passing the exam, it was *you*."

Valmont was glaring furiously at Henry, as though Henry ought to have known. As though Henry had purposefully taken away his glory and honor, relegating him to one of the late-admit spots based on family connections, stealing his place as a golden boy and demoting him to the role of Theobold's second in command, when back at the Midsummer School he had had cronies of his own.

"So *that's* why you hate me?" Henry asked, surprised. "Because I stole your glory by passing the exam back at Midsummer?"

"Obviously," Valmont sneered.

"Could you *be* any more selfish?" Henry accused.

"You're here anyway, aren't you? Do you know what would have happened to *me* if I'd failed the exam? I'd still be a servant scrubbing pots in the kitchens, eating cold scraps of leftovers, and sleeping in an unheated attic in the winter. So I didn't steal your glory or whatever it is you think I did. I gave myself a future, and what's more, I deserved it."

Henry had never been so angry, had never loathed Valmont so much as he did in that moment. Valmont was without a doubt the most ungrateful, spoiled, self-centered brat he'd ever met.

"I know," Valmont said.

"What?" Henry unclenched his fists and looked up.

"I know that, all right? That's what makes it so much worse. Because I'm not allowed to be mad at you. It's not like Harisford or some other boy from Midsummer passed the exam instead of me. No, it was the brilliant servant, the downtrodden orphan whom everyone felt so sorry for and let take the exam because of a loophole. For five years I'd been promised admiration and awe, and then a charity case came along, and what did it matter about *my* breaking some stupid curse when *you* changed five hundred years of history."

Henry didn't know what to say. Valmont was, well,

a person. He wasn't just some horrible monster sent specifically to torment Henry. From Valmont's perspective, it was rather the reverse. But he was still Valmont—none of this changed anything. He still called Henry and his roommates servant boy, Jewish boy, and Indian boy. He'd still tripped Henry in the hall and told everyone that Henry used to sleep in the barn with the pigs, and he'd still hurt Henry's arm with the bandage that first day in medicine. But now Henry knew the reason.

"I hope this doesn't mean we're friends," Henry said.

"Good. Me neither," Valmont spat.

"Good, because we're not."

"This doesn't mean I like you," Valmont said.

"Obviously," Henry returned. "Is Sick Matron going to let you out by supper?"

"She said she would. Why?"

"Chess rematch after," Henry said. "Or you could just concede victory now and save yourself the rather public humiliation."

"All right, I admit it," Valmont said, rolling his eyes. "You're better than me at chess."

The rest of the week was devoted to frantic preparations for the Inter-School Tournament, with little time for anything else. Professor Turveydrop was beside himself in protocol, drilling the boys on Nordlandic table manners ("Fork tines *up*, boys, not *down!*") and phrases ("Refer to all professors with the title Compatriot, never Lord or Sir"); Sir Frederick spent a rather welcome lesson reminiscing about his years of hospital work in the Nordlands and completely forgot to assign homework; Professor Lingua glared at Henry as though he wished he could take back his earlier words and force Henry to enter the French oratory competition; Lord Havelock recruited Theobold, Valmont, and a rather horrified Luther Leicester to undertake the novice military history quiz; Adam sulked constantly; Edmund, who had joined the choir at his elder brother's behest, forever had his nose buried in sheet music; and the fencing master took aside two pupils, Rohan and James St. Fitzroy, and devoted all of his attention to their form, leaving the other students to "practice what they'd learnt."

Rohan spent his evenings in the armory, leaving supper deep in conversation with James about feints and passes, and the library was empty most nights, giving Henry and Adam the luxury of sprawling their books while they worked—if they could concentrate despite the noise in the corridors. Jasper Hallworth and his crowd of "devil may care" second years were taking underground bets on the tournament and had set up shop in the annex across from the library. Boys in Henry's year, in a desperate attempt to learn more about the tournament, had adopted the habit of loitering outside the third years' common room. And two third years had been banned from the tournament for selling a cheat pamphlet, which, despite booming sales, turned out to be full of rubbish.

Henry didn't mind that he wouldn't be competing in the tournament. He didn't need the whole school counting on him on top of everything else he had to worry about. He didn't need the pressure, and he certainly didn't want the glory. Even though nowadays his classmates were quite civil, he still remembered those first few days all too well, when eating his supper felt like an examination that could be failed by his dropping a knife or using the wrong fork.

"I still don't see why Professor Lingua won't take it back and let us compete," Adam complained the night before they were to leave, with a glare in Rohan's direction.

"At least *you* don't have to worry about anything happening during the tournament," Rohan said severely.

"*I* could be disqualified at any moment for who knows what. *I* could be expelled."

"You could also slaughter those smug Partisan students," Adam wailed.

"It's only novice level," Henry said consolingly. But Rohan did have a fair point—the three of them weren't exactly lucky when it came to being around swords.

Rohan sighed.

"Henry's right, you know," he told Adam. "It's only first years—we don't count toward the overall tournament score. I doubt anyone will even notice the outcome. Besides, you *might* be relieved that you won't be calling attention to yourself."

Henry frowned. What was Rohan talking about?

Rohan indicated Adam's yarmulke.

Of course.

Henry had become so used to his friend's small, circular head covering that he barely noticed it anymore. But the Nordlandic people weren't known for their religious tolerance, and even though Henry was certain the tabloid stories were nothing more than gross exaggerations, they were certainly based on *some* truth.

"Er, Adam?" Henry said. "Maybe you should, you know, not wear—"

"I'm *not* taking off my yarmulke!" Adam protested. "Absolutely not. I should never have taken off my *necklace*, and you know what happened with *that*."

"Suit yourself," Rohan said calmly, "but don't say I didn't warn you. I, for one, am glad that I'll be competing in a masked event, and after it's over I intend to stay well out of the way."

Henry shot Rohan a sympathetic look. Being adopted by a duke couldn't change the fact that Rohan was brown-skinned and foreign-looking. And for all the Nordlands' boasting that they'd done away with their aristocracy, the Nordlandic people were known to be fiercely antiforeigners.

Ironically enough, for the first time since Henry had gone away to school, he wouldn't feel like a lowly commoner. And yet, he would have traded all that in a moment if it meant that his friends could feel less anxious about their visit.

The next morning, the bells sounded at far too early an hour even for Henry. And just before dawn, the red-eyed, half-asleep Knightley Academy students boarded a specially reserved train at Avel-on-t'Hems station express to the Nordlands.

The journey took most of the morning and afternoon. Adam sprawled out over a whole bench in their compartment and promptly began to snore. Rohan sat reading a book without turning the pages, and whenever Henry asked him a question, Rohan looked up blankly and said, "Pardon?"

Henry studied a Latin book he'd brought along, reviewing the declinations until he gave himself a headache from reading on the train.

By midafternoon, the train was hurtling through the northern reaches of the country, an area that Henry had never seen. He stared out the window of their compartment, fascinated.

Outside, he could see the coast, dotted with sturdy fishing boats and quaint seaside villages. Swelling beyond the occasional lighthouses was the channel, a murky gray expanse. Soon the train tracks veered further inland, revealing hills cresting so high that Henry at first thought they had to be mountains, before he remembered his geography. They passed stone castles and the crumbling remains of old military fortresses, and suddenly, they passed nothing at all but rocky land covered with an early layer of frost.

"Nearly there," Rohan said blandly, checking his pocket watch.

A half hour later, they'd reached the border, and the train came to a screeching halt outside a squat gray building.

"*This* is Partisan?" Adam asked, unimpressed.

The door to the building opened, and six Nordlandic patrollers in two neat rows marched smartly toward the train, their breath clouding in the cold northern air. Henry and his friends watched as the Nordlandic patrollers, their green-coated uniforms made of thick winter wool, stepped onto the train for inspection. The Patrollers wore tall furry hats, and at their hips, alongside their peacekeeper's swords, were nasty-looking wooden batons covered with metal spikes.

When a patroller opened the door to Henry, Adam, and Rohan's compartment, Henry and his friends surged to their feet and met him with a sturdy salute, as Professor Turveydrop had taught them.

Their patroller was barely out of Partisan, from the looks of him, his face still cragged with acne beneath his tall hat. He frowned at Rohan, but returned their salute and then marched smartly from the compartment.

After the patroller left, Henry let out a breath he hadn't realized he'd been holding.

It wasn't as though he'd expected something horrible to happen, but Henry was surprised to recognize that when it came to the Nordlands, he was curious, yes, but also . . . afraid. And he rather suspected his friends felt much the same.

Henry watched as Adam guiltily removed his school uniform hat and turned it over and over in his lap, as though the inside of that hat held the answer to what he should do about his yarmulke.

Each of them lost in thought, Henry, Adam, and Rohan said nothing until the patrollers had exited the train and the steam engine again lurched to a start.

The sky had started to darken during the patrollers' inspection, and as the train continued its journey, the scene outside their compartment window was one of midnight blue mountain silhouettes and faraway lights of distant towns.

"Blimey, can you believe we're in the *Nordlands*?" Adam finally asked, breaking the contemplative silence.

Henry shook his head, too mesmerized by the view out the window to reply.

"I hope we haven't missed supper," Adam added. "And I hope it isn't that rubbish food Sir Frederick was going on about—raw fish and meat jellies and that sort of thing."

"With our luck," Rohan said with a small smile, "it will probably be nothing but bacon."

And despite their anxiety, the three friends grinned.

They reached Partisan nearly a half hour after the border inspection. The rail station sat at the foot of a hill, at the top of which loomed the Partisan School castle, known as Partisan Keep. A moat gone to sewage encircled the hill, and a fat stone bridge flanked by two crumbling watchtowers was the only way across.

The Knightley students were forced into two-by-two rows by Lord Havelock, and the first years were the last group to cross. Henry walked alongside Edmund, who hummed his choir section under his breath.

The Partisan School was an ancient stronghold left over from the days of the Sasson conquerors, with slits for windows to deflect the course of harmful arrows. Everything about the place was eerily antiquated. Instead of modern electric lighting, Partisan used old-fashioned torches, which lit the way up dozens of worn stone steps and through an enormous wooden door that rather resembled a drawbridge.

"Spooky, isn't it?" Adam whispered to Rohan.

Henry, who was behind his friends, tried not to smile as Rohan elbowed Adam in the side.

But it *was* spooky, Henry had to admit. And freezing. Trying to keep his teeth from chattering, Henry followed the line of students through the drafty corridors and into Partisan's Great Hall.

Checked banners bearing the Partisan crest (an equal-armed cross inside a diamond) and the Nordlandic crest (three serpents and a star) billowed from the elaborate ceiling beams. The Partisan students stood in neatly formed squadrons, their thick wool uniforms trimmed with fur and gleaming with badges.

Henry's heart thundered with excitement and awe as he marched behind his friends. They came to a halt at the far end of the hall, where the High Table stood resplendent in front of an enormous stained-glass window that depicted victorious crusaders on horseback. They formed the lines from Professor Turveydrop's drills, and at their year monitor's count, saluted.

Henry was glad for his height, as from his place he could see Headmaster Winter step forward and embrace the Partisan headmaster, a short, plump man in a fur-trimmed military-style suit so heavy with brocade and badges as to render the color of the fabric unrecognizable.

Headmaster Winter, Henry noted with some amusement, had spilled tea down the front of his shirt on the journey—but at least his cravat was done and he'd remembered to replace his bedroom slippers with proper shoes.

The short, plump man saluted Headmaster Winter, kissed him warmly on either cheek, and stepped up to a lectern. Immediately the hall quieted.

"Welcome, Grand Chevalier Winter, Knightley Academy students, and distinguished staff," he said in his thick Nordlandic accent, which butchered the vowels in a way that fascinated Henry. "I am head of Partisan School, Dimit Yascherov, and I cannae tell ye how glad I am to host this year's Inter-School Tournament here at Partisan Keep."

Henry and the rest of the students clapped politely, and Henry couldn't shake the feeling that he'd heard Yascherov's name somewhere before.

The feeling nagged at him all through Yascherov's speech about the tournament festivities, which would begin the following morning with both levels of fencing and choir, to be followed by mock treaty and quiz, then oratory and composition.

Finally Headmaster Yascherov bade the students to sit for supper at their year tables, which had been extended specially for the occasion. Henry stuck by Adam and Rohan as they walked toward the first-year table, which seemed nearly long as a train. Henry felt ridiculous in his formal jacket and especially in his rarely worn school hat, but was glad enough that they'd been forced to wear them, as it gave Adam some anonymity. Rohan wasn't as lucky. The Partisan students stared.

Their expressions, Henry noticed, were nothing like the surprised-but-resigned-to-being-polite looks that the other students had given Henry and his friends during their first week at Knightley. No, the Partisan students' faces looked almost . . . disgusted.

Rohan smiled bravely and pretended to ignore it, but Henry could tell that his friend was on guard. Henry didn't blame him—even though he, Henry, looked unremarkable to the Partisan students, he was still guarded as well.

They took seats at the farthest end of the joined-together tables, away from the Partisan students. As if prompted by some invisible cue, the Partisan students removed their hats and bent their heads, joining hands.

Henry exchanged a look of horror with Adam.

Wordlessly, Adam removed his hat along with the rest and joined hands with Henry and Rohan.

The Partisan students recited a short thanks for the meal, gratitude for their strength and courage, and the hope that a common good would prevail.

As the prayer subsided, Adam reached up and pulled the yarmulke from his head, stuffing it into his pocket.

Henry didn't blame him.

The meal was served family-style, in large, plain bowls to reflect the lack of a class system, but Henry wasn't fooled. When the Partisan School staff emerged from the kitchens with the heavy bowls and platters, Henry could see deep chilblains across their hands, and noted that their uniforms were of thin cotton that provided little, if any, warmth.

"Looks like we've got purple soup," Henry said, ladling a small amount into his bowl and passing the large pot and ladle down the table.

Sir Frederick had warned them about the purple soup, but Henry didn't think it was half bad. Then again, Henry had never had the opportunity to be a picky eater.

Adam, to no one's surprise, groaned when he saw their starter.

"It's *beetroot*," he said. "My gran used to serve something like this, and it's bloody awful."

Rohan, who put down his spoon after one mouthful, had to agree.

Thankfully, the rest of the meal was less alien: roast beef with small, hard potatoes, and a clear jelly for dessert.

"It isn't *fish*, is it?" Adam asked, staring at the quivering blocks of jelly.

Henry bravely took a bite.

"Some sort of fruit," he said.

Adam still made no move to try it.

"Honestly, it's nice," Henry said.

"Just checking, mate," Adam said, finally taking a piece. "I mean, you *did* like the soup."

After the meal, the Partisan students put on a small exhibition. There was traditional Nordlandic dance (which, per Adam, looked like a lot of pointless hopping and clapping), a student who juggled daggers, an original orchestral composition by some of the third years, and a masked pantomime done in an Eastern style, which seemed to be a parable about listening to one's elders.

Adam, despite sleeping for most of the day on the

train ride up, yawned through the last half of the panto-mime. Henry was tired as well. There was something about sitting for vast quantities of time that was even more exhausting than fencing.

Finally, the exhibition concluded and a Partisan fourth year whose uniform was more heavily deco-rated than the rest showed them where they would be sleeping.

Henry nearly laughed at the expression on Rohan's face when they had a look at their sleeping conditions. Sleeping sacks had been laid out on the floor of a cavern-ous hall, like an enormous indoor camping ground.

Well, Henry thought, it wasn't as though there were seventy-five extra beds to accommodate the Knightley students, never mind their headmaster or heads of year.

Henry and his friends chose sleeping sacks next to one another, changed into their pajamas, and climbed in.

Candles were blown out, and gradually, the hall filled with soft snores and even softer whispers.

Henry stared up at the high stone ceiling for ages, unable to sleep.

"Hey, Rohan," Adam whispered.

"What?"

"How do you like sleeping on the floor?" Adam asked.

Henry tried not to smile.

"I'd like it better if you weren't keeping me awake," Rohan snapped.

"Oh, that's right, you've got your big fencing match tomorrow," Adam said.

"Stow it, Adam." Rohan sighed.

"Sorry," Adam said, and then, "Hey, Rohan?"

"What?"

"Do you reckon Henry's asleep?"

"I'm not," Henry said.

"Oh . . . well, hey, Henry?"

"Yes?" Henry asked, resisting a very strong urge to sigh.

"I wish Frankie were here."

"Me too," Henry said with feeling, knowing that somehow Frankie would have made them laugh over the purple soup and the pantomime, over the sneering Partisan students and their pompous headmaster. "Me too."

20

KNIGHTLEY VERSUS PARTISAN

Henry had meant to stay awake until the other students had fallen asleep, and then to have a look around the deserted corridors, but somehow, despite the hard ground and his desire to find out what really went on in the Nordlands, he'd fallen asleep after all.

Angry at himself because of it, Henry buttoned his shirt in silence alongside his classmates in the cavernous hall the next morning.

Rohan looked horrible as they dressed for breakfast, his face a greenish gray.

"You all right, mate?" Adam asked, knotting his tie. "Because you look a bit peaky."

"I'm perfectly fine," Rohan snapped.

"Because if you're ill," Adam continued, "I could take your place in novice foil."

"I'm just nervous, that's all," Rohan said, straightening his cuffs. "*You* would be too if everyone stared like *you* were some sort of heathen."

Adam reflexively raised his hand to the back of his head, which he'd left bare.

Theobold, who was lacing his boots nearby, looked up.

"You're *both* heathens," he said. "Coming here will do you well to remember it."

Adam clenched his fists. "It's *your* fault I got banned, Theobold. You *know* Henry and I weren't cheating."

"To each what he deserves," Theobold said, and then narrowed his eyes at Henry. "Why so quiet, Grim? Shouldn't you jump in to defend your friends like you always do?"

"From what?" Henry asked, rolling up his sleeping sack. "*Your* words?"

"Remember your place, Grim," Theobold hissed.

"Leave it alone," Valmont said, buttoning his jacket. "It's not worth it."

"Well *I* say it is," Theobold challenged. "Anyway,

Beckerman, what's happened to your little hat?"

"Last call for bets on the tournament!" Jasper Hall-worth said, interrupting. "How about you, Grim?"

"Him?" Theobold scoffed. "He hasn't a penny to bet with."

Henry shook his head.

"No, thanks, Jasper."

"Worth a try," Jasper said, shrugging. "Knightley's a sure thing this year, especially with yours truly fencing sabre."

"I really can't," Henry said firmly.

When Jasper left, Adam whispered, "I didn't bet either. Somehow, it isn't as much fun when you're not participating."

At breakfast they encountered the dreaded fish gelatin, which the Partisan students were enthusiastically spread-ing on their toast.

There were great quivering blocks of the stuff, inside of which were suspended tiny chunks of fish, including heads and tails, waiting on the tables.

"Eat up," Henry joked, sipping his tea. "Big day ahead."

"You first, mate," Adam said.

Even Henry ate his toast dry that morning.

After breakfast, all of the boys who meant to compete went off to rehearse or review, and Henry, Adam, and a handful of others were left to help with last-minute preparations.

Lord Havelock had volunteered Henry to squire the fencing match, and so Henry missed the opening remarks, instead double-checking that every sword in the fencing anteroom met regulation standards.

"I'm certainly glad to see you," Rohan said, sitting down next to Henry with some difficulty, as he was already wearing full fencing gear, including the mask.

"Yeah, well, I've made sure to put you down for the sword with the loosest bell guard and worst balance," Henry teased, trying to make Rohan relax.

Rohan's right leg was bouncing from nerves.

"So everything's in order?" Rohan asked.

"Just about," Henry said, ticking a box on his checklist. "How are you holding up?"

Rohan glanced around. The other fencers were congregated on the opposite side of the room, swigging water, doing extra stretches, or pantomiming sword passes.

The older boys, who could elect foil or sabre, were

particularly terrifying, practicing moves that looked set to chop an opponent's head off.

"Is it just me," Rohan asked, "or are the Partisan students rather . . . large?"

Henry's first thought was that Rohan was imagining things, but sure enough, when Henry looked again, he did notice that the Partisan students seemed a bit hulking, especially next to their Knightley challengers. Then again, they *were* from a different country.

"Don't worry, you'll be brilliant," Henry assured his friend, and then hefted the huge bag of swords. "I have to report to the tournament master with these before we start, but I'll see you after."

"Right. After," Rohan said, looking as though he doubted he'd survive that long.

"I'd wish you luck, but you won't need it," Henry said, staggering out of the room under the weight of the swords.

The fencing was set up in a large tournament hall, with spectators from Knightley along one side and spectators from Partisan along the other. Above their respective sides were school banners, and the Partisan students had made pennants, which they waved merrily, cheering for their own.

The two schools' fencing masters were set to referee, with Henry handling the scoreboard. A Partisan squire was situated at the opposite end of the hall with a large megaphone, interpreting the judges' calls and announcing the contestants.

Henry sat behind a large wooden scoreboard. Nearby he had set aside the first two foils to wait for their respective contestants. He stared out at the Partisan crowd in their fur-trimmed uniforms, waving their pennants, and at the Knightley students, cheering and clapping in their stiff, formal coats and caps. He spotted Adam standing with Luther and Edmund, applauding along with the rest.

Somehow, without their noticing, they had become part of Knightley, Henry thought. And then, turning his attention back to the scoreboard, Henry waited, his heart pounding, for the games to begin.

"And now, in novice fencing," the Partisan squire called, and the first contestants stepped forward, accepting their designated swords from Henry, "James St. Fitzroy of Knightley Academy against Luon Muirwold of Partisan School, fencing foil to five hits."

James and Luon took their places across from each other on the piste, waiting for the signal to start.

Henry's view at the scoreboard was from behind

James, and the match began so quickly that Henry nearly missed it, with James and Luon meeting at the center of the piste, and James landing a quick hit.

Knightley cheered, and Henry hung a "1" on the scoreboard for James.

The players returned to their ends of the piste and went again, but it wasn't much of a contest—Knightley continued cheering as James swiftly dispatched his opponent with a final score of 5–1.

Henry reset the scoreboard to 0–0 as James and Luon shook hands and returned their swords.

"Well done," Henry whispered to James, and James, his blond hair matted to his head with sweat, smiled.

Henry readied the swords for the next pair, and when the Partisan squire called, "Rohan Mehta of Knightley Academy against Volomir Dusseling of Partisan School," Henry clapped his hand on his friend's shoulder and wished him luck.

Volomir, Henry noticed, was one of the larger Partisan students, and Henry wouldn't have thought him to be a first year.

Still, Rohan took his place opposite his hulking opponent, giving a curt salute and waiting for the call to begin, never betraying his fear.

Henry wished he were allowed to cheer along with his schoolmates as Rohan quickly landed a hit to Volomir's stomach.

With the scoreboard changed to 1–0, Henry turned his attention back to the match. Rohan, although not quite as flawless in form as Adam, was light and quick on his feet—amazingly so. He was nothing but a blur to Henry, while Volomir seemed to stand still, his sword darting dangerously around him.

Volomir landed a hit high on Rohan's target zone, and Henry changed the scoreboard, hoping fervently that Rohan would win.

It was close, with a final score of 4–5, but the match went to Volomir.

Rohan removed his mask and shook hands with his opponent, and Henry watched Volomir pander to the Partisan crowd, pumping his fist in triumph, and then galloping toward Henry and throwing down his sword.

Rohan smiled ruefully, his chest heaving and his face trickling with sweat.

"You almost had him," Henry said, and Rohan nodded seriously.

"Next year," Rohan swore.

The fencing competition turned to the main attraction now that the novice fencers had gone, and Henry felt as though he was constantly hanging numbers on the scoreboard as the older boys' swords clashed and hit to deafening cheers.

Henry realized what Rohan had meant about the Partisan boys seeming so much bigger than their Knightley opponents, and as he watched Jasper Hallworth land a crushing blow to the side of a Partisan student's mask while fencing sabre, comprehension dawned. It wasn't that the Partisan students were taller or heavier, it was that they all looked like athletes, their muscles thick and their hair cropped short. The Knightley students spent their free hours sitting around their respective common rooms in front of chess and checkerboards, and they looked it.

Finally, after Henry was long sick of hanging numbers over the scoreboard, the last fencers shook hands at the end of their match, and the Partisan squire called the end results: Partisan led by two bouts.

Bad luck, Henry thought as the other students went off to watch the choirs compete, and he stayed behind to account for the swords.

Henry busied himself with his checklist, watching the Partisan squire on the other side of the anteroom do the same with the masks and gloves. The last of the expert sabre fencers were toweling off, and the room had a musty, postsport smell that Henry hoped wouldn't cling to his clothes.

"Hallo," the Partisan squire called, nodding at Henry.

"Hello," Henry said back.

"Rum luck we've got here," the Partisan squire said, indicating the boxes of gear he had to sort and account for. "Whadya do?"

"Sorry?" Henry asked.

"Whadya do, t'get stuck with equipment duty?" the boy asked in his Nordlandic accent.

"Nothing." Henry said, surprised. "At least, I don't think I did. But my head of year isn't particularly fond of me."

"I'm Meledor," the boy said, and Henry couldn't tell if it was his first or last name, but didn't think it polite to ask.

"Henry," Henry said, dragging the equipment over to Meledor's side of the anteroom. "What did *you* do, then?"

"What ha'eñt I done?" Meledor laughed darkly. "Ten demerits this week at inspection."

"Inspection?" Henry asked.

As they sorted through the work, Meledor told Henry how he'd failed to tuck the corners of his sheets, correctly stow his spare uniform, iron the wrinkles from his trousers, tidy his work space—the list went on exhaustively. It seemed that Partisan was far stricter than Knightley, and with more severe punishments.

Henry listened sympathetically. He was fascinated to learn the differences between the two schools, to find out that Partisan admitted students who were members of the Morsguard—a sort of student scouts who sang songs about their chancellor, marched in parades, and took Sunday lessons in making the right choices.

"I cannae fathom how ye get on with that brown student," Meledor said while Henry helped him finish sorting the gloves by size.

"Rohan?" Henry said, puzzling through Meledor's slightly foreign way of talking. "He's one of my good friends."

"And yor folk at home don't mind?" Meledor asked.

Henry tallied the last of the large gloves and marked down the figure.

"Why should they?" he asked.

"Round here we call them heathen and leave them to their own, those who don' keep the same god."

"Well, that's a rather narrow way to live," Henry said angrily, shaking his finished tally to dry the ink. "You should get to know a person before you judge him."

Meledor finished his own count and followed Henry to hand in the lists to the tournament head.

"Why don't you educate women?" Henry asked daringly.

"Women learn from the world," Meledor said. "No need to fill their heads with troubles they may never encounter."

"Troubles like reading?" Henry asked skeptically.

"If a man wants his wife to read, he teach her and then she reads," Meledor answered, leading Henry through a narrow stone passageway.

"And if she wants to learn but he won't teach her?" Henry asked.

"An' if a servant in *your* country wants to learn but his master don't teach him?" Meledor accused.

"That's different," Henry said. "It isn't illegal to educate the lower classes. Your government's given privileges to half its subjects and taken them away from the other half for no good reason."

"All men in the Nordlands are equal," Meledor answered.

"Not having titles doesn't make everyone equal," Henry said. "I doubt you'd be friends with a boy who worked in the kitchens."

"If we are both ill, a hospital treats him who arrived first. If we are both hungry but cannae afford food, the chancellor provides us the same bread."

"But you would not be equally ill, or equally hungry," Henry said, thinking of the thin uniforms for the school staff.

"We are all born the same, what happens after is free will," Meledor said, pushing open a swinging door and signaling the attention of the tournament head.

After Henry was relieved of his squire duties, the choir competition had already ended in Partisan's favor, and Henry found his friends consoling Edmund.

"It's a cheat," Edmund wailed over the meat puree and carrots they'd been given for their afternoon meal.

"Actually, I thought Partisan was quite good," Adam said, causing Rohan to elbow him in the side.

"What are we watching next?" Henry asked. "Quiz or treaty?"

"Quiz," Rohan said promptly. "I want to see Valmont and Theobold embarrass Lord Havelock."

But Theobold, Valmont, and their teammate Luther didn't make fools of themselves at all.

By the end of the first round, they led by three points.

"Round two, where every question is worth double," Compatriot Quilpp, the quiz master, called. "At what age did pre–Longsword Treaty conscription laws bind boys to military service?"

Luther rang the bell first.

"Knightley?" Compatriot Quilpp called.

"Thirteen," Luther said.

"Correct. Two points to Knightley."

The audience applauded.

"What ancient weapon is said to be a cross between a pike and a scythe?"

Partisan rang first.

"A gisarme."

"Correct. Two points to Partisan."

Henry played along with the quiz in his head as he watched with his friends. It was strange rooting for Valmont. Not that he was rooting, exactly. But from his conversation with Meledor, Henry was becoming less and less a fan of Partisan School. Knightley had to win the tournament. Come on, Henry thought fiercely, win!

"What was the title of the boy who carried the banner of a knight?" the quiz master asked, and Knightley promptly rang in.

"A standard bearer," Luther answered.

Knightley was still up by three.

"Which ancient knight was famous for his orders to massacre every occupant of castles taken by force?" the quiz master asked.

Partisan took the point on this one, and the crowd cheered, as the whole match now depended on the next— and final—question.

"Final question," the quiz master said. "Which ancient order of knights is responsible for the idea of the 'note of hand'?"

Henry nearly laughed aloud. Knightley had this!

Valmont hit the bell.

"Knightley?" the quiz master asked.

"The Knights Templar," Valmont answered.

"Correct!" the quiz master said. The room erupted in cheers.

Henry grinned and clapped along with his friends, even though the results didn't matter to the overall tournament score, even though it was just novice level and they weren't particular friends with the boys on the team.

Valmont, at the front of the room with the rest of the quiz team, was smiling hugely, as though he were back at the Midsummer School for Boys all those months ago and his name had just been called on that fateful morning in the dining hall.

21

THE SECRET OF
PARTISAN SCHOOL

The announcement was made just before dinner, and no one was surprised that Partisan had won the Inter-School Tournament.

"They bloody cheated," Adam grumbled.

"At what?" Rohan asked, clapping along politely with the rest of the Knightley students.

"How should I know?" Adam whispered back.

Henry didn't mind that they'd lost. Of course he'd wanted Knightley to win, wanted it very badly, but the more he thought about Meledor and his ten demerits, about the depressing food and the Morsguard, he had to admit, the Partisan students could use something to celebrate.

But then, come to think of it, so could he.

Because those rumors, the ones in the gossip magazines that he'd always been certain were nothing more than gross exaggerations? Now he wasn't so sure. Being there in the Nordlands, and seeing just a small piece of how things were, Henry could easily believe that anyone caught educating women would be given three years' forced labor or that shopkeepers would be required to display portraits of the chancellor in their windows.

As the students got ready for bed, Henry couldn't wait to get back to Knightley Academy in the morning. He wanted to make sure Frankie hadn't killed her grandmother, for one thing, and he wanted to see Professor Stratford and tell him about the Nordlands.

"Our last night in these sleeping sacks," Rohan said cheerfully, pulling the top half up to his chin.

And finally, with much whispering, and hushing of the whisperers by those who were trying to sleep, the hall quieted.

Henry turned over onto his side, watching the silhouettes of the other sleeping boys rise and fall in the gray-blue darkness. But he didn't close his eyes or try to fall asleep himself. Instead, he waited until he was certain that no one would notice, and then, as quietly as he could, Henry slipped out of his sleeping sack.

With his boots in his hands, he tiptoed through the sleeping minefield of students and crept carefully into the hallway. He didn't know what he was looking for, or what he expected to find. He just knew that there was something off about the Partisan School, and something oddly familiar about their headmaster.

The corridors were frigid at night, and Henry followed the clouds of his breath down the corridor, toward a faint glow in the distance.

The glow, when he reached it, turned out to be a spluttering candle lighting the way down a stairwell—a maids' stairwell. He stayed to one side of the stairs so they wouldn't creak. At the bottom was a cabinet of bells and pulleys, each neatly labeled with a corresponding room. And beyond that, a smoky hearth and a threadbare armchair.

All of the doors were locked, and so Henry crept back up the stairs and went in the other direction down the corridor.

He'd found the classrooms.

Scarcely daring to breathe, Henry turned the knob on one of the doors and pushed it open.

It was just a classroom, nothing special, although

instead of desks, the seating was arranged in the style of an amphitheater, in raised levels. The textbooks on the master's table were plain old military history, the same as he'd seen on Lord Havelock's bookshelves.

Henry sighed.

He could be caught at any moment, and he had no idea what he was looking for—if there even was anything to *be* looking for.

Feeling foolish, Henry closed the door to the classroom and headed back down the corridor in the direction from which he'd come.

But he could have sworn he'd never passed that suit of armor before, and that it had been a portrait, not a landscape, hanging above the stair. It was late, though, and he hadn't slept . . . probably it was just his imagination running wild.

Henry made the left turn that would bring him back to the servants' staircase.

And then he panicked. He'd found the entrance to the school library. Which meant that he was completely and utterly lost.

Trying to keep calm, he went back the way he'd come, attempting to find something he recognized. But the long corridors of endless doors all looked the same, and it was as though the eyes on the portraits followed as he made wrong turn after wrong turn. At every step, he half expected to be caught out of bed—rather, out of sleeping sack—or worse, to be stuck wandering Partisan Keep all night, trying to find his way back to bed.

Finally, Henry found a part of the castle that he thought he recognized. That door there could have been the supply room from the fencing that morning, and that stained-glass window looked vaguely familiar.

But what was *that*?

What seemed at first to be an innocent-looking decoration in the wall paneling turned out to be a hidden doorway, left ajar.

The Knights Templar had been fans of secret passages, allowing them a safe getaway from invaders, and clearly Partisan Keep had been built with the same idea in mind. It was probably nothing more than a small hiding chamber barely large enough for two people. Nonetheless, something made Henry push open the panel and step inside.

The hidden chamber was cavernous.

A torch flickered in one of the two holders along the far wall, sputtering its last sparks of light, and in the dim light Henry could make out a cabinet full of weapons.

Not blunt-tipped fencing foils or sabres, but real, true weapons, the kind you saw depicted in gruesome battle scenes on woven tapestries or stained-glass windows. The sorts of weapons that had been illegal for the past hundred years.

On the left wall: burlap-covered mannequins with red targets painted across their chests. And on the right wall a neat row of charts hung from rusty nails. Henry stared at the first chart, marked HAND-TO-HAND COMBAT, reading the list of names, looking for one he knew. There! Volomir Dusseling, the hulking first year who had beaten Rohan in foil fencing, marked as number six.

Number six what? Henry wondered, and then he realized what this place was: he'd found a room that wasn't supposed to exist—the place where Partisan students were trained in combat!

It was illegal! It was beyond illegal; everyone knew that combat training was forbidden by the statutes of the Longsword Treaty, that so long as no citizens were trained in combat, there would be peace between all countries that had signed the treaty.

And the Nordlands had broken it—this room was definite proof of that.

His heart pounding, Henry tried to think what he

should do. He needed proof. One of those lists should work nicely . . . but did he dare take one?

If he did, it would be instantly obvious that someone knew about the combat training. He could inadvertently start a war.

But would anyone believe him without proof?

Suddenly, Henry heard footsteps in the corridor, footsteps getting louder.

He pressed himself against the nearest wall, trying not to make a sound. There was a good chance that whoever was coming down the hall would pass right by.

The footsteps stopped, and Henry heard a flurry of furious whispers:

"You're certain you dinnae remember to lock it?"

"Aye."

"How could you be so stupid?"

"I thought I heard—"

"Thought you heard what? Knightley students creepin' up behind ye?"

Cruel laughter.

Henry peered out into the corridor.

Two huge Partisan boys were at the far end, arguing.

And just a meter away from where Henry hid was a staircase. If he could only make it unobserved . . .

Holding his breath, Henry leaped around the corner and, still barefoot, ran furiously down the staircase.

It was a mystery to Henry how he finally made it back to his sleeping sack, or how he even fell asleep at all, but the next thing he knew, he was opening his eyes to the gray light of early morning and to the other students packing their belongings.

Henry rolled up his sleeping sack, his head fuzzy from lack of sleep. And then the past night came rushing back to him: the combat training, the treaty, and how, in the panic of almost being caught, he had left the room with only his word as proof.

After a breakfast of tasteless porridge, Henry and the other Knightley students weren't particularly heartbroken to board the train back to their school.

Henry, Adam, and Rohan found an empty compartment, and Henry could hardly wait to tell his friends what he'd discovered.

"You're being quiet," Rohan said, narrowing his eyes at Henry. "What aren't you saying?"

"Oh, sorry." Henry hadn't realized he was so obvious. "It's just, I have something huge to tell you."

And then the door to their compartment opened.

"Hallo," Edmund said cheerfully, holding a deck of cards. "Luther's already fallen back asleep. Mind if I join you?"

Henry gave his friends a desperate look. He couldn't tell them what he'd found out if Edmund was in their compartment!

Rohan, to his credit, cleared his throat in the awkward silence and said, "Feel free, although I should warn you that I'm having horrible indigestion from the Nordlandic food." Rohan made a pained face and pressed his hands to his stomach.

Henry recognized the signs that Adam was about to start laughing, so he stamped on Adam's foot.

"Think I'll pass, actually," Edmund said, edging toward the door.

When Edmund had gone, Henry breathed a sigh of relief. "Thanks," he told Rohan.

"Don't mention it," Rohan said.

Adam made a farting noise with his mouth against his arm and then burst out laughing.

"Pity there wasn't a competition in that," Rohan said.

"In what?" Henry asked.

"Pure stupidity." Rohan rolled his eyes at Adam.

Adam composed himself, only to burst out laughing once more.

"Get over it, Adam," Henry snapped, and then said, "Sorry. It's just that I found something quite serious last night."

"Last night when you were wandering around Partisan Keep instead of being asleep?" Rohan asked, his face impassive.

"You knew?" Henry asked, shocked.

"I heard you get up," Rohan said. "But I wasn't going to follow you and get expelled."

"You could have taken *me* with you," Adam whined.

"Well, I didn't know that I'd find anything," Henry said.

"We still don't know what you found," Rohan said pointedly. "And I've just embarrassed myself over it, so this better truly be huge."

"It is," Henry said. "I found this door hidden in the wall paneling near that fish statue on the first floor. Anyway, the door led to this huge room full of practice weapons and charts."

"What, like fencing?" Rohan asked.

Henry shook his head. "The Partisan students are being trained in combat."

"What?" Rohan practically yelled.

"Shhhhh!" Henry said.

"Sorry." Rohan lowered his voice. "Proper combat? You're certain?"

Henry nodded and told his friends the rest of it: what he'd seen in detail, how he'd almost been caught, and how he'd escaped without any proof.

"We have to tell someone," Adam said.

"Wait here. I'll get Lord Havelock," Rohan said dryly.

But then a thought occurred to Henry.

Lord Havelock. Military history.

Yesterday's quiz question: *"At what age did pre–Longsword Treaty conscription laws bind boys to military service?"*

And the answer: *thirteen.*

"Wait," Henry said, realization dawning.

"I wasn't really going to get Lord Havelock," Rohan said with a puzzled look in Henry's direction.

"No, not that," Henry said. "Conscription laws. No one's changed them since before the Longsword Treaty. If we go to war with the Nordlands, every boy over thirteen will have to fight."

"But I thought those laws were just ancient history," Adam said nervously.

"Well, that's what *I* thought about war," Henry said. "And now Partisan is training its students in combat. I'm certain of it. And if we tell anyone about this, there's going to *be* a war."

"There's going to be a war anyway," Rohan said. "Why else would you train in combat?"

Henry hadn't thought of it that way. But then he thought of something else.

"I don't know," he said, "but do you remember the first lesson we had in military history? Adam got kicked out because he didn't know the answer and—"

"Oi, watch it, mate!" Adam said.

"Sorry," Henry said quickly. "But, Rohan, you remember, don't you? What Lord Havelock said?"

Rohan nodded gravely. "Commoners captured in battle rot in prison cells. Only nobility are ransomed."

"We're going to *rot* in *prison cells*?" Adam whined.

"No, we're not," Henry said firmly. "Because there's not going to be a war. Someone will draw up a new treaty and everything will be fine."

"I don't know," Rohan said. "It seems to me that the Nordlands have been wanting a war for a long time."

And even though he didn't want to admit it, Henry knew that his friend was right. War was coming with the force of a tempest. War against the Nordlands, the likes of which they had only read about in history books.

And they would have to fight.

And so would every other boy over thirteen—unless there was something they could do to stop it.

"Sir Frederick will know what to do," Henry said.

Comforted by the thought, he stared out the window at the passing landscape, trying not to picture the frosted ground littered with the fallen bodies of his classmates, or packed fresh with their unmarked graves.

22

A STORY WITHOUT PROOF

Henry, *Adam, and Rohan had barely opened the door to their room before Frankie was tossing rocks at their window.*

Exhausted from the journey and the walk back from the train station, Henry wanted to do nothing more than stretch out on his soft bed and fall asleep. Instead, he pushed open the window.

"Come outside," Frankie shouted merrily.

It was getting colder on the school grounds, and brightly colored leaves that had crunched under their feet only a week ago were now turning to soggy mulch.

The four friends met by the bench outside the entrance to the hedge maze, stamping their feet to keep warm.

"I'm only free until supper," Frankie said hurriedly. "My grandmother's gone shopping and taken Professor Stratford along to carry her purchases."

"I'll bet he loves that," Henry said wryly.

"She's never leaving," Frankie said with anguish. "I swear she isn't. Every day I think it's her last but she just *stays*, like my personal circle of infinite hell."

"Well, your grandmother is the least of our worries," Henry said, and quickly filled Frankie in on what he'd found.

"You're certain?" she asked. "Of course you're certain. But what are we going to *do*?"

"Personally, I've always wanted to command a squadron of soldiers," Adam joked, and then cringed at the looks everyone shot in his direction. "Sorry."

"I was thinking that we go to Sir Frederick directly after supper," Henry said. "Tell him what we've found, ask for advice, see what he thinks we should do."

"What about my father?" Frankie asked.

"Do you think he'd believe us?" Rohan asked.

"I'm not sure." Frankie bit her lip, lost in thought. "I just can't imagine . . . I mean, everyone's been saying for ages that we're close to war, that Chancellor Mors has secret armies or new technologies to use against us, but I never thought it would be *now*."

"My father always says, 'When you expect something, you never see it coming,'" Rohan said.

"Your father is friends with my grandmother," Frankie reminded him.

And even though it felt as though they were on the brink of war, as though they weren't allowed to be happy, the four friends shared a brief smile at the thought of anyone being friends with Grandmother Winter.

Henry knocked nervously on the door to Sir Frederick's office after supper, suddenly regretting his decision to talk to the medicine master alone. But then, it was his responsibility; after all, he'd been the one to discover the secret room.

"Yes?" Sir Frederick called through the door.

"It's Henry Grim, sir," Henry said.

"Come in."

Henry opened the door and found Sir Frederick puzzling at a slide through his microscope, his desk littered with papers.

"I hope I'm not disturbing you, sir," Henry said.

"Not at all."

Sir Frederick waved a hand dismissively and pushed the microscope aside.

"Well," Sir Frederick prompted, "what did you think of the Nordlands?"

Henry smiled weakly.

"It was different," Henry said truthfully. "And Partisan seemed much more strict than Knightley. Actually, sir, I wanted to talk to you about something I saw at Partisan."

Sir Frederick leaned back in his chair, took out his pipe, and told Henry to go ahead.

"Well," Henry began, "last night I found this room where the Partisan students are trained in combat."

Sir Frederick choked on his pipe smoke and Henry waited until his professor's coughing fit had subsided.

"Go on," Sir Frederick said. "You think you—ahem! Ahem! Sorry about that—found a room where Partisan trains its students in combat?"

"I don't think, sir," said Henry, "I'm certain of it. There was a wardrobe filled with weapons, and practice dummies with painted-on targets, and charts ranking the students in different forms of fighting."

Sir Frederick was very quiet for a long while after Henry finished explaining what he'd seen. Finally, when

Henry was afraid Sir Frederick would continue to sit there and say nothing at all, the professor cleared his throat and said, "I assume you have proof?"

Henry's cheeks flushed. "No, sir."

"Is it possible," Sir Frederick asked, "that you simply had a bad dream and woke up believing it was true?"

"I know what I saw," Henry said stubbornly.

"But you have no proof."

"No," Henry said again, staring at his lap.

"And you've told your friends about this, I'd assume."

"Yes, sir."

"But no one else?"

Henry shook his head.

"Here is what I think," Sir Frederick said, tapping his pipe on the edge of his desk. "I think the Partisan students wanted you to believe they were being trained in combat. I think it was a prank."

"It's not very funny, sir. No offense."

"Nordlandic humor," Sir Frederick said with a shrug.

For a moment Henry considered that it could have been a prank. That the students had set the whole thing up just to see who might be gullible enough to fall for it.

But of course that was ridiculous. It had been real.

Henry knew what he'd seen. Those mannequins painted with red targets had been used—and recently. The lists were too meticulously kept to be anything but real. And those weapons. Even now, the gruesome blades made Henry shudder just thinking of them.

"I don't think it was a prank, sir," Henry said. "The Nordlands have broken the Longsword Treaty. Partisan is training its students in combat. I'm certain of what I saw."

"Henry," Sir Frederick said kindly. "I want to believe you. Truly, I do. But what you're telling me is that you just happened to be wandering around out of bed, and you just happened to walk down a corridor and find a room full of weapons, and you don't have any proof or any witnesses, but according to you, the Nordlands are preparing to go to war against us."

Henry sighed. He knew it sounded impossible, but he'd thought Sir Frederick would believe him. "Basically, yes," Henry said.

"I'm sorry," Sir Frederick said, "but it's just a lot to accept based on a schoolboy's testimony."

"But it's true," Henry insisted.

"I know you think you saw this room," Sir Frederick said, "but if you ask me, they've been working you boys too hard to prepare for the tournament. You look exhausted. Get some sleep. Think on it. Maybe in the morning you'll change your mind about what you saw."

"Maybe," Henry muttered, although he doubted it.

Henry stared dully at his prayer register the next morning, not even bothering to mouth the words.

Sir Frederick hadn't believed him.

Of course, it *was* a lot to believe, but he had no reason to make up a story like that, nothing to gain from false accusations or lies.

Henry watched Theobold deface his prayer register with a pen from his school bag until the service ended.

Breakfast had never smelled as good as it did that morning.

The table was piled high with smoked fish and scrambled eggs, pots of jam and plates of toast, and fresh-baked scones with little mounds of sugar crystals on top.

As Henry buttered a hot scone, he thought about the Nordlands, and how the students had probably been up for hours, awaiting inspection. He thought of them eating lumpy porridge and then going off to learn combat in their secret training chamber, preparing for war, believing so strongly that their way of life was the only way—the right way—that they had to fight for other people to see it.

Henry hardly paid attention in medicine, and he practically sleepwalked from Sir Frederick's classroom to Lord Havelock's military history tower.

But he forced himself to attend to Lord Havelock's lecture, in which Lord Havelock held up crumbling artifacts like black-tipped spearheads and statuettes and spoke of what they could learn about past military conquest from archaeological digs.

Lord Havelock passed the artifacts around, and they were no more interesting up close, but Henry turned them over in his hands anyway, taking notes as he was expected to do.

Finally, Lord Havelock had them pass the artifacts up to the front of the room.

We should talk to Professor Stratford during our free hour, Henry wrote out on the bottom of his notebook and tilted the page toward Adam and Rohan.

His friends nodded.

Up at the front of the room, Lord Havelock frowned.

"I have only thirteen artifacts, what has happened to the fourteenth?" Lord Havelock asked.

Everyone shuffled through the things on their desks, but no one could find it.

"This is not a game," Lord Havelock sneered. "We will all sit here until the talisman is returned. And yes, I am aware that you will be missing your luncheon."

But five minutes later, no one had made any move to return the missing object.

"Stand up!" Lord Havelock barked. "Behind your chairs, all of you. Satchels open on your desks, jackets off, trouser pockets turned out."

Feeling foolish, Henry turned out his trouser pockets and stood behind his desk like the rest of his classmates.

"What do you think's going on?" Adam whispered.

Henry gave a tiny shrug in response.

Because the truth was, Henry half expected that Lord Havelock would find this missing object inside of his own bag. After all, there was no reason for their saboteur to suddenly stop his efforts toward getting Henry and his friends kicked out of the academy just because he hadn't struck while they were away at Partisan.

There had been so much going on with the tournament and discovering the combat training room over the past few days that Henry had nearly forgotten that he and his friends still didn't have any idea who might be out to get them—besides Lord Havelock, that was.

Lord Havelock glared inside of Theobold's bag and then came to Henry's row.

Henry held his breath as Lord Havelock rifled his satchel, which contained nothing but notebooks, pens, and embarrassingly, half a scone left over from breakfast, wrapped in a napkin.

"Saving this for a rainy day, Mr. Grim?" Lord Havelock asked with a mocking smile.

Henry's cheeks reddened.

But mercifully, Lord Havelock moved on to Adam's bag, which was stuffed full of chewed pen nibs, scraps of paper, a handful of pennies, crumbs, a tattered envelope, notebooks, pens, textbooks, and a deck of cards tied together with Frankie's blood-splattered hair ribbon from all those weeks ago.

"Nice one," Henry whispered to Adam about the hair ribbon, not caring that Lord Havelock could hear him. Adam made a face and shrugged.

Lord Havelock was stopped in front of Rohan's desk, peering into Rohan's satchel.

And then Lord Havelock's expression changed to a

dangerous sneer as he removed his hand from Rohan's satchel, his long, pale fingers closed tightly into a fist.

"Mr. Mehta, would you care to explain this?" Lord Havelock asked.

"Explain what, sir?" Rohan asked, puzzled.

Lord Havelock opened his fist.

Lying in his palm was a tiny obsidian statuette, the missing artifact.

"I didn't . . . ," Rohan began, "I mean . . . you can't possibly think that I would . . . this is absurd."

Lord Havelock stared down at Rohan, his mouth a thin, hard line, his eyes glittering treacherously. "Mr. Mehta, I think that you should come with me. The rest of you are dismissed."

"He didn't do it, sir," Henry said. "I was here the whole time; I would have seen something."

"Are you implying that you *helped* Mr. Mehta to steal this object?" Lord Havelock asked.

"No, he didn't," Rohan put in quickly. "Henry, Adam, go on. I'll be all right."

Henry gave Rohan what he hoped was an encouraging smile and trudged out into the hall along with Adam.

Neither of them ate anything in the dining hall that afternoon. Henry sat staring at the doorway, waiting for

Rohan to walk through any moment and say that everything had been sorted, and did anyone happen to save him a roast beef and cress sandwich?

But he didn't.

Finally, with just ten minutes before they needed to leave for their next class, Henry and Adam slipped out of the dining hall and opened the door to their room.

Rohan was inside, standing over his open school trunk, eyes puffy as though he'd recently been crying.

"Well?" Henry prompted.

"I've been expelled," Rohan said tightly, tossing an untidy ball of shirts into his trunk.

"What?" Henry asked.

"But you're innocent, mate," Adam said.

"Tell that to bloody Lord Havelock," Rohan said, throwing his books into the trunk on top of the mountain of shirts. "He dragged me off to see Headmaster Winter. 'This boy was caught red-handed,' he said, 'stealing a valuable Nordlandic artifact from my lesson. He was given ample time to come forward and return the item, yet he chose to see if he could get away with it.'"

"Surely Headmaster Winter didn't believe him," Henry said.

Rohan smiled sadly. "What choice did he have? It

was our head of year's word against mine. Lord Havelock was dead set that he'd caught me stealing, and without any reason for doubt, they didn't even need to gather the trustees for a vote on my expulsion."

"But anyone could have planted it in your bag," Henry said desperately.

"Lord Havelock didn't think so," Rohan said sadly. "In fact, after making me out to be a thief, he rather blamed the headmaster for all of this, because what did he expect would happen if he let commoners into the academy?"

"This is what Professor Stratford warned us about," Henry said. "That if we do anything wrong, Headmaster Winter could be fired. . . . Not like you did anything wrong, though."

"Well, it's as good as if I had," Rohan said bitterly.

"You can't leave," Adam wailed, sitting down on his bed and putting his head in his hands. "Not *now*!"

"It's not as though I was begging to be expelled," Rohan said with an odd little laugh. "But my father might be able to convince them to take me back. Build a new library. Or how about some nice combat training rooms?"

"How come it's funny when *he* jokes about it?" Adam whined.

Henry swallowed, his throat tight. Rohan was expelled from the academy. He couldn't believe it.

"I don't know what we're going to do without you," Henry said quietly.

"I do," Rohan said firmly. "Find out who's behind all this. Convince someone of what you saw in the Nordlands. Fix this."

"I'll try," Henry said doubtfully. It wouldn't be the same without Rohan as the calm voice of reason by his side.

"When are you leaving?" Adam asked.

"Now," Rohan said. "On the next train to Holchester. They want to keep this quiet, since I've apparently broken the Code of Chivalry and all."

Rohan smiled sadly and reached into his trunk. He took out his stack of leather-bound adventure novels and his gold pocket watch.

"Here," Rohan said, handing Adam the novels. "Take them."

"I couldn't," Adam protested.

"Please."

Adam accepted the books quietly and, with a crooked grin, gave Rohan a salute.

Rohan turned to Henry, who shook his head. "You'll be back," Henry said.

"Keep this for me until then," Rohan said, giving Henry the pocket watch. And even though they were fourteen, and far too old for anything besides a handshake, Henry gave his friend a hug good-bye.

"Aren't you going to be late for ethics?" Rohan asked.

Henry shrugged, and then pulled the watch out of his trouser pocket and checked.

"Maybe a bit," he admitted.

"Go," Rohan said.

Henry bit his lip.

Adam scuffed the toe of his boot at the floor.

"'Bye," Henry said.

"Good-bye," Rohan said, smiling bravely.

Reluctantly, Henry and Adam headed to their next lesson, just the two of them.

"Pssst! Grim!" Theobold said after the lesson. "Where's your friend?"

"Shove off, Archer," Henry said miserably. He didn't want to talk about it.

"Did he get expelled?" Theobold pressed. "Is your friend a nasty little thief?"

Henry started forward, but Adam grabbed his arm and held him back.

"Really?" Theobold said, delighted. "You're going to fight me for *that*? Well, have at it, Grim. I've not got all day."

And as much as Henry wanted to, as dearly as he wanted to punch that smirk right off Theobold's face, he didn't quite dare. Because if he got expelled too . . .

"I'm waiting, Grim," Theobold said, stifling a fake yawn.

"You're not worth it," Henry told him, wishing he could think of something better to say. His blood was boiling with hatred toward Theobold, who knew perfectly well that Rohan had been expelled, and probably knew just as well that Rohan was innocent of his accused offense.

Henry hated to walk away, but he needed to talk to Professor Stratford during their hour free, and he didn't want to waste his time with Theobold.

"Come on, let's go," he told Adam.

Ellen glared when they showed up at the door of the headmaster's house, but Henry was getting used to it.

"Miss Winter is having her piano lesson," the maid said severely.

"We're here to see Professor Stratford, actually," said Henry with his most winning smile.

The door slammed shut in his face.

"Frankie's rather horrible on the piano, isn't she?" Adam commented while they waited. Through the front door, Henry could hear the faint tinkle of terrible piano music. He had to agree.

The door opened.

"Professor Stratford will see you in his study," Ellen sniffed, and Henry and Adam followed her—up the main staircase this time—to the professor's study.

"Henry!" Professor Stratford cried, delighted to see his former pupil. "And Adam! Come in, come in! But where's Rohan?"

"He's been expelled," Henry said darkly, slumping into a chair.

"You *can't* be serious."

"Afraid so," Henry said. "Someone made it look as though he'd stolen . . . well, I'm not sure what it was exactly. Some sort of good luck talisman from Lord Havelock's archaeology lesson."

Professor Stratford shook his head. "This is terrible," he said. "I'm so sorry."

"Yeah, well, so are we." Adam pouted.

"No, I mean, this is really terrible," Professor Stratford said. "It's precisely what I warned you about; Headmaster Winter's competency could very well be questioned for letting common students into the school."

Henry exchanged a look with Adam.

Professor Stratford groaned. "Already?" he asked. "Someone has said something already?"

"Lord Havelock," Adam said, pulling a face.

"But that isn't even the half of what's happening," Henry said miserably.

"There's more?" Professor Stratford asked with a grimace.

Henry told the professor what he'd seen in the Nordlands—the battle training room, the weapons and lists—and how he'd nearly been caught and hadn't managed to take away any evidence.

"I told Sir Frederick," Henry said, "but he didn't believe me. He said that it was a prank, or that I was mistaken, but I know what I saw."

Professor Stratford was quiet for a long time. He

chewed the corner of his mustache and drummed his fingers on the table and had a faraway look in his eyes.

"I believe you, Henry," the professor finally said. "I don't know what good it does, but I do."

"I knew you were always reading those inane gossip magazines for a reason," Henry said.

"There's truth to every rumor," Professor Stratford said, in the old way of almost quoting that made Henry nostalgic for a time in his life he thought he'd never miss.

"What should we do?" Henry asked.

"The best thing that you can do right now would be to stay out of trouble," Professor Stratford said. "And I mean it. Clearly, Rohan was set up, and whoever wanted him gone will be looking to get rid of the two of you next. Stay out of trouble, and I'll see what I can do."

It wasn't what Henry wanted to hear, but he had to admit that Professor Stratford had a point—and that, thankfully, the professor had believed him. But then, Professor Stratford didn't teach at Knightley. He was just a tutor, just a friend.

But he was all they had.

23

LIFE WITHOUT ROHAN

*S*upper that evening was horrible. *The feeling that they were eating upon a stage had returned—and tripled.* Everyone knew that Rohan had been expelled, and Henry and Adam put up with curious stares and whispered conversations that stopped immediately as they walked by.

"Poor Rohan," Henry said, pushing peas around on his plate.

"I know," Adam said.

"Can you imagine?" Henry asked. "I mean, really *imagine* being expelled from Knightley?"

The possibility had been there ever since Henry's quarter-term essay had gone missing, but it hadn't truly seemed real until that afternoon, until they'd seen Rohan standing over his trunk, packing his things to go home. And now it was all too real and all too looming—like the threat of war.

"We have to tell Frankie," Adam said, shredding a slice of bread.

Frankie caught up with them after supper.

"What's going on?" she asked. "Where's Rohan?"

"Holchester, wherever that is," Henry said.

"He's been expelled," Adam said.

"Is this true?" Frankie asked Henry.

Henry nodded. And caught sight of Frankie's grandmother marching toward them.

"What for?" Frankie asked.

"Stealing," Henry said.

"*Stealing?*" Frankie asked, raising an eyebrow. "*Rohan?*"

"I know," Henry said with a sigh. "And your grandmother's spotted us."

"Drat," Frankie said. "Come on." She ducked around the corner.

"Where are we going?" Adam asked, amused.

"Away from my blasted grandmother," Frankie said.

"She had me playing piano all afternoon. *Piano*. Thank goodness Professor Stratford has come around and is letting me do Latin."

"Right, because *Latin* makes up for *piano*," Henry said sarcastically.

Frankie pushed open a door to the school grounds.

"We're going outside?" Adam asked.

"We can hide in Professor Stratford's study," Frankie said.

"Yeah, small problem with that," Adam said. "What if Professor Stratford is *using* his study?"

Frankie bit her lip. "Do you have a better idea?"

"The library?" Adam suggested.

"The librarian's still at supper," Henry reminded them.

"Common room?" Frankie asked.

"We can't talk there," Henry said, shaking his head. They might as well duck into the armory. At least no one would look for them there.

The armory! Henry thought suddenly. They were down for fencing tomorrow, and the only left-handed foil in the armory had been missing at the last lesson.

"You wouldn't happen to have a private store of foils, would you?" Henry asked.

"And this is relevant how?" Frankie asked, raising an eyebrow.

"I need to borrow a left-hander's foil for tomorrow," Henry said. "Mine was missing last lesson, and I don't want to take any chances."

"Hmmm," Frankie said, biting her lip. "Well, she'd never look there. I'm certain of it. All right, onward."

Henry and Adam followed Frankie across the quadrangle and through the back door of the headmaster's house. Putting a finger to her lips in warning, Frankie led the boys down a stairwell and into the basement, which had been converted into a regulation fencing piste.

"This is brilliant," Adam said, his mouth falling open in awe.

"Well, it's for my father, not me," Frankie said sourly. "The advantage of being headmaster."

Frankie opened an impressively inlaid cabinet and took out a foil.

"We're both left-handed," Frankie said, testing the balance. "And honestly, he never uses this one, so he won't notice if it's gone."

She made sure that the tip had been blunted and handed the sword to Henry.

"Thanks," he said, trying a few passes.

"Don't mention it," Frankie said. "So what ever happened with Sir Frederick?"

"He didn't believe me," Henry said.

"What are you going to do now?"

"We told Professor Stratford," Adam said.

"Well, what did he say?"

"To let him handle it and to stay out of trouble," Henry said sourly. "As though we can control that sort of thing. I mean, it wasn't as though Rohan *planned* to get expelled. Trouble just seems to find us."

"If by trouble, you mean Lord Havelock, I'd agree," Frankie said.

"How do you mean?" Adam asked.

"He never took his eyes off the two of you at supper," Frankie said. "It was bizarre. I only noticed because I was seated two down from him at the High Table, but it was really strange."

"Lord Havelock's the one who found the artifact in Rohan's bag," Henry said. "He's the one who went to the headmaster about it."

"I'll bet my father loved that," Frankie said wryly. "He can't stand Lord Havelock."

"Well, who can?" Adam asked. "Horrible git, if you ask me."

And the one behind all of this, the three friends thought but didn't say.

"I just wish we had proof," Henry said. "Of anything."

"Yeah, well, we're supposed to stay out of trouble," Adam said.

"Since when do we *ever* do what we're supposed to?" Henry asked.

"True enough, mate," Adam agreed.

And then, all at once, the three of them realized that Rohan really had gone. Because there was no one to talk sense. No one to tell them not to. No advice, no voice of reason, no disapproving stare or exasperated sigh.

"Thank you for the sword," Henry said.

"Any time," Frankie said.

"You should probably find your grandmother and convince her that you haven't died," Henry said.

"If she thought I had, do you suppose she'd go home?" Frankie asked.

"Maybe you could fake your own death anyway," Adam suggested.

"If you need a blood-soaked hair ribbon, just ask Adam," Henry said with a small smile.

"Hey!" Adam protested.

"What *are* you talking about?" Frankie asked, wrinkling her nose.

"Never mind," Henry said quickly. "See you tomorrow."

"If I haven't perished," Frankie called merrily.

Henry tried not to stare at Rohan's bare desk as he studied that night. He tried not to stare at Rohan's empty bed or the gaping space in the wardrobe where Rohan's clothes had been.

The room felt too big now for just the two of them.

Adam mentioned this as he and Henry got ready for chapel the next morning.

"I know," Henry said, checking Rohan's pocket watch. "Come on, we don't want to be late."

"Speak for yourself," Adam said, stifling a yawn. "Because I, for one, would love to be late for chapel, or perhaps to miss it all together."

Henry rather felt the same. Especially since the priest chose that morning to give a lengthy sermon about stealing.

"Well, that was subtle," Henry joked on the way to breakfast.

"What was subtle?" Adam asked.

Henry laughed. "Exactly," he said.

"No, seriously, what was subtle, mate?"

Henry shook his head. "Never mind. I'm going to dash back to the room and grab Frankie's foil. I'll meet you at breakfast."

It was fortunate that Henry had borrowed the foil from Frankie, as the left-handed equipment was once again missing from the armory.

Pleased he'd managed to thwart their saboteur, Henry put on his glove and lined up with the rest of the intermediates.

The fencing master, to his credit, tried not to mention Rohan's absence.

"I'll be assigning pairs today," the fencing master said. "Five touches per usual, and report back to me with the results. I'd like to get an idea of whether we should add an advanced level to the class."

Adam grinned at the news of an advanced level, and continued grinning as he was matched up to fence Max Pearson, one of James's friends whose lunges were always crooked.

"Grim, you'll be fencing Archer," the fencing master said.

Henry tried not to sigh. Was he always destined to go up against Valmont and Theobold in foil? He took his place across from Theobold and gave his salute, which Theobold made no move to return.

"You're supposed to salute," Henry called.

"And *you're* supposed to scrub the floors," Theobold returned.

Henry sighed.

Ever since he'd come to a sort of understanding with Valmont, Theobold had, if anything, become worse, focusing all of his hatred on Henry and his friends now that Valmont had backed down.

Edmund had been right—Theobold *was* the worse of the two.

"Let's just go," Henry said, still crouched in an "on guard" position.

Henry easily scored the first touch.

He hadn't fenced Theobold before, but he could certainly see what Adam had meant about Theobold's form. Instead of working on improving, Theobold fought as though winning were the most important part, as though every practice match was a bloody battle that had to be won.

If Henry just slowed down for a moment and looked

for an opening or an advantage, he always found one.

Henry scored the second touch as well.

Theobold was overconfident, striking out without making certain that he could protect the outside—a foolish move, especially with Henry's being left-handed.

"Two-zero," Henry called, returning to his end of the piste.

Theobold snarled and they went again, Henry angling right for the outside and scoring his third hit.

"Three-oh," Henry called.

"Wait," Theobold said, reaching out and grabbing at Henry's sword. "What's this?"

"Left-handed foil," Henry said with a shrug.

"No, it's not. Let me see it."

Before Henry could protest, Theobold had grabbed the bell guard and pulled the sword from his hand.

"It's a left-handed foil," Henry said, trying not to let doubt creep into his voice. What else *could* it be?

Theobold called for the fencing master, and Henry suddenly had a very bad feeling.

"What seems to be the problem?" the fencing master asked.

"Grim's sword," Theobold said, handing the weapon

to the fencing master, who turned it over in his hands with a deep frown.

"What's wrong with it?" Henry asked.

"For one thing, it doesn't belong to this armory," the fencing master said, indicating the stamp on the bell guard. "This is world standard, with the Ecks Caliber mark here."

"So it's stolen," Theobold said with an enormous grin.

"No, it isn't," Henry said. "It's borrowed. I'm sorry, I didn't realize there was anything wrong. It's just, the left-handed sword has been missing a lot of the time, and I didn't know what to do, so I asked to borrow a spare."

"From whom?" the fencing master asked, raising an eyebrow.

"Fra— I mean, Miss Winter," Henry said.

"I find it hard to believe that Miss Winter would loan a schoolboy she hardly knew a sword of this quality."

Henry bit his lip.

"Mr. Grim?" the fencing master pressed.

"We're friends," Henry said.

"Friends. Ah." The fencing master didn't believe him. Henry could see this at once.

"Mr. Archer," the fencing master said. "Can you please run to the headmaster's house and tell Miss Winter that I would like to see her in my office immediately?"

"Yes, sir," Theobold said with a nasty smile.

Henry had never been to the fencing master's office before. It turned out to be a tiny, cramped room located behind the armory, most of its space taken up by a large trunk bursting with equipment in need of repair.

Henry sat in the hard wooden chair across from the fencing master's desk, still in his fencing kit. His leg bounced nervously.

There was a knock on the door.

"Come in," the fencing master called.

Frankie burst through the door, out of breath and carrying an embroidery sampler. "Yes, maestro?" she asked, bobbing a curtsy.

"Can you please describe the object that Mr. Grim has in his possession?" the fencing master inquired, waving Frankie into the empty chair.

A beat too late, Henry wondered if he ought to have stood in Frankie's presence to make a better impression.

"He's just borrowed a foil," Frankie said with a frown. "A left-handed foil."

"From your father's private stores?" the fencing master asked mildly.

"Yes," Frankie said.

"I see."

"Is something the matter?" Frankie asked.

"Are you often in the habit of loaning out world standard Ecks Caliber foils with platinum inlay and custom maker's marks?" the fencing master asked.

"No one was using it," Frankie said with a shrug.

"Are you aware of the cost of a sword like the one you so casually loaned Mr. Grim?"

Frankie ventured a guess.

The fencing master laughed and told her it was worth at least ten times that amount.

Henry nearly gasped. The sum seemed enormous. Enough to buy a house, perhaps. Certainly more than Professor Stratford made in a year.

"Um," Frankie said. "Probably should have given you one with a worse balance, then."

"Don't worry about it," Henry muttered.

"Actually," the fencing master said, putting up a hand. "I'm not concerned about the sword, rather with what it implies."

"And what might that be?" Frankie asked, daring the fencing master to say it.

"That there are . . . improper relations between the two of you."

Frankie snorted. "That's ridiculous," she said dismissively.

"We're not having—erm, doing—anything like that," Henry said, his face flushed with embarrassment.

"I am merely concerned for Miss Winter's reputation," the fencing master said. "After all, she is nearing marriageable age, possibly preparing for her first City Season."

Frankie sighed, not wanting to be reminded. "Truly, Henry was helping me with my French. You can ask my grandmother all about it."

"I have heard other rumors of your . . . improper behavior," the fencing master continued as though Frankie had said nothing at all. "I seem to remember at the beginning of the term some of the boys voicing doubt about your . . . propriety."

Henry cringed, remembering Valmont's cruel taunts on the first day of fencing that an educated woman was a ruined woman. Had the fencing master overheard him? Apparently so.

"There's nothing of the sort going on here," Henry said firmly. "Fra— Miss Winter loaned me a sword and even admits that she had no idea of its value. It's simply a misunderstanding."

The fencing master looked back and forth between Henry and Frankie, and finally shook his head in defeat.

"From now on, Mr. Grim, in my class you will use swords from this armory, swords that I have given to you expressly for training purposes. Do you understand?"

"Yes, sir," Henry said.

"And Miss Winter," the fencing master continued. "Really, do try and behave yourself. Or at least think of what impressions your actions might give."

"I'll try," Frankie said doubtfully. But even Henry could tell she didn't mean it.

24

WHAT SIR FREDERICK FOUND

Their midday meal was half finished by the time Henry changed back into his uniform and made it to the dining hall.

"Where *were* you, mate?" Adam asked, making room for Henry between himself and Edmund.

"Being lectured by the fencing master." Henry sighed.

"Yeah, what was that about?" Adam asked.

"The foil Frankie loaned me," Henry said. "Didn't you notice anything unusual about it?"

"Besides it's being bloody expensive?" Adam asked.

"You *knew* and you didn't say anything?" Henry asked, nearly dropping his juice glass.

Adam shrugged. "Sorry. I mean, a foil's a foil, right?"

Henry lowered his voice and told Adam what had happened. Adam burst out laughing.

"It's not funny," Henry said.

"Actually, mate, it kind of is."

"Well, I don't think so," Edmund put in. "I mean, it must have seemed a bit suspicious to the fencing master, for him to call you into his office like that."

"But no one thinks . . . I mean, no one's said anything about it, right?" Henry pressed.

Adam was suddenly fascinated by a fleck of dirt on his juice glass.

Edmund coughed and looked away.

"Awwww, come on!" Henry said. *"Really?"*

"No one saw what happened," Edmund said. "One moment you were fencing Theobold and the next moment the fencing master had sent him off to find Francesca and dragged you into his office."

Henry winced.

He couldn't win. Someone steals the left-handed foil to ruin him, but when he brings in one of his own, he gets in trouble anyway.

"Hey, Grim," Theobold hooted. "Are you just after

her money, or do you actually find that sort of girl attractive?"

Valmont laughed. "Or maybe Grim just likes it when she bosses him around," Valmont put in with a nasty smile. "After all, he *likes* taking orders, what with being a servant and all."

Henry gritted his teeth and forced himself not to respond.

He never should have borrowed that sword. It had seemed such a small favor at the time, but if Rohan had been there, he would have pointed out the impropriety or recognized the cost of the weapon.

But Rohan was gone. Expelled. And Henry was left to navigate his friendship with Frankie by himself.

Valmont whispered something to Theobold and the two of them laughed uproariously and glanced in Henry's direction.

Henry sighed.

Hopefully they'd have gotten over it by supper.

They hadn't.

Finally unable to take any more teasing, Henry made his excuses and left his supper half-eaten on his plate.

Back in his room, Henry took out his new Latin

exercise book and forced himself to slog through the homework, knowing that he'd have to help Adam with it later.

The exercise was ridiculously simple, as they'd just begun the Latin unit, and Henry, who had already studied this the year before, had a hard time paying attention.

He kept thinking of Lord Havelock's triumphant sneer when he accused Rohan of stealing and about how he, Henry, was ever going to prove that all of the horrible things that had happened were part of Lord Havelock's evil master plan.

Because they had to be.

Even Valmont had implied that Lord Havelock was willing to manipulate the results of the Knightley Exam back when he'd been chief examiner.

If Henry could just *prove* what Lord Havelock had done, then Rohan might be able to come back, and Headmaster Winter could keep his job, and then Frankie would stay, and they'd all get to remain at the academy for another year.

He banged his fist against his exercise book in frustration.

"Whoa, take it easy," Adam said, standing in the

doorway. He put a napkin filled with sugar biscuits on the edge of Henry's desk.

"Thanks," Henry said.

"Don't mention it. Although, I wouldn't mind a favor in return."

"Latin homework?" Henry asked knowingly.

"It's really awful. Worse than French," Adam complained, taking out his own exercise book.

"Don't copy," Henry snapped, and then he sighed. What did it matter, anyway? "You know what, go ahead."

"Really?" Adam asked suspiciously. "Why?"

Henry shook his head.

"I hate this," he said simply. "I hate that I hate this, but I do. Rohan's gone and Lord Havelock's after us and there's a war coming that only Professor Stratford knows about, but what's *he* going to do about it? I am just so *sick* of *everything*."

"I know how you feel," Adam said, putting down his pen. "But at least you're good at school. I've got all of that, and I'm having to sit here and copy your bloody Latin."

There was a knock at the door.

"Hello?" Henry called.

The door opened a crack. It was Frankie.

"Can I come in?" she asked.

Henry looked to Adam. Adam shrugged.

"We could be expelled, you know," Henry reminded her.

"No one ever checks," Frankie said. "And I *don't* want to go to the library. Everyone's staring at me funny."

"At least all *you're* getting are funny stares," Henry said darkly.

Frankie shut the door behind her. "Who?" she demanded. "Valmont?"

Henry nodded.

"And Theobold," Adam put in. "Mostly Theobold."

"I detest Theobold," Frankie said. "He's exactly the type who spent his childhood burning ants with a magnifying glass and bragging about it to his tutors."

"He *is*!" Adam hooted.

"Shhhh!" Henry cautioned. "Frankie, I really think you should go."

"Fine." Frankie pouted.

Henry sighed. "You're not allowed to be in here. You *know* that."

A knock at the door. Everyone froze.

"Who is it?" Henry called.

"It's Sir Frederick. I've come to see how you're getting on without your friend."

Henry gulped. Frankie looked around wildly, as
though she planned to hide, and Adam began to unlatch
the window.

And then, as if in slow motion, the doorknob turned.

"Good heavens," Sir Frederick said, standing in the
doorframe in his tweeds, carrying that day's newspaper
under his arm and a pipe in his hand. "Francesca."

"I was just leaving," Frankie said, attempting to
escape.

"Not so fast," said Sir Frederick.

Henry exchanged a horrified glance with Adam.
"Not so fast" was practically code for "not so good."

"Is there a problem, sir?" Henry asked, hoping Sir
Frederick would just laugh and pull out a tin of biscuits,
or tell a story, or ruffle their hair in that absentminded
way he had.

But Sir Frederick smiled sadly. "I'm afraid so," he
said. "You boys know the rules."

Henry hung his head.

"They asked me not to come in," Frankie said. "They
told me it wasn't allowed, but I ignored them. This isn't
their fault."

"Whether this is your fault or theirs, girls are not allowed in students' chambers," Sir Frederick reminded them. "Now grab your coats. We're paying a visit to the headmaster's office."

The walk down the corridor was excruciating; the other boys were on their way back from the dining hall and gave Henry and his friends curious glances as they streamed in the opposite direction.

"There goes your reputation," Henry whispered to Frankie.

Adam, who'd overheard, snorted.

The door to the headmaster's office, when they reached it, no longer seemed comically large. Instead, it seemed horribly looming.

Sir Frederick rapped smartly on the door, and Headmaster Winter opened it, clearly having just returned from supper himself—there was a wet splotch on his shirt where he'd been trying to rub out a food stain.

Headmaster Winter raised a ginger eyebrow at the crowd assembled outside his door and ushered them inside.

The office was just as messy and scatterbrained as ever, except instead of cheerful and welcoming, now the clutter appeared sad and neglected.

"What can I help you with?" Headmaster Winter asked, lowering himself into his imposing chair with an audible sigh.

Unsure how to navigate the squashy sofa that bore the only empty seats in the room, Sir Frederick, Frankie, Adam, and Henry remained standing.

"Anthony, I'll get straight to the point," Sir Frederick said. "I stopped by Mr. Grim and Mr. Beckerman's room after noticing that they'd left supper early, and I found your daughter inside."

Headmaster Winter groaned. "*Really*, Francesca?"

Miserably, Frankie nodded. "They told me not to come in," she said. "I just . . . didn't listen."

"You *never* do," Headmaster Winter said plaintively. "But this time, no matter who's to blame, I'm afraid it's consequences all around."

Henry and Adam hung their heads.

"Girls are not allowed," Headmaster Winter continued, "in dormitory rooms. This is a clear rule, and there is a clear consequence."

Henry and Adam exchanged a look of horror.

Henry's heart clenched. This was it, there was nothing the headmaster could do or say to change the fact that he, Henry, had caused his own downfall. His own expulsion. The one thing he'd been worried about, the one thing he'd fought so hard to prevent, and he'd gone and brought it on himself. The irony was unbelievable.

"But, sir," Adam began, "isn't that rule supposed to be about, you know, *kissing* girls?"

Slowly, the headmaster nodded.

"Therein lies the problem," Headmaster Winter said slowly. "There are not usually girls at Knightley Academy. If a boy were caught in a room alone with a girl, clearly her reputation would be scandalized. How had she gotten there? Where was her chaperone? What were her intentions allowing herself to go into a boy's room? But none of the reasons surrounding this rule apply here, and I am loath to give a punishment that is meant for a different, and far more severe, offense just because the circumstances are similar."

At this, Henry allowed himself a small hope that perhaps all was not lost.

Headmaster Winter turned to Frankie. "Honestly, Francesca, you've given me no choice."

"But, Papa—," Frankie began.

"I'll have to tell your grandmother what has happened and let her punish you as she sees fit," Headmaster Winter finished.

Frankie went pale. "No, please. I promise, I'll be good."

"It's too late," Headmaster Winter said, holding up a hand. "I don't enjoy my mother's company either, but she's a good influence on you and seems to be the only one who can keep your behavior in check."

Frankie pouted. "I'm *not* going back to Maiden Manor," she said. "She'll make Headmistress Hardwicke take me back, but I'm not going. I'd rather run away and join an acting troupe. Or the circus. It's not fair. They only teach poetry and painting and French, no matter what we want to learn. All I want is to be a—"

"You're *not* a boy, Francesca," Headmaster Winter said tiredly. "No matter how persistently you try to be one. You are a lady, and you'd better start acting like one. Now *go to your room* until I send for you."

"Yes, Father," Frankie said, all of the fight gone out of her. "And by the way, if you expel my friends, I shall never speak to you again."

Satisfied, Frankie flounced out of the room.

The headmaster sighed and raked a hand through his hair.

"What am I going to do with you?" he said, half to himself and half to Henry and Adam.

"Overlook this one, sir?" Adam asked, and Henry promptly elbowed him.

A smile flickered over the headmaster's lips.

"I think the three of us are all right here," Headmaster Winter said to Sir Frederick.

Sir Frederick inclined his head and left.

"Take a seat," Headmaster Winter said, indicating the squashy sofa. Henry and Adam sank into it, peering at the headmaster from between their knees.

"It's unfortunate that the evidence against your friend was so compelling," Headmaster Winter said. "There was no choice but to expel him, you know."

Henry and Adam said nothing. What was the headmaster going on about?

"I like this job," Headmaster Winter continued. "I truly believe in this school, and I'm hoping to do some good here, to update Knightley's long-standing traditions. But I can't do much good if I'm no longer headmaster, which is exactly what would happen were I to expel the two of you—and which might very well happen anyway, what with the events of this evening.

"I can't see you turned out on the street, or sent home in shame. Not when the offense is so gray and so muddled. I know my daughter, and I have no doubt that she did as she wished, no matter what you told her. And I can't in good conscience ruin all three of our lives because of her actions."

"So we're not expelled?" Henry asked, hardly daring to believe it.

"Suspended," Headmaster Winter said. "Pending a hearing with the board of trustees. It's the best I can do without seeming to favor the two of you, do you understand?"

"Yes, sir," the boys chorused gratefully.

"You will also be serving all-day detention with your head of year until the board can gather for your hearing."

Henry's hope gave way. No, they weren't expelled, but was this truly any better? Suspended. Not allowed to go to class. All-day detention with Lord Havelock.

"Sir?" Henry began. "What are the odds that the board of trustees will let us stay?"

Headmaster Winter shook his head. "I can't say. Of course, I will speak in your defense, and you are welcome to ask any of your professors for character recommendations. But all hope should not be lost, do you understand? I'm certain you boys will find a way to fix this, to put everything back together as it should be."

Henry frowned. It sounded as though Headmaster Winter was talking about something else besides their suspension. As though the headmaster knew about the sabotage, or guessed. As though the headmaster was on their side, or as far over the line of adult impartiality as he dared to step.

And that gave Henry renewed hope.

"Thank you, sir," Henry said.

"Yes, thank you," Adam echoed.

"Now, you're to attend chapel in the morning, eat your breakfast in the kitchen, and then report to Lord Havelock in his office. Is that clear?"

"Yes, sir," the boys mumbled.

"Hope! Vigilance! Truth!" the headmaster called as they wrenched the heavy door closed behind them.

"This is horrible," Henry muttered as they headed back to their room.

"My parents are going to kill me," Adam moaned.

"Yeah, well, at least you've got somewhere to go home to if we are expelled," Henry said quietly.

"Right. Sorry," Adam murmured, embarrassed. "I'm sure my family would love you, though."

"Thanks for the offer." Henry shook his head sadly.

He'd failed, and Lord Havelock had won. How was he possibly going to gather evidence that Lord Havelock had been sabotaging them while serving detention under Lord Havelock's disapproving stare?

But then, what did it matter anymore, anyway?

25

FEELINGS OF
FAILURE

Adam wouldn't sit still. He prowled their room that evening, pacing back and forth until Henry threw down his book and said, "Would you calm down?"

"I can't!" Adam cried miserably. "Rohan's expelled and Frankie's going off to finishing school and we've got a death sentence, in case you haven't noticed."

"I've noticed," Henry said darkly.

"How can you just lie there?" Adam accused.

"I dunno," Henry said sarcastically. "Maybe because I'm too afraid to do anything else?"

"Let's go and see Professor Stratford," Adam whined.

Henry sighed and shook his head.

"Why not?" Adam pressed.

"He lost his job," Henry said quietly. "He lost his job at the Midsummer School so I could come to Knightley Academy. I can't very well go tell him that I've been suspended—possibly expelled—and everything he did for me is wrecked."

"He'd probably prefer to hear it from you, mate," Adam said.

"You just want to see Frankie," Henry accused.

"And what if I do? She's in as much trouble as we are, maybe more. If you've already given up, why not go say good-bye?"

"I haven't given up," Henry said. "I just need some time."

"Well, take all the time you want," Adam said angrily. "Meanwhile the Nordlands are invading with their combat-trained army, but never you mind, just sit there and read a book."

Henry sighed.

How could he explain to Adam that the only reason he'd been reading a book was to try and escape into another story, one that didn't involve his being on the brink of expulsion from Knightley and the end of everything that had ever made him happy?

"I'm sorry," Adam said. "I know you're just trying to cope with all this. I shouldn't have yelled."

"Don't worry about it," Henry said. "I'm sorry too. And you're right, we should go to see Professor Stratford. And Frankie."

Henry put on his coat and began lacing his boots.

Triumphantly, Adam did the same.

"You're just in time," Ellen said when they turned up at the doorstep of the headmaster's house.

"In time for what?" Henry murmured as she led them up the back staircase to Professor Stratford's office.

The door was ajar, and Ellen left Henry and Adam without bothering to announce their presence.

"Hello?" Henry called, pushing open the door.

Professor Stratford had a suitcase open on his desk and was busy piling books inside of it.

Henry felt as though the floor had given way beneath him, as though he were falling and had no idea if the landing would be soft—or if he even wanted it to be.

"What's happened?" Henry asked.

"Been fired," Professor Stratford said with a sad smile.

"What for?" Adam asked boldly.

"Oh, what I'm always fired for," Professor Stratford said. "Have a seat. I'd like the company, if you've nowhere else to be."

"Nowhere else," Henry said, daring Adam to tell the professor the whole of it.

"Lady Winter recently discovered that I was teaching her granddaughter Latin, that I allowed her granddaughter to read the Greeks instead of pretty little novels, and that, generally, I am 'exactly the sort of bad influence that encourages Miss Winter's frightful behavior.'"

Professor Stratford frowned sourly and put a spare pair of shoes into his suitcase.

Henry sighed.

"I don't think you're a bad influence at all," Henry said. "What are you going to do now?"

"Back to the City," Professor Stratford said. "Find work tutoring for the rest of the term, if I can. It's not as though I have any letters of recommendation from my last two employers."

"I'm really sorry," Henry said.

"It's nothing I haven't brought upon myself," the professor said. "I'm always overstepping. First with you, and now with Frances—with Frankie."

"When are you leaving?" Henry asked.

"Last train of the night is at half nine. I should just catch it," Professor Stratford said.

"I've been suspended," Henry blurted, and then hung his head. "Adam and I both. And possibly expelled, pending a hearing with the board of trustees."

"Oh, Henry," the professor said sadly. "And Adam."

"I tried so hard not to, but I failed anyway," Henry said.

"You haven't failed," Professor Stratford said. "You're still here, aren't you? You've just got less time than you'd thought. But you have to show everyone that you *were* being sabotaged, that the headmaster wasn't wrong about you."

"How?" Henry asked miserably.

"You'll think of something," Professor Stratford said. "I have no doubt."

"But what about the Nordlands?" Adam asked.

"That too," Professor Stratford said. "It's all on your shoulders now to let everyone know what's coming. Sometimes the hardest thing isn't making people believe what they don't want to believe, but *whom* they don't want to believe."

Henry smiled sadly.

Professor Stratford, who always sounded as though he was quoting, who had risked his job so Henry could attend Knightley, who had been the closest thing to family Henry had known, was leaving.

"I don't want you to go," Henry said.

"Everything will turn out all right," Professor Stratford said bravely.

"What about Frankie?" Adam pressed.

The professor winced and looked away.

"What?" Henry asked.

"She'll be going away to school," Professor Stratford said.

"She hated that school," Henry protested. "And I don't blame her; it sounded horrible."

"Actually, Lady Winter has arranged for Frankie to attend a reformatory in the Alpine Mountains."

"A reformatory?" Henry repeated, stunned.

"In the Alpine Mountains?" Adam echoed.

Professor Stratford nodded. "I'm afraid so."

"But Frankie doesn't belong at a reformatory," Henry cried. "The girls who go to places like that have done terrible things! It's hardly better than a jail!"

Professor Stratford shook his head. "In Lady Winter's

opinion, it is the only option they have not tried. Frankie leaves in three days. They are arranging her passage as we speak."

Henry and Adam exchanged a horrified look.

Frankie was really going off to a foreign reform school. Professor Stratford was fired. Rohan was expelled. And they were the last two standing, but not for much longer, if the board of trustees had anything to say about it.

"Don't despair," Professor Stratford said. "Find whatever happiness you have left and hold on to it, do you hear me?"

Henry nodded. Adam bit his lip and tucked his hands into his pockets.

"I'll try," Henry said bravely. "I'll try to fix this. After all, there's nothing left to lose, is there?"

Professor Stratford smiled crookedly. "That's the spirit."

And with a tearful round of good-byes, Henry and Adam left Professor Stratford and his half-packed suitcase, trying to find the tiniest pinpoint of happiness in that disaster of a week.

Henry fell asleep still trying.

"Still here, then?" Theobold asked at chapel the next morning.

"Why wouldn't we be?" Henry returned.

"No reason," Theobold said, turning back around in the pew with a knowing smirk.

"I really hate him," Adam whispered.

Henry rolled his eyes in agreement.

And just then, the priest launched into a not-very-subtle sermon on the virtues of keeping a good reputation.

Henry headed for the kitchen after chapel with an odd sense of déjà vu. After all, there he was once again in the halls of a boys' school, forbidden from attending class with the other students.

"This is just like that night we snuck down here for strawberry tarts," Adam said, pushing open the door to the kitchen.

Well, that was one way of thinking about it.

The kitchen was boiling, and Henry immediately began to sweat beneath his tightly buttoned collar and tie.

The cook, a man as wide as the stove, whistled as he scrambled a massive pan of eggs. In the corner by the crockery, a group of maids were setting up the tea services for professors who had elected to take that morning's meal in their offices.

Their old friend Liza looked up from sorting a pile of silverware and grinned. "Well, if it isn't Master Henry and Master Adam!"

"Hello," Henry said, uncomfortably aware that every member of the serving staff was either obviously watching or obviously listening to this exchange.

"I tol' Mary 'bout it bein' *you* in the library that night," Liza continued, wiping her hands on her apron. "An' she laughed and laughed because she'd swore it was a ghost."

"I did no such thing, Liza!" Mary protested from next to the china cupboard. "I was terrorfied, I was!"

"Right," Henry said shyly.

In all the excitement of the past few weeks, he'd forgotten about Liza. But there she was, as cheerful as ever, and it made Henry feel guilty that he hadn't even bothered to stop in and say hello.

"So wot brings the two o' you to the kitchen this mornin'?" Liza asked.

Henry blushed. It seemed the rest of the kitchen staff was rather wondering the same thing. Two of the serving boys had given up all pretense of arranging the breakfast platters and instead were staring warily at Henry and Adam.

"Oh, er—," Henry began.

"We're in loads of trouble," Adam said happily, unaffected by their audience. "Heaps. So we're to eat breakfast in the kitchen today."

"An' they were going to tell us about this *when*?" Liza said angrily. "Well, come on, dearies, grab some toast and jam before the boys take 'em to the tables."

Henry took a few slices of toast and began buttering them.

He tried to imagine what it would be like to work in the stifling kitchens again, hastily eating a slice of bread before serving hot meals to the boys who sat in their uniforms, laughing and joking at the tables. Surely a few months at Knightley hadn't changed him too much to humble himself with servants' work, studying his books in the evenings.

But as soon as he thought this, Henry wondered if he was going mad. Things couldn't go back to the way they were before Knightley. He *had* changed. And no one would ever believe the truth about the Nordlands if he were nothing but a lowly servant.

No, it would be horrible if he and Adam were expelled. Not just horrible but catastrophic.

Henry passed half of his stack of toast to Adam, and said, "Let's go."

"We can't eat here?" Adam whined.

"We're in the way," Henry said. "And anyway, we need to see Sir Frederick."

"What for?"

"Character recommendations for our hearing."

"Oh, right," Adam said with a longing glance at the teapot.

"I can take the service to Sir Frederick's office, if he's ordered one," Henry told Liza, knowing that Sir Frederick rarely ate his meals at the High Table.

"Well, I never!" Liza said, putting her hand to her chest. "If that ain't the kindest thing."

Henry took the tea service from Liza and promised to come back and visit soon, though he doubted he'd be around long enough for that.

Sir Frederick was in his office when the boys arrived, sorting a box of microscope slides.

"Come in, boys," Sir Frederick said, and Henry set

the tea service on the professor's desk with a bow, just as he had at the Midsummer School.

Adam snorted.

"What seems to be amusing, Mr. Beckerman?" Sir Frederick asked, squinting at a glass slide.

"Nothing, sir," Adam said. "Well, it's just, Professor Turveydrop used to yell at Henry for bowing like—"

"Like a servant bringing in the tea," Henry finished with a smile. It *was* funny, come to think of it.

Sir Frederick took an austere sip of his tea and raised an eyebrow. "How can I help you boys?"

"We were hoping for character recommendations," Henry said. "We've been suspended, and the board of trustees makes the final ruling as to whether we're to be expelled."

"I'm aware of that," Sir Frederick said, clattering his teacup into its saucer. "But I am also a member of the board of trustees, and that capacity prevents me from being able to speak in your behalf."

Henry tried not to let his despair show. He'd been counting on Sir Frederick to help them.

"Thank you anyway," Henry said. "We should be getting to our detention."

"The common good will prevail," Sir Frederick called after them.

In the hallway, Henry groaned.

"Sorry it didn't work out, mate," Adam said. "What about Professor Lingua?"

"Forget it," Henry said moodily.

"It was just a suggestion," Adam huffed, handing Henry his napkin-wrapped stack of toast. "Now eat your breakfast. I'm sick of holding it."

Henry bit into a piece of toast. It had already gone cold.

Not like it mattered.

26

THE SABOTEUR
REVEALED

Lord Havelock smiled nastily when Henry and Adam turned up at his office.

"Ah, yes," he said, his dark eyes glittering. "The two detainees. I can't say I'm surprised."

With a sweep of his master's gown, Lord Havelock rose from his chair and glared down at Henry and Adam. "Come with me," he said, marching smartly down the corridor. "And don't"—he cringed—"slam the door."

"Sorry," Adam said.

Lord Havelock sneered.

"I have other priorities besides babysitting the two of you," Lord Havelock continued. "You will do as I say, and you will do so diligently. If you cause trouble, I will see to it that you *are* expelled, do you understand me?"

"Yes, sir," the boys chorused.

Lord Havelock stopped abruptly outside the library. "In," he said.

They went in.

Lord Havelock led them up to the small reading room, and suddenly Henry had a very bad feeling.

"Lines," Lord Havelock demanded, slamming two small, dusty clothbound books onto the table.

"How many, sir?" Henry asked, staring dubiously at the books.

Lord Havelock produced a sheaf of paper and two pens from a fold in his master's gown. "By this evening I shall expect not two but four copies of that book."

Adam's mouth fell open in protest.

"Is there a problem, Mr. Beckerman?" Lord Havelock demanded.

"No, sir," Adam mumbled.

"I didn't think so," Lord Havelock continued. "You shall be fed again when you've finished. And if there is so much as a comma out of place, you'll redo the section, is that clear?"

"Yes, sir," Henry and Adam said miserably.

"Well, what are you standing around for?" Lord

Havelock asked nastily, sweeping out of the room and slamming the door behind him.

"The whole book," Adam moaned. "We have to copy a whole book."

"Could be worse," Henry said. "He could have given us the dictionary."

Adam picked up one of the books as though it were a particularly rotten piece of meat.

"'The Rules and Regulations Concerning the Governance and Operation of Knightley Academy,'" he read.

Even Henry made a face. The rules of the school. There couldn't be anything more boring.

"Well, it *is* detention, what did you expect?" Henry asked.

Adam shrugged.

With a sigh, Henry uncapped his pen and began to copy the first page. Grudgingly, Adam did the same.

Hours passed. Henry's stomach grumbled, but he ignored it.

Adam, however, moaned about how hungry he was and how boring the lines were and how his hand had cramp.

"Do put a lid on it," Henry said. "At least *we're* not being sent to a reformatory."

"Poor Frankie," Adam said.

"Well, there *is* a bright side," Henry continued with a sardonic smile, turning his book to the next page. "Frankie will be all the way in the Alpines when the Nordlands attack."

"Good for her," Adam said sourly, peering at Henry's page number. "Oi, slow down, mate. You're making me look bad."

"Sorry," Henry said.

And then someone knocked on the door.

"Yes?" Henry called.

The door pushed open a crack, and Sir Frederick peered inside.

"Hello, boys," Sir Frederick said. "Lord Havelock sent me to check how you're getting on."

"Page twenty-three, sir," Henry said.

"Well done," Sir Frederick said, holding out a stack of paper. "I've brought this in case you're running out."

"Not quite," Adam said.

"Right, well, I'll leave you to it," Sir Frederick said, fumbling the door shut behind him.

"Oh good, more paper," Adam said sourly.

Henry reached for a sheet with an apologetic smile. "Don't give me that look. I've run out."

Adam gave a frustrated sigh. "'Provisions for three late students to be admitted to the first-year class pending special circumstances,'" Adam read disgustedly. "What does that even *mean*?"

"It goes faster if you don't read it," Henry said.

"You mean I've been *reading* this dreck for no reason?" Adam asked.

"Afraid so," Henry said, frowning at the page in front of him:

That—the—chief—examiner—replaces—the—headmaster—until—a—suitable—replacement—can—be—unanimously—elected—by—the—board—of—trustees, Henry wrote, his index finger keeping place on the page.

He hadn't been reading, just brainlessly copying, but somewhere in the back of his head, he'd linked the words together. And their meaning gave him pause.

"Wait a minute," Henry said, picking up the book and flipping to the previous page.

"I thought you said it went faster if you *didn't* read," Adam whined.

Henry's eyes went wide.

"Did you make a mistake?" Adam asked, passing over a fresh sheet of paper. "Bad luck, mate."

"No. Wait," Henry murmured, rereading what had to be an error in the print.

"What?" Adam asked.

Henry looked up from the book, hardly daring to believe it.

"If Headmaster Winter is fired, Sir Frederick becomes the new headmaster."

"So what?" Adam said.

"It doesn't make sense," Henry said. "Look. Page twenty-three. Sir Frederick is on the board of trustees. It takes a unanimous vote to choose the next headmaster. So, hypothetically, Sir Frederick would be in charge of the school for however long he wanted."

"But I like Sir Frederick," Adam said.

"Right, but *Lord Havelock* doesn't."

"And?" Adam prompted.

"Lord Havelock wouldn't sabotage us knowing that Headmaster Winter's job was at risk—not if it meant Sir Frederick would become the new headmaster indefinitely."

Henry frowned. If Lord Havelock wasn't behind all of the sabotage attempts, then who was?

"So it's not Lord Havelock?" Adam asked.

Henry shook his head. "I don't think so. I mean,

obviously Lord Havelock doesn't like Headmaster Winter, because the headmaster let commoners into the school. Well, Sir Frederick was the one who started it all when he let me take the exam."

"But Lord Havelock found that whatever-it-was inside Rohan's bag," Adam said. "Lord Havelock lost your essay. And, I mean, he's *Lord Havelock*."

"I *know*," Henry said, biting his lip. He was missing something big, something important.

"If it's not Lord Havelock, then who?" Adam asked.

"That's the question," Henry said.

Suddenly, Adam cursed.

He'd been pressing the tip of his pen against the sheet of paper so hard that it had burst, splattering ink all over his hands.

"Bad luck," Henry said sympathetically.

"I'm going to wash up," Adam said, his non-ink-splattered hand on the doorknob. And then he stopped.

"What?" Henry asked.

"Is the door supposed to be locked?" Adam asked.

"No," Henry said, trying the knob himself. "I mean, Sir Frederick was just—"

Sir Frederick!

But no, that was impossible. Sir Frederick was their friend.

But then, the more Henry thought about it, the more sense it made. Sir Frederick would become the new headmaster if Headmaster Winter were fired. Sir Frederick hadn't believed Henry about the combat training in the Nordlands and had tried to convince Henry that what he'd seen was a prank. Sir Frederick had found Frankie in their room the other night and had promptly dragged them off to see the headmaster instead of looking the other way. Sir Frederick had asked what page Henry was on before shutting the door, had known what Henry was about to find.

"Hello, Henry?" Adam asked.

"Sorry," Henry said. He was still holding the doorknob and had been staring off vaguely in the direction of the ceiling. "Sir Frederick."

"What about him?" Adam asked.

Henry gave the doorknob a last, desperate shake. "He's locked us in, if you haven't noticed."

"Right, but *why*?"

"Adam," Henry said evenly, "I don't think Sir Frederick is on our side."

"What?"

"Think about it," Henry said, the words tumbling out of him. "He's been behind everything—getting me into Knightley in the first place and giving Headmaster Winter the idea to admit commoners, which of course meant that Headmaster Winter could be fired. And then he would be the new headmaster."

Henry frowned.

It was like a riddle he'd only half figured out. Everything still wasn't connected, but he'd at least decoded part of it.

"But why would Sir Frederick go to the trouble of getting us into Knightley just to turn around and make sure we got kicked out?" Adam asked, scratching his head. "He can't want to be headmaster that badly, can he?"

Henry shook his head. He was as baffled by their new knowledge as Adam.

"We need to see Sir Frederick," he said. "I have to hear it from him. I just . . . I mean, I'm certain it's Sir Frederick. He's the only one who stands to gain anything by any of this, but I just can't believe some of those things he did: your necklace, the nuts in Rohan's muffin, the unblunted sword."

Sir Frederick had seemed so kind. That day when he bandaged Adam's arm, when he'd given them biscuits and tea, the way he ruffled Henry's hair and called him "my boy." Had it all been a lie?

Henry felt sick. His stomach heaving with revulsion, he kicked the door in anger. "How are we going to get out of here?" he asked, turning around and glaring at the room.

"The window?" Adam asked sarcastically. They were on the third story of the main building. "Naturally you'd go first."

"How can you joke at a time like this?" Henry asked.

"The same way you can sit calmly and read a book when we're suspended," Adam returned, prowling the room and prodding at the bookshelves.

"What are you doing?" Henry asked.

"It's different here. The design. Don't you see?"

Henry looked. There was a break in the paneling on the bookshelf, but that could have been from anything.

"Maybe," Henry said doubtfully.

"No, I'm serious," Adam said. "Look. You can see light through here, and why else would there be only two dictionaries on this shelf?"

Adam pushed and prodded at the bookshelf, convinced that it was a secret passage. Finally, he slammed his hand against the larger of the two dictionaries in disgust.

"I give up," Adam said, as the bookshelf clicked open, revealing a passage.

Henry stared.

"Impossible," Adam breathed.

"Adam, you've done it," Henry said.

"I have my moments," Adam said with a self-satisfied grin.

Behind the bookshelf was a rickety stairway leading upward.

Henry followed Adam up the stairs, which were lit dimly by a single electric wall sconce. The stairwell was steep, and the climb exhausting.

Suddenly, in front of Henry, Adam gave an odd little laugh. "I don't believe it!"

"What, you've found a hidden combat training room?" Henry asked, half joking.

"It's that gruesome unicorn tapestry," Adam said.

The stairwell filled with light.

Henry frowned. What was Adam going on about?

He found out soon enough.

The exit to the hidden stairwell was located behind that horrible tapestry outside Lord Havelock's tower classroom—hence the steep stairs.

"I knew I always liked this thing," Adam said, dusting off his uniform and giving the unicorn tapestry a friendly pat back into place.

Henry nearly laughed. "It's still creepy, if you ask me. Let's go."

"Remind me again," Adam panted, following Henry down the proper stairwell, "why we're going to seek out Sir Frederick now that we've decided he's evil?"

"I have to hear it from him," Henry said. "I have to know why. It just doesn't add up. We're missing something."

"Can't we just miss it all together and, I dunno, not accuse Sir Frederick of sabotaging us since he could, you know, hurt us?"

"Don't you want your necklace back?" Henry asked.

"Too right, I do." Adam said. "Lead on."

Henry led on.

It was nearing the end of second lesson, according to Rohan's pocket watch. They should make it to Sir Frederick's office just as that day's hour free began.

Sure enough, as Henry and Adam crossed the quadrangle and pushed open the door of the thatch cottage that held Sir Frederick's office, boys spilled out into the corridors, filling the main building with noisy chatter that filtered through the half-open windows.

Henry ached to join the other students. To spend his hour free in the first-year common room and bet silly trinkets on the outcome of a checkers game. To stand on the sidelines before a cricket match and hope to be chosen toward the beginning. To have a laugh with his roommates and sneak down to the kitchens for extra tarts and try not to snicker at the boys who fell asleep in chapel. To put on his fencing mask and wield a practice sword at lessons. To have his favorite pudding at supper, and earn a perfect mark on an essay. To be normal.

But that door had long closed and left him standing on the outside of those happier school days, carrying around an unwanted and unasked for burden.

Henry stopped outside Sir Frederick's office, wishing he just had a simple question about that day's lesson.

"Go on," Adam urged.

With a deep breath, Henry raised his fist and knocked.

"Come in," Sir Frederick called.

Henry pushed open the door and Sir Frederick paled as though he'd seen a ghost—two ghosts.

"How—," Sir Frederick began, and then composed himself and said, "have you run out of paper again?"

"Not quite," Henry said, "although you might ask how we let ourselves out of a locked room."

"Ah," Sir Frederick said. "How clumsy of me. Had Lord Havelock not locked the door?"

"Neither this time, nor the last," Henry said with a small smile.

"What is it you've come to see me about?" Sir Frederick asked, his eyes glittering, daring Henry to say the words out loud, to give them power, to make it real.

Adam coughed and looked away. Henry bit his lip.

"I was, er, reading page twenty-four of the rules of the school," he began. "And it occurred to me—to both of us—that you would become the next headmaster if Headmaster Winter lost his job."

"That's true," Sir Frederick said with a wary frown.

"It also occurred to us that, well, the person who has been doing all of these things, sabotaging us . . ." Henry stopped. There was no use being polite. Not now. It was too late, and he was in this too far to turn back. "That it was you," Henry finished.

Sir Frederick didn't deny it.

"And why would I do that?" Sir Frederick asked mildly, but his gaze betrayed his indifference, and for the first time, the medicine master looked sinister.

"I don't know, sir," Henry said.

"A clever boy like you," Sir Frederick said, as though scolding a small child, "and you can't even venture a guess?"

"I wouldn't know where to begin, sir," Henry said. "I was hoping you'd tell us the reason for the letters and my being locked inside the library overnight and the nuts in the muffin and the unblunted sword and stealing Adam's necklace—which, by the way, he'd like back. Because we *trusted* you. I *confided* in you. And I can't imagine *why* you'd betray us like this."

Henry stopped to catch his breath, his chest heaving with anger. He stared down at his boots, and when he looked up again at Sir Frederick, he forced his mouth into a thin, determined line and willed his eyes not to show uncertainty—or fear.

"You boys are so selfish," Sir Frederick crooned. "It's always about *you*, isn't it? All your little problems and disasters, and you never think that maybe this is part of something bigger."

"Like what?" Adam asked with a derisive snort. "The Nordlands?"

Sir Frederick's eyes narrowed.

"Perhaps," Sir Frederick allowed, but Henry could

see that Adam's offhand comment had landed perilously close to the target. "What you boys need to do is consider the greater good, to think of what it would *accomplish* if you were expelled."

"Let me think for a moment," Henry said, his voice dripping with disdain. "I'd be out on the streets, Adam would disgrace his family, but oh, *you'd* be headmaster."

"Precisely," Sir Frederick said with a dangerous smile that forcibly reminded Henry of Lord Havelock. "Because once I am appointed headmaster, I will completely open Knightley to common students. Think of it: a new era of Knightley Academy, where the school is no longer a bastion of the elite but an attainable prize for smart, ambitious boys. Boys like yourself."

"But Headmaster Winter would open the exam to everyone if we succeeded," Henry said with a frown.

"Would he?" Sir Frederick asked, raising his eyebrow. "Would he *really*? Or wouldn't it just be two or three places reserved for commoners, a good show put on for the trustees?"

"Headmaster Winter would take everyone who was qualified," Adam said with a frown, as though already unsure.

"You poor, ignorant boy," Sir Frederick said, shaking his head sadly, his gaze filled with pity. "Headmaster Winter is unprepared for what's coming. His motivation for opening the exam is all wrong."

"And how is *yours* any different?" Henry retorted.

Sir Frederick smiled serenely and held up his hand. "Patience, my boy. Do you remember what you told me about the Nordlands? About the boys of Partisan School being trained in combat?"

"You said you didn't believe me," Henry accused.

"I lied." Sir Frederick shrugged. "A war is coming, and those who can't see it are blind to the ways of the world. War is inevitable, yes, but it is also for the best."

Henry raised an eyebrow and exchanged an incredulous glance with Adam. How could war *ever* be for the best?

"Look what the Nordlands have done," Sir Frederick continued. "Look at the wonderful world they've created. No aristocracy! All men as equals! The Nordlandic cause is worth fighting for. Imagine this tired, set-in-its-old-ways country led into the new century by a man like Yurick Mors!"

Henry gave an involuntary shudder. He could imagine it, all right.

Imagine it the way he dreamed up nightmares the night before an exam, the way he dreamed up horrible things he wished he could forget.

"And *we're* to be the sacrifice?" Henry asked.

"Of course not," Sir Frederick said. "I'm *protecting* you the way I'd protect my own sons. If you stayed at Knightley, you'd have to fight. And surely Lord Havelock has told you what would happen then."

Henry knew all too well what Sir Frederick was talking about.

"Commoners captured in battle can be killed or tortured, while members of the aristocracy have to be ransomed and treated according to their status," Henry said, as though in the classroom, reciting back what Lord Havelock had taught them on the first day of class.

"I'm saving you," Sir Frederick insisted. "Giving you the opportunity to come over to the right side before it's too late."

"It's already too late," Henry said.

"We could run a military hospital," Sir Frederick continued. "On the front lines. We could save lives."

"Whose lives?" Henry insisted. "Boys our own age who have been plucked from their classrooms and forced to fight by ancient conscription laws? Or an army of

Knightley students, all commoners, all sent off to command their peers, slaughtered on the battlefield while their aristocratic schoolmates are captured and given feather beds?"

"The greater number of common students we have at Knightley, the easier it would be for a Nordlandic victory," Sir Frederick urged. "Don't you want to be part of it all? To tell your grandchildren that you built their world, that you abolished the tired aristocracy and had a hand in making all men equal?"

Henry and Adam exchanged a horrified glance—Sir Frederick was talking about killing Knightley students, about making it *easier* to kill them.

"Actually, sir, with all due respect, I'd rather not," Adam said.

"What?" Sir Frederick asked.

"I'm with Adam," Henry said.

"I can see to it that you boys make history," Sir Frederick growled, "but I can also see to it that you wish you'd never refused my generous offer. I can ruin you so much worse than you could ever imagine. Make those acts of 'sabotage,' as you call them, seem like a holiday."

Henry gulped. How could he have ever been so

wrong about Sir Frederick? How could Sir Frederick be so wrong about the world?

"Go ahead," Henry said bravely. "Do your worst."

"Oi, watch it, mate," Adam murmured.

"No," Henry said. "Because I know that the Nordlands have got everything wrong, and that I would never in a million years of a million threats support them—or Chancellor Mors. Because the Nordlands may not have an aristocracy, but they still have a ruling class—men restricting women from reading and writing is a step backward, not progress. The Nordlanders don't tolerate anyone who's different. They'd call Adam and Rohan heathens and sentence anyone who tutored Frankie to three years' hard labor.

"So, no, I won't join you, and I think that your ideas about the way the world should be are the most unchivalrous thing I've ever heard. It's never right to exclude anyone in order to include someone else. That's elitism and snobbery and the opposite of everything we're taught here at Knightley. The Code of Chivalry teaches us to do right by everyone, not to force the world to take on a different shape that looks good from far away but up close is a bleak and utter disaster."

Henry's fists were clenched, and his eyes were narrowed, and he couldn't believe he'd just said all of those things aloud.

"I won't let this war happen," Henry said, more calmly this time.

"Oh, really?" Sir Frederick asked nastily. "You and what credibility? Because what I see here are two common little boys who think they're too good to fight for the Nordlands, who believe in a tired aristocracy because it's been good to them, and who no one will ever listen to, because this afternoon, I will personally see to it that you are expelled from this academy and that a war with the Nordlands is brought down with swift and sudden force."

"We'll find a way," Adam said. "Professor Stratford believed us."

"Ah, yes, that gullible tutor of yours. Pity he's been fired from his last *two* jobs, was it? Such a credible source."

Sir Frederick patted his waistcoat pocket and removed a small, glittering charm on a chain—Adam's necklace.

"Such a pretty little charm," Sir Frederick said. "I wonder how much this would fetch if I melted it down?"

"Don't you dare," Henry said.

At the same time Adam exclaimed, "My necklace!"

"Of course," Sir Frederick continued, dangling the necklace from his fist, the charm swinging back and forth pendulously, "you could have this back if you changed your mind."

The look on Adam's face was one of pure torture.

At that moment, the door burst open, and Lord Havelock stood there, his master's gown swirling around his ankles, his cheeks peppered with stubble, a horrible sneer stretching over his lips. "I'll thank you to stop distracting these boys from their detention," he snapped.

"Come, now," Sir Frederick said with an indulgent smile. "Surely their detention can wait."

"Can it?" Lord Havelock asked, his sneer growing so large that it rather resembled a snarl. "And how about your plans for a war with the Nordlands, and your little ambitions to be headmaster? Can those wait, as well?"

Sir Frederick's face twitched.

"Ah, yes, Frederick," Lord Havelock continued. "I've heard everything."

Henry experienced a momentary disorientation. He was so used to fearing and loathing Lord Havelock and feeling grateful to Sir Frederick, but now everything was reversed.

"Have you?" Sir Frederick asked nervously.

"You see, I think we have a bit of a misunder-standing here," Lord Havelock continued, his voice dangerously calm. "I agreed to help you rid the acad-emy of these commoners and of our pesky, idealistic new headmaster, but had I known that you planned to take over this school by turning it into a military command center filled with commoners, to end the Hundred Years' Peace and go to war with the Nord-lands, I would have turned you in to the authorities for high treason and sheer stupidity."

"Would you really, Magnus?" Sir Frederick asked, and it took a moment for Henry to realize that Lord Havelock had a first name.

"Do not test me, Frederick," Lord Havelock threat-ened.

The tension in the room thickened, and the silence that followed Lord Havelock's threat was ominous indeed.

Despite all this, Henry's mind whirled to process what he'd just heard. Lord Havelock had been helping Sir Frederick. It *had* been Lord Havelock sabotaging Henry and his friends after all! It hadn't been his imagi-nation; it had been real. More real than Sir Frederick playing the role of a sympathetic mentor and confidant, anyhow.

Sir Frederick and Lord Havelock were shouting now. Calling each other horrible names that Henry didn't think even Valmont would dare to use.

Henry exchanged a glance with Adam. It rather seemed as though, at any moment, it might come to blows between Sir Frederick and Lord Havelock.

And then there was a knock at the door.

Sir Frederick stopped shouting midsentence. Lord Havelock composed himself.

Sounding just like the confidant and friend he had once been, Sir Frederick called, "Who is it?"

"Augusta Winter," was the haughty reply.

Without waiting for an invitation, Grandmother Winter opened the door and stared reproachfully at the crowd she found inside Sir Frederick's office.

"The rest of the trustees have arrived," she said primly, her mouth set in a disapproving frown. "I was hoping to have a few words with you before the hearing, but I can see that you're quite busy."

"Unfortunately so," Sir Frederick said with a sheepish grin, lapsing back into the role of the kindly medicine master.

"Thank you, Augusta," Lord Havelock said, giving a small bow. "I'll see to it that the boys are prepared for their hearing."

As soon as Grandmother Winter had shut the door, Lord Havelock grabbed Henry and Adam by their wrists. "Come on," he said, and then turned to Sir Frederick. "Don't test me, Frederick. Don't even think of it."

27

THE HEARING

H alf an hour later, Henry and Adam had combed their hair, washed beneath their fingernails, and shined the scuffs from their boots.

Nervously, they stood outside the door to a room in the main building they'd never before entered, in an out-of-the-way wing of the second story. Lord Havelock, his glare so intimidating that it noticeably lowered the temperature in the corridor, stood beside them, keeping watch.

Adam rubbed mournfully at the ink stain on his hand, which, despite a good ten minutes of scrubbing, had barely faded.

"Stand still," Lord Havelock hissed.

"Sorry, sir," Adam whispered.

The door opened, and a tiny, wizened old man in an expensive pin-striped suit peered out, clutching his bowler hat to his chest.

"Ah, Lord Havelock," the man said.

"Lord Ewing," Lord Havelock said, inclining his head.

"Are these the boys?" Lord Ewing asked.

"Naturally. Shall I lead them inside, Ewing?"

"Yes, quite," Lord Ewing mumbled in his stiff-lipped, aristocratic way.

"Walk," Lord Havelock sneered, prodding Henry and Adam in the back.

Henry nervously flattened his hair as he entered the room.

It was a large parlor, with tall windows shrouded by heavy velvet curtains that had been drawn closed, casting the room in shadow. A vast, circular table took up most of the space, and around the table sat an assortment of glaring, important-looking men—the board of trustees.

But Sir Frederick was missing.

Henry looked around uncertainly.

"Mr. Grim, Mr. Beckerman," Headmaster Winter said, rising from his seat at the table. "Please, come in and stand near the brazier."

Henry, his heart pounding furiously, did as Headmaster Winter asked. Adam took his place next to Henry and clasped his hands behind his back to hide the ink stain.

Lord Havelock closed the door.

Headmaster Winter frowned. "Is Sir Frederick not coming?"

Lord Havelock gave the Headmaster a significant stare. "I have not seen him. In fact, I assumed he was already here."

Headmaster Winter's frown deepened. "Strange," he mumbled.

"Won't Sir Frederick be joining us?" Lord Ewing asked, taking his seat.

"Evidently not," Lord Havelock said. "But thankfully, with twelve members of the board present, you have a quorum and can rule on student cases."

Lord Ewing nodded slowly. "We can indeed," he said, "although it is regrettable that Sir Frederick cannot join us. Now, to the proceedings."

"Of course," Headmaster Winter said. "This meeting of the board of trustees is now called to order on this the, er . . ." Another member of the board helpfully supplied the date, and Headmaster Winter nodded his thanks. "At, right, half five in the evening," Headmaster Winter continued, glancing at his pocket watch. "We're here to rule on the cases of Misters Adam Beckerman and Henry Grim, both first-year students who are currently serving suspensions and are here facing the prospect of expulsion from the academy."

"Can you please explain the circumstances that led these boys to receive suspensions?" The man seated to the left of Lord Ewing called, frowning as he scribbled notes into a ledger, playing the role of secretary.

Headmaster Winter inclined his head. "Last night after supper, Sir Frederick found my daughter in their room."

Collectively, the board of trustees frowned and shifted uneasily in their seats.

"My daughter," Headmaster Winter continued, "does not always exercise the best judgment, and claims that she entered their room even though they told her not to do so. These boys have become friends to her, and her intentions in entering their bedchamber were innocent. She has been duly punished, but as the case is not black-and-white, I felt these boys did not deserve to be expelled on the spot, despite expulsion being the usual punishment for the offense."

"How has their performance been otherwise?" Lord Ewing asked, glaring at Henry and Adam.

Headmaster Winter shuffled a sheaf of papers.

"Ah, yes. Mr. Beckerman's marks are average in ethics and protocol, below average in languages and military history, and excellent in fencing. Mr. Grim's marks are excellent in every subject except protocol, in which he is average."

"And have the boys received any previous disciplines?" Lord Ewing inquired.

"Misters Grim and Beckerman were both banned from participation in the Inter-School Tournament."

Henry's mouth went dry.

"And why was that?" Lord Ewing asked.

"Professor Lingua issued the punishment after the boys found a cheat page in one of their assignments and did not come forward immediately."

Henry and Adam exchanged a look of horror.

They were done for, Henry knew. Imperfect marks, previous disciplinary actions, and not one professor to speak on their behalf.

"Misters Beckerman and Grim have also been the object of theft on two separate occasions," Headmaster Winter continued.

"Regrettable, certainly regrettable," Lord Ewing muttered, scribbling notes onto a third sheet of paper. "Am I to take it that these boys are generally disliked by their fellow students?"

"They are not popular students, no," Headmaster Winter conceded, "but they are friends with my daughter, Francesca, and also with former first-year student Rohan Mehta."

"Former?" Lord Ewing asked.

"He was expelled last week after being caught stealing by their head of year," Headmaster Winter said. "Surely you received my letter of concern over the incident."

"Wait," Adam said. Henry stared curiously at his friend.

Lord Ewing harrumphed.

"Yes, Adam?" Headmaster Winter said.

"About what you just said, sir," Adam continued, swallowing nervously, "about Rohan? He didn't steal anything. He was set up. And so were we, with the cheat page in Professor Lingua's class."

"It's true, sir," Henry said.

"And why would someone do that?" Lord Ewing asked doubtfully.

"Because," Henry said, knowing that it was then or never, that this very well might be his final chance to be believed, "they stood to gain if we were expelled from the academy. At least, that was the reason at first. But then we saw proof when we were in the Nordlands that the Partisan students are being trained in combat, and it became even more important to discredit us so that no one would believe the truth: sir, the Nordlands have violated the Longsword Treaty."

Shock played over the faces of the members of the board of trustees. Lord Ewing dropped his pen in surprise.

"Why didn't you boys come to see me about this?" the headmaster asked.

"I spoke with Sir Frederick first," Henry said, "and he didn't believe me. I thought no one would believe me if Sir Frederick didn't. I also told Professor Stratford."

"Sorry, which professor?" a sallow man with a large, pitted red nose asked.

"Stratford," Headmaster Winter said, wincing. "My daughter's tutor. He was fired last night and has already left the school grounds."

"How convenient," the man with the nose that rather resembled a strawberry said, "that these boys have devised an excuse for their behavior, the validity of which rests on the shoulders of two men who are currently impossible to track down."

"I'm not making it up," Henry said. "There's a combat training room at Partisan, in the first-floor corridor, hidden in the wall paneling near the fish statue. It's full of illegal weapons. Halberds and crossbows and who knows what else. They have dummies with targets painted on and charts ranking the students in different types of combat. I saw it myself."

As Henry spoke, the members of the board exchanged nervous glances. Because this boy in front of them, his cheeks scrubbed pink and his nerves on display, seemed absolutely confident about what he had seen, and where. The level of detail with which he spoke about this combat training room was troubling. And it wouldn't do if they dismissed what could be their only warning before the beginning of a fearsome and terrible war . . .

"Stuff and nonsense," the man with the strawberry-shaped nose said dismissively, but the other members of the board did not seem to share his sentiments.

"I've never known Mr. Grim to be anything but truthful," Headmaster Winter said with an encouraging smile in Henry and Adam's direction.

"Perhaps," Lord Ewing said, his voice coming out

in a squeak, "we should send someone to the Nordlands to verify Mr. Grim's claims. If there *is* a violation to the Longsword Treaty, that's serious news indeed."

"Pish posh, Ewing!" the man with the strawberry nose said, sniffing loudly. "I'll go myself. I wager there's nothing to see, but at least I'll put an end to this rubbish."

"Viscount DuBeous has volunteered to journey to the Partisan School this evening to investigate claims of combat training," Headmaster Winter said. "Does anyone on the board object?"

Silence.

"Permission granted, Viscount," Headmaster Winter said. "And now, we'll recess this meeting of the board until the viscount's return—hopefully by tomorrow afternoon, hmmm?"

"If it takes that long," Viscount DuBeous said with a dismissive sniff of his massive red nose.

Henry looked to Adam and breathed a sigh of relief. The decision on their expulsion would have to wait another day. And perhaps in that time, Henry's discovery of the combat training at Partisan would not only save the two of them from being expelled but save them all from being unprepared for war.

Still, waiting was never easy, and without schoolwork as a distraction, the next twenty-four hours promised to be excruciating.

When Henry and Adam returned to their room that evening, the window was open, and a small clothbound book sat on the windowsill.

The book, when Henry examined it, turned out to be a collection of poetry. And written in the inside cover was this message: *I sat in a clearing two hours after sunset and waited to say good-bye.*

Frankie.

Henry showed Adam the inscription. Adam, who had been in the middle of taking off his coat, shrugged back into it. "Let's go," he said.

And they did.

There was a layer of frost on the bench by the hedge maze, as though discouraging their clandestine meeting. The trees, which had been full of brilliantly hued leaves only weeks before were now picked-over bones, skeletons of their former glory.

In the faint moonlight, Henry shivered and drew his wrists deeper inside the sleeves of his jacket.

Suddenly, they heard footsteps crunching over the icy grass.

"Hello?" Frankie called.

"We're here," Adam called back.

She was just a shape in the distance, and then she was there, grinning at them from beneath a fur wrap, her blue eyes determined.

"Hullo," Henry said.

And it shouldn't have been uncomfortable, the three of them, but it was.

"We heard about the reformatory," Adam said. "Bad luck."

Frankie shrugged and smiled ruefully. "It's not so bad. At least the girls there won't giggle incessantly."

But Henry could tell that Frankie was just as scared as they were about the reformatory.

"So, what was the verdict?" Frankie asked. "Are you expelled?"

Henry and Adam exchanged a look.

"Come on, tell me!" Frankie pleaded.

"Not exactly," Henry said.

"Oh, well, *that* clears things up," Frankie said with a snort.

"Sir Frederick's evil!" Adam blurted.

"Nice one," Henry muttered.

"Well, he is," Adam insisted. "Frankie doesn't know what happened. We can't very well start at the end."

"The end?" Frankie asked, arching an eyebrow and drawing her wrap tighter around her shoulders.

"Adam's right," Henry said. "Sir Frederick is the one who's been sabotaging us and doing all of those things. Well, Lord Havelock helped, but it was mainly Sir Frederick."

"Sir Frederick?" Frankie asked skeptically.

"Really," Adam said. "He'd be headmaster if your father got fired. And he's a maniac. Completely off his nut. He wants us to go to war with the Nordlands so the Nordlands can win."

"What?" Frankie asked.

And so Henry explained. He told Frankie how Sir Frederick had spoken reverentially of the Nordlandic cause and Chancellor Mors. How Sir Frederick had asked them to help run a military hospital. How Sir Frederick believed in abolishing the aristocracy no matter that the alternative was worse, and how Sir Frederick had threatened them and nearly come to blows with Lord Havelock.

"I just can't believe it," Frankie said, shaking her head as though stunned.

"That's not the best part," Henry said wryly. "Sir Frederick didn't show up to our hearing. So we told the board of trustees what I'd seen in the Nordlands, and they sent this one man, Viscount Something-or-other, to see for himself before they decided anything."

"But if he does find evidence of combat training, then what?" Frankie asked.

"Dunno," Adam said with a shrug. "But maybe we won't be expelled. And they could rewrite the Longsword Treaty."

"And rename it the Grim-Beckerman-Mehta Winter Treaty," Henry joked.

"Oi, how come *your* name's first?" Adam complained.

"Francesca!" Grandmother Winter's voice trilled, and all three friends groaned.

"No," Frankie said angrily. "Let her find us here. I don't care."

"When are you leaving?" Henry asked.

"Day after tomorrow," Frankie said, trying to sound brave.

"We could take the train into the City together," Henry said with a sad little smile.

"And join the circus," Adam joked. "Run away. Disappear into the backstreets and alleyways, travel with the freak show."

"Maybe just you," Frankie teased.

Henry laughed.

"Francesca Winter, you shall catch your death of cold!" Grandmother Winter shrilled, and in the distance, Henry could make out her silhouette marching angrily through the grass.

"You'd better go," Henry said.

"I don't know," Frankie demurred, "catching my death of cold sounds like an awfully big adventure."

"Please, no more adventures," Henry said with a groan.

"Define 'adventure,'" Adam said. "Because joining the circus, for example—"

"Do shut up, Adam," Henry and Frankie said at the same moment.

And then, without really saying good-bye, Frankie ran off into the night, toward the scolding sound of her grandmother's voice.

28

NEWS FROM THE NORDLANDS

Henry Grim stood at his bedroom window the next afternoon, watching a sleek black car follow the twists and turns in the driveway of Knightley Academy. On his bed sat his suitcase, fully packed, just in case. Adam was sprawled on the floor, playing a complicated game of solitaire with a deck of cards that turned out to be missing the king of diamonds.

"Stupid cards," Adam muttered, smearing the columns of cards into a pile.

"Someone's coming," Henry said.

Adam looked up. "Viscount Whoever?"

Henry nodded, and Adam joined him at the window.

Their breath fogged the panes of glass, and Henry wiped away the condensation.

Outside, the driver of the automobile hopped out and opened the door for Viscount DuBeous, helping the pale and trembling man onto the front steps.

"Oi, what's wrong with him?" Adam asked.

Henry shrugged, remembering the Viscount's red nose. "Caught a chill?" he suggested.

"Maybe."

"Well," Henry said, smiling tightly, "shouldn't be long now until our hearing."

And it wasn't. Within the hour, Lord Havelock rapped smartly on the door to their room.

"Ah," Lord Havelock said, frowning at Henry and Adam. "I see you've packed your things. Given up already?"

"Preparing for the worst, sir," Henry said, straightening his tie in the glass.

"They're ready for you. Come along," Lord Havelock snapped, turning on his heel.

The board of trustees sat around the same table as they had before, and if anything, their disapproving frowns had deepened.

Headmaster Winter resumed the hearing with all

of yesterday's formalities, and then turned to Viscount DuBeous, who looked as though his chill had become flu.

"Erm, right," said the viscount. "The Nordlands."

And then he broke into a fit of coughing.

"I found no evidence of combat training," the Viscount said with a shudder. He put a hand to his forehead, exposing a wrist chafed raw and encrusted with blood.

"What's this, DuBeous?" asked Lord Ewing, seizing the viscount's arm and pushing back his sleeve. "These look like rope marks."

Viscount DuBeous shuddered again, his right eye twitching.

"What's going on here?" Headmaster Winter asked with a frown.

"I found no evidence of combat training," Viscount DuBeous repeated, tugging his sleeve down over his wrist.

"How about evidence of torture?" Lord Ewing squeaked, revealing a matching raw band around the viscount's other wrist.

At the word "torture," the room buzzed with furious whispers, and Henry caught the name Dimit Yascherov as it passed between Lord Ewing and the storklike gentleman to his right.

Suddenly, Henry remembered where he'd heard the head of Partisan School's name—in that very first newspaper clipping he'd received about the Nordlands. With some concentration, Henry dredged the passage out of the recesses of his memory:

> According to High Inspector Dimit Yascherov of the Nordlandic Policing Agency, and head of Partisan School, the women and children were half frozen, and nearly all suffered from terrible dysentery, and preparations were immediately made for transport to a nearby hospital. Despite the inspector's claims, the hospital holds no records of treating any women or children who match the description.

"Well, Viscount, is this true? Have you been treated poorly during your journey to the Nordlands?" Headmaster Winter asked.

Viscount DuBeous stared at his lap. He bit his lip. The dark circles under his eyes seemed to deepen, and the cracks in his dry lips seemed to spread as he shook his head.

"Right," Headmaster Winter said. "Lord Havelock, can you please take the viscount to see our sick matron and make certain he is looked after?"

"Of course," Lord Havelock said with a bow, helping Viscount DuBeous to his feet and leading the man from the room.

As the door clicked shut, the remaining members of the board of trustees sat in silence, and Headmaster Winter sighed and rubbed at his ginger beard.

"Can anyone tell me," Lord Ewing asked, breaking the silence, "what has happened to Sir Frederick?"

Henry and Adam rather wondered the same thing.

Headmaster Winter shook his head sadly. "Sir Frederick has disappeared without explanation, no doubt to tend to some emergency."

Henry exchanged a significant look with Adam. Emergency indeed. Sir Frederick had fled, fearing exposure.

"That's not true, sir," Henry said, unable to stop himself.

"I beg your pardon?" Headmaster Winter asked with a frown.

"I'm sorry, sir," Henry said, "but that's not true, what you said about Sir Frederick. Yesterday, Adam and

I confronted Sir Frederick, and he admitted to plotting against us and trying to get us kicked out of the academy."

"'Plotting against you?'" Headmaster Winter asked.

"It all started with the threatening newspaper clippings in the morning post," Henry began, listing their grievances against Sir Frederick, and ending with Sir Frederick locking them inside the library reading room.

Finally, Henry turned to Adam and asked, "Have I missed anything?"

"That about sums it up," Adam said.

The board of trustees was very quiet. They looked to one another, at a loss for what to say or do. Because, clearly, *something* was happening in the Nordlands. And it was unlike Sir Frederick to disappear so suddenly, without even a hint as to his whereabouts.

"Surely you can't believe these boys, Headmaster?" Lord Ewing said.

"I can confirm their story myself," said a deep, sneering voice. Lord Havelock had returned from the sick bay.

"Truly, Magnus?" Headmaster Winter asked.

"I'll admit that it is a bit hard to believe," Lord Havelock said, striding to the center of the room, his master's gown swirling around the legs of his best tweed suit, "but it is true, every word. I myself heard Sir Frederick admit guilt yesterday, and I had wondered why these boys seemed to have such particularly bad luck. Naturally, I told Sir Frederick that he had committed high treason and I planned to turn him in to the authorities, but with your arrival, gentlemen, things became a bit, dare I say, muddled."

Lord Havelock clasped his hands together and smiled dangerously, then continued. "I planned to accuse Sir Frederick at the hearing yesterday, but he never arrived. Guilty conscience, I can only surmise. But the matter on the table is not Sir Frederick's betrayal and, might I add, subsequent disappearance, but rather the expulsion of these two boys."

Henry caught Adam's eye and gave his friend a small, brave smile. This was it.

"Taking into consideration all of the facts," Lord Havelock continued, "I believe it would be an enormous error to expel Mr. Beckerman and Mr. Grim from the academy. If anything, they have shown an excess of chivalry in handling the unfortunate incidents Mr. Grim has just described. They are neither of them at the bottom of their year academically, and I am to understand that

Mr. Beckerman shows great promise in fencing, while Mr. Grim has remarkable facility with languages. It is unfortunate, yes, that Miss Winter was found in their room, but as there is no indication of any impropriety, I recommend, as both their head of year and as their professor, that these boys be allowed to stay on as students at Knightley."

Henry had never thought he would feel gratitude toward Lord Havelock, but at that moment, he nearly threw his arms around their head of year. Adam looked as though he felt the same.

"Thank you, Lord Havelock," Headmaster Winter said. "It takes a majority vote exceeding two-thirds for expulsion. We will vote now, first in the case of Mr. Adam Beckerman. All in favor of expulsion?"

One gentleman promptly raised his hand. And another. And another. And no one else.

Adam grinned.

"Mr. Beckerman, I expect to see you at chapel bright and early tomorrow morning," Headmaster Winter said with a small smile.

"Yes, sir," Adam said, beaming.

"And now," Headmaster Winter continued, "all those in favor of the expulsion of Mr. Henry Grim?"

Again, three hands.

"The same goes for you, Mr. Grim," Headmaster Winter said, and Henry sighed with relief.

He was allowed to stay at Knightley!

But there was just one thing.

"Sir?" Henry said. Headmaster Winter looked up. "What about Rohan?"

Headmaster Winter frowned.

"I mean," Henry continued, emboldened, "Rohan should be reinstated, as his expulsion was due to Sir Frederick's sabotage. Rohan's no thief, and Lord Havelock might be willing to take back the accusation in light of recent evidence."

Everyone in the room turned to stare at Lord Havelock, who frowned distastefully at the attention, his mouth a thin, angry line. And just when Henry had nearly given up hope, their head of year cleared his throat.

"The act did seem a bit out of character," Lord Havelock said. "Not to mention that no student would dare to steal from me, especially a worthless trinket such as the one I found in Mr. Mehta's school bag. I hereby revoke my accusation against him."

"Very well," Headmaster Winter said. "A majority

vote, I believe, in this case? Mr. Mehta was expelled on the spot, with the evidence against him so compelling that there was no need for a vote, but now that he was evidently made to look guilty for a crime that was not his, I put it to you: All those in favor of reinstating Rohan Mehta to the first-year class and removing the offense from his school records?"

Slowly, Lord Ewing raised his hand.

And then the storklike man next to him.

And the man with the mutton-chop whiskers.

And the portly man who smelled of snuff.

And the man to his left.

And the man to *his* left.

And finally, Headmaster Winter.

"A majority," Headmaster Winter said. "Rohan Mehta is officially pardoned and reinstated as a member of the first-year class."

Henry and Adam grinned triumphantly.

Headmaster Winter's eyes twinkled as he said, "Sir Roberts? Can you please send a telegram to Holchester informing Mr. Mehta and his family of the good news?"

And with much good cheer, the hearing came to a close. The members of the board rose from their seats and offered their hands to Henry and Adam in congratulations. The room emptied, until only Lord Havelock, Henry, and Adam remained.

"Are you meaning to stand there all day?" Lord Havelock asked. "Or were you planning to unpack your things in time for supper?"

"Sorry," Henry murmured, and then, knowing that it had to be said, added, "and thank you, sir."

"Whatever for?" Lord Havelock asked with an all-too-familiar Havelook of Doom.

"Speaking on our behalf," Henry said, "and on Rohan's."

Henry elbowed Adam.

"Right, thanks," Adam said.

"There are *some things* that need not be mentioned," Lord Havelock said with a significant look at Henry and Adam. "Gratitude, in this case, is *one* of them."

Lord Havelock swept out of the room, his master's gown billowing behind him.

"What was that about?" Adam asked, frowning.

"A bribe," Henry said, making a face. "Lord Havelock had been helping Sir Frederick to get us kicked out of the academy, remember? But now that Lord Havelock has spoken on our behalf to make things right, we can no longer accuse him of anything without seeming horribly ungrateful. Think about it."

"You're right," Adam said. "The git is blackmailing us."

"It's not blackmail," Henry said with a sigh, "not when both sides benefit. It's more like . . . an understanding."

On the way back to their room, Henry and Adam ran into Valmont coming the other way down the corridor.

"Why haven't you been at lessons?" Valmont demanded.

Henry shrugged. "We were suspended."

"Right," Valmont said. "I heard about the hearing from Theobold. Are you really expelled? For trying to steal from the headmaster's armory?"

"What?" Henry protested. "That's ridiculous."

"I *told* Theobold I didn't believe him," Valmont said, scuffing the toe of his boot into the carpet.

"Well, the board voted, and we're not expelled," Henry said.

"Really?" Valmont asked, surprised.

"And Rohan's coming back," Adam blurted.

"Congratulations," Valmont said sourly.

"Listen, mate, can I ask you something?" Adam asked. "Why are you being, well, *nice*? Nicer than usual, anyhow."

Valmont scowled. "Uncle Havelock told me to."

"Oh," Adam said.

But Henry wasn't so sure that was the reason. He remembered how Valmont had laid off tormenting them over the past few weeks. How Valmont had nearly stuck up for them at Partisan.

"Just because I'm being nice doesn't mean I like you," Valmont said.

"Good, the same goes for us," Henry said, edging past Valmont in the hallway.

"Chess match tonight?" Valmont called after him.

"Only if you're prepared to lose," Henry called back.

When Henry and Adam returned to their room, there was someone waiting for them.

Headmaster Winter stood, hands clasped behind his back, staring out the window. When the door opened, he turned.

"Hello, sir," Henry said with a frown. "Everything all right?"

"Not really, no," Headmaster Winter said, looking around for a place to sit and finally giving up. "Viscount DuBeous has been taken to the hospital. He's covered in bruises, and a fever has made him delirious."

"I'm sorry to hear that," Henry said, nudging Adam, who mumbled his agreement.

"Whatever the viscount saw in the Nordlands," Headmaster Winter continued, "he has not confirmed evidence of combat training or this room of which you spoke."

"But it's true, sir," Henry said.

"True or not," Headmaster Winter said with a sad smile, "without proof that the Nordlands have violated the Longsword Treaty, there is nothing we can do at the present time."

Henry could hardly think, he was so upset with the headmaster's words. Viscount DuBeous had to have seen *something*, whether or not he would acknowledge it. Why didn't the headmaster send someone else to the Nordlands? Of course, Partisan would have removed the evidence, moved their combat training equipment to another part of the castle now that they knew the room had been discovered—but sit and do nothing? Ridiculous.

"So we sit here and wait for them to attack," Adam muttered.

"There are worse places to sit and wait," the headmaster said.

"Like reformatory schools?" Henry asked before he could stop himself.

"Ah," the headmaster said, his smile tightening into a grimace, "that."

"Frankie doesn't want to go, in case you haven't noticed," Adam said. "She likes it here. She has friends here. And she's learned what happens when you break the rules. Please, sir, you can't send her away. If you're going to send *anyone* away, *my* vote is for Grandmother Winter."

Henry nearly laughed out loud. Even Headmaster Winter seemed amused by Adam's outburst.

"I'd been thinking that the decision was a bit rash," Headmaster Winter admitted.

"Sir," Henry said, "it doesn't seem fair that our punishment was two days' suspension, and Frankie's is to be sent away for good."

"No," the headmaster said, tugging at his beard, "it doesn't. In any case, I'll leave you boys to it. I just wanted to make certain that you understand about the Nordlands."

"Without proof, it's as though what I saw never

happened," Henry said sourly, wishing it didn't have to be that way. He'd fought so hard to be believed, and now it didn't even matter. It was as though nothing had happened at all. An army was sharpening its swords and preparing its attack, and those with the power to stop it were content to sit and wait.

"Right you are," the headmaster said, taking out his pocket watch. "I'll see you at supper in . . . goodness, can it be forty minutes?"

It felt strange going back to the dining hall and the first-year table, even though it had been only two days.

As Henry and Adam took their seats, the whole of the dining hall craned their necks to stare.

Well, Henry thought wryly, *staring is becoming a common occurrence these days.*

"You're back!" Edmund said, scooting over to sit with Henry and Adam.

"Yeah, we are," Adam said with a grin. "Got out early for good behavior."

"Actually, Edmund, can we copy your class notes?" Henry asked.

"Oi, how can you think about schoolwork at a time like this?" Adam asked.

"A time like what?" Henry frowned. And then he realized what Adam was going on about.

Rohan stood in the cavernous entrance to the dining hall, his grin nearly as wide as the set of double doors.

"Oh good, the thief is back," Theobold said with a sneer.

But Henry hardly heard him. He was too busy giving Rohan an enormous hug.

"It's jolly good to see you too," Rohan said stiffly.

"Sit down and have some potatoes," Adam said, pulling Rohan into the seat next to his.

"I almost forgot," Rohan said with a frown. "I found this in the pocket of my school blazer."

It was the king of diamonds, the missing playing card from Adam's solitaire game. "Brilliant, thanks," Adam said, pocketing the card.

"What have I missed?" Rohan asked.

Henry and Adam exchanged a glace.

"Oh, nothing much," Henry said.

"Really?" Rohan asked skeptically.

"Well, we were suspended," Adam said, his mouth full of potatoes. "And then Sir Frederick was evil, and Lord Havelock was on our side, and we had a hearing, actually two hearings, and we're not expelled, and

Professor Stratford was fired, and Sir Frederick has disappeared, and Viscount Someone-or-other was tortured, and Frankie may or may not be sent to a reformatory."

"Okay, Henry, what have I *really* missed?" Rohan asked.

Henry bit his lip, suddenly overcome by a fit of laughter.

"Are you trying not to laugh?" Rohan accused. "Honestly, what's funny?"

Henry's shoulders shook, and he had to fight to swallow a mouthful of juice. Because it *was* funny, come to think of it, in a tragic sort of way: so much had happened, yet so little had been accomplished.

Rohan finished unpacking his things after supper, while Henry and Adam sat on their beds and filled their friend in on what he had missed.

"I'm sorry," Rohan said, locking his trunk, "but we're friends with *Valmont*?"

"Not friends," Henry clarified. "Just, well, not-enemies."

"Yeah, if only it were so easy with the Nordlands,"

Adam said sarcastically. "Oi, my uncle said I have to play nice, so no more war."

"That *would* be nice," Henry said quietly.

And, just then, a pebble smacked against their window. Rohan pushed up the windowpane and stuck his head out. There was a muffled thwack.

"Owww, that's my face!" Rohan complained, as Henry and Adam rolled with laughter.

"Sorry," Frankie called. "Anyway, good to see you, Rohan."

"The pleasure is all mine, Miss Winter," Rohan teased.

"Well, guess what?" Frankie called.

"What?" Henry asked.

He and Adam had joined Rohan at the window.

"I'm not going to a reformatory," Frankie said, grinning in the moonlight.

"Well done!" Henry said.

"Brilliant," Adam said.

"Your father can't be letting you stay here?" Rohan asked with a frown.

"He is!" Frankie said. "My grandmother is packing her things now. She says the house will be too cramped with all the tutors."

"Tutors?" Henry asked, hardly daring to believe it.

"Well, obviously they've hired some silly *nursemaid* to teach me elocution and painting and piano and those sorts of rubbish things I'll be horrible-on-purpose at learning, but Professor Stratford is coming back to teach real subjects—on the condition that I behave. And my father mentioned something about Professor Stratford supervising Sir Frederick's second years until they hire a proper replacement."

The mention of Sir Frederick's name caused the four friends' smiles to fall. Because they remembered all too well how they had trusted Sir Frederick—and how he had betrayed them. And how war, whether they had proof or not, was looming just beyond the horizon every morning when they dressed for chapel in the gray dawn.

"Want to come play cards in the common room?" Adam asked. "Because it's bloody cold out, and I'm not keen to keep shouting through the window."

"What's the wager?" Frankie asked, hands on her hips.

"There's always a wager with you, isn't there?" Adam accused.

"Makes things interesting," Frankie said.

"Good, because things need to be *more* interesting around here," Henry said.

And with a grin, Henry loosened his tie and prepared to spend an evening in the company of his friends.

MARION COUNTY PUBLIC LIBRARY
321 MONROE STREET
FAIRMONT, WV 26554